THE GOLDEN KEY

MARIAN WOMACK

TITAN BOOKS

THE GOLDEN KEY
Print edition ISBN: 9781789093254
E-book edition ISBN: 9781789093261

Published by Titan Books
A division of Titan Publishing Group Ltd
144 Southwark Street, London SE1 0UP
www.titanbooks.com

First Titan edition: February 2020
10 9 8 7 6 5 4 3 2 1

A CIP catalogue record for this title is available from the British Library.

Printed and bound by CPI Group (UK) Ltd, Croydon, CR0 4YY

To Oliver Julius Womack Via

*There was a boy who used to sit in the twilight and
listen to his great-aunt's stories.*

*She told him that if he could reach the place where the end of
the rainbow stands he would find there a golden key.*

*'And what is the key for?' the boy would ask.
'What is it the key of? What will it open?'*

*'That nobody knows,' his aunt would reply.
'He has to find that out.'*

GEORGE MACDONALD,
The Golden Key (1867)

Who has not experienced the burning heat of the sun
that precedes a summer's shower?

EUNICE FOOTE,
'Circumstances Affecting the Heat
of the Sun's Rays' (1856)

CHAPTER ONE

There are many ways of getting lost. Breadcrumbs can sink into the snow, be eaten by rooks.

You can be sucked in by the marshes, lose your way on the flatlands. Be spirited away from the narrow footpaths. You could get confused at the imagined frontier of impenetrable dusk that hangs over the Fens, lose sight of the realm of the tangible.

Samuel Moncrieff had never been lost. For as long as he could remember he had been graced with the intuition that, if you got lost, you might never come back.

It almost happened once. He felt it, a strange force that pulled at him from the lane that cut between the flatlands. He had gone out for a walk; he could smell the cold, the wet leaves. The little shoots of frozen grass crunched under his feet, and the ground was white with frost.

Ahead of him, the dark agricultural fenland stretched,

eerily flat. For a second the world had lost some of its gravity, its weight.

He felt suddenly alert, and turned back, pulling with all his might.

He could not blame the fog, for it happened in that uncertain November twilight, impossibly heavy under its many layers of dusk. One step out of place, that's all it would have taken. Later, he would hear the expression 'being pixie-led'; but he himself had no words for such a portent, not then at least. Except for the notion of falling into an inescapable void, the unmistakable sensation of darkness advancing in his direction, intent on devouring him. Like drowning in a pool of stagnant water.

That day, the day he had almost got lost.

Was that the day he first saw it, the ruined house that had haunted his childhood dreams?

The dismal construction had been such a fixture of his nightmares for so many years, and yet had disappeared all of a sudden as soon as he put Norfolk behind him, went off to be educated. Almost every night he had traversed its corridors, looked up at the sky through the collapsed ceiling, dreading, always dreading the approach to that mouldy room at the passage's end. The house stood on a flat stretch of yellow land. The formal garden had run wild, overgrown, and he could hear a faint murmur of water. Some of the outer walls were blackened, and part of the ceiling was gone. The dim light, flat as the land itself, drew endless unmoving shadows.

It was a hollow carcass, home to foxes and mice, and to the jackdaws that flew to and fro around its triangular gables. Branches were overhanging the opened rooms, the floors covered in brown dirt, stones, broken pieces of flint. The dreary salons and bedchambers were all livid with mould, so that the fireplaces looked as if they had been painted in many shades of green by a madman. Ivy had crept in through the windows, and fungi of many different colours, shockingly vibrant, spread their silent empire over the walls, painting maps to unknown realms.

The house spoke of lives coming to abrupt ends, of broken promises. It spoke of endless possibilities, both seen and unseen. Its layers of unmoving time made him uneasy: there was something odd, slightly off-key. You could not hear the birds, the wind rustling. Like a place neither here nor there.

Why had it reappeared now, after all these years, with the inopportune insistence of a long-lost friend one has no time for?

He knew, deep down, what the house meant. A place to escape to, it came back to him during those first feverish hours without Viola, with its faint aura of a long-lost memory; the river accident had triggered its return. Just as mould and decay covered its imagined walls, so the memory of the house had silently conquered his nightmares, leaving no place for Viola, for the treacherous Isis.

What Sam could not remember was whether the building was a true memory, or something that he had imagined, part of some vivid childhood make-believe, a long-forgotten game of hide-and-seek with the shadows. He had no recollection of the property existing in this world. But then, he had been there once, had he not? He could not simply have imagined it, not in all its sumptuous decaying detail.

Samuel Moncrieff had never been lost, and had never wanted to be. It was different now.

Sam's arrival in London coincided with the first signs of Christmas. Little lights charmed passers-by from behind cloudy shop windows, and Albert trees sprouted here and there. The festivities welcomed him with their air of a season out of time, and came and went quickly; a sad, subdued affair.

'Samuel, my boy. The only thing we ought to concern ourselves with is your health. I have instructed Mrs Brown to provide for your every need.' Sam's godfather, Charles Bale, had a house in Saffron Hill Road, a large number of friends associated with the Spiritualist cause, and too much time on his hands. His robust disposition, cheerful eyes and fondness for amusing company were at odds with his prominent position in one of those societies occupied with exploring the darkest corners of our universe. Bale was one of the most senior members of The New Occultist Defence League, funded some years previously to 'defend those interested in Spiritual communion from the misunderstanding or aggravation caused by the non-Spiritualist-minded'. Showing a rare delicacy, the older man had not been inquisitive about the tragic accident that had brought Sam to his door. He had asked no questions, and demanded no answers. And so Sam had the chance to gather his breath. London, even if looked out upon from a window, did not look back at him with reproach: a welcome change. College life lay behind him, forever gone. He was capable of admitting that much to himself.

A few weeks after Sam's arrival, the Queen's passing changed the mood of the capital once more. To his godfather's delight, advertisements now kept sprouting everywhere for lectures on Mesmerism in working men's clubs, or for assemblies and raffles to gather funds for séances. Victoria's death had suddenly rekindled the interest in their dusty cause: most of the papers proclaimed new ghostly sightings and bewildering phenomena, usually involving the departed monarch.

'Who knows?' Charles took to saying with a smile. 'Her Majesty may, even now, be looking at us from The Beyond.'

Most visitors to Saffron Hill Road interpreted the black ribbon on Sam's arm as a mark of respect for Victoria, and he did not set them right. He often heard Charles and his friends discussing what they called the Queen's 'promotion', and admiring the symbolism of her final journey: the crowds in dark mourning, the bright white horses. The monarch had famously made all the preparations herself, in accordance with her well-known interest in the fanfare of death.

Sam avoided seeing the ominous procession. The incident in the river, still an open wound in his mind, meant that he was not in a humour to witness such an event. And then there was the house: the crumbling walls, soft with lichen; the dense silence welcoming him back. At night he turned in bed left and right, until a feverish sleep found him. And what came to his rescue but this ruin, this *thing*? It was all there again; so unreal, so recognisable, bringing back no memories, but dark premonitions from the past. Then nothing: his mind filled with black water. Sam longed for only one thing: a night of untroubled sleep. It was one of his uncle's Spiritualist gazettes that proposed the notion, imbued with dark meaning, of what might be happening, bringing to mind at once the ruined house, the river, Viola, as a melange of connected possibilities:

TWENTIETH-CENTURY CURE. MAGNETISM IS LIFE!

 WRITE AT ONCE.

MARVELLOUS CURES.

**ALL SUFFERERS FROM LOSS OF MEMORY,
SADNESS, AND ALL NERVOUS AILMENTS,
INCLUDING SLEEP ILLNESSES**

Sleep illness. Could *that* be his affliction?

What he needed wasn't a cure for his nightmares, but a potion to help him forget. He knew people who had wandered down to the canalside in Oxford, where the slow Chinese barges sometimes came up from London. They had spoken to him of medicines that could calm the busiest brain, but for some reason he had always rejected these out of hand. What he ought to do was give himself over to the dedicated task of changing the fog inside his head for the London fog, like a self-induced trance. But he wondered: would he be able to do that alone, or would he need a light to guide him? Samuel Moncrieff felt irrevocably lost, for the first time in his life.

It was in this particular mood that Sam re-encountered his Oxford friends Frederick Edgington and James Woodhouse. They passed each other one morning on a busy street during one of Sam's endless wanderings without direction, zig-zagging through the labyrinth of the city. Someone shouted his name and he stopped, unsure if this was happening in real life, or if the sound was coming from somewhere further away, the ruins of his vivid dreams. It was only Freddy, and Viola's cousin, Jim. They greeted each other, Freddy rather more warmly than quiet Jim. They both wore black armbands. For the Queen? For Viola, in Jim's case? It was impossible to know, and Sam preferred to avoid the issue. Shortly afterwards they were partaking of a hearty lunch in the booth of a Holborn tavern, thick with wolfish lawyers and monkish clerks. Sam half-listened to Frederick's assertion that he wasn't in London illicitly, far from it. His tutor, it appeared, had contracted such severe melancholia after the passing of the monarch that he had taken an indefinite leave of absence, and Freddy had been left to his own devices.

'Taken to his bed, if you please! And so here I am, waiting on what they decide to do with me. A lost Hilary term is the least of it,' he explained, smiling through his pork pie. Sam said nothing, and took a long draught of his ale. He eyed Jim over his cloudy glass, thankful that Viola's cousin had chosen not to mention the recent events. Jim had given no explanation for why he had come to the capital. Thankfully, they both seemed to have reached the tacit agreement of allowing Freddy to speak to his heart's content.

'And what do you gentlemen intend to do?' asked Sam.

'Dine in style, get acquainted with pretty young things, enjoy the theatres and music halls.'

After dinner they walked down to the river, and on the embankment they took a tram to the Lambeth Road, where stood one of the seedy establishments upon which Freddy bestowed his patronage. The bright lights of the Waterloo Variety poured their inconsiderate gaudiness over everything, even Sam's misery. He felt dreadful, seeing the theatre for what it really was. The velvet curtains were black with grime, the floor was littered with cigarette ends. People were loudly chatting, drinking, smoking, clapping. They were coarse people, biting hard on their cigars and laughing too loudly, sipping the bright gilt liquid as they crashed their cheap champagne glasses together. The light and the smoke hung in the air like a shroud. Sam sucked deeply on a cigar he didn't want, and observed the young women: mostly chancers clad in imitations of expensive outfits, with make-up covering their faces like a carnival mask, and smiles showing rotten teeth. Out of the corner of his eyes Jim moved here and there, talking to people, never going very far from Sam, hovering around him.

But Freddy had correctly judged the effect this place might have on his friend's sinking spirits. Barely an hour after crossing the Waterloo's threshold, Sam was sipping his third glass of sparkling alcohol (it would be a sin to call it champagne). He was convinced that he wouldn't stay long, that nothing could possibly fill the emptiness inside him; the emptiness from which, before Viola, he had been so blissfully free. But he forced himself to drink up. He allowed Freddy to guide him backstage, where he was introduced to a number of chorus girls. Everywhere there were smiles and noise and thick lavender smells and big teeth. Among the noise, the cigarettes and the pots of cold cream, alcohol and other drugs flowed freely, and he accepted another drink. It was brandy. A little smile tried very hard to curve Sam's mouth, almost succeeding. He had forgotten this, but he remembered now: there existed very few pains, great or small, that the London night could not muffle.

It would be backstage at the theatre, of all places, where he would come to meet her, this particular girl who mildly intrigued him. He grew used to finding her in the dressing room, standing very straight among the comings and goings. What had struck him was how elegant she looked under the old-fashioned gas lamps, but he had also detected something slightly off-key about her, something that didn't quite ring true. She was a seamstress who appeared never to mend anything. No, it wasn't that, exactly. She was a seamstress who looked like somebody dressed up as a seamstress: the neatness of her clothing, the 'correctness' of her demeanour, like a child playing at a profession. One evening, to his surprise, he found the girl sneaking into one of the managers' offices, opening the door after a careful inspection of the corridor.

Curiosity won over, and Sam moved slowly towards the slightly opened door to peep inside. The seamstress was diligently going through a sheaf of papers. What could she be doing? Sam's logical assumption was that she was looking for something to steal.

He pushed the door open and slowly entered.

'May I ask what you're doing, miss?' he interrupted her.

To his surprise she didn't have the grace to act like

someone caught red-handed. On the contrary, she seemed vexed to see him.

'And you, sir?' came the astonishing answer. Perhaps even more astonishing was the clear-cut authority of her response. Sam hadn't had the chance to speak to her and her looks had made him expect an accent of some sort.

'Excuse me? It is you who have crept in here like a sneak, rummaging in this poor fellow's private documents.'

To his surprise, the young woman rolled her eyes, sighed deeply, and composed the shadow of a patient smile.

'I am sorry, I truly have no time for this,' she said, and instantly resumed her search. Sam felt unsure how to continue. That wasn't the reaction he had expected.

'My dear woman! May I remind you that this is a private office? I will have no compunction in calling a constable right now!'

The false seamstress stopped what she was doing, turned to look at him, and said:

'Sir, you are misinterpreting this scene wildly; you know nothing of what is going on here.'

'Then, pray, illuminate me,' he said, his voice slightly mocking her. She looked briefly amused, but the emotion passed over her face like a cloud, as she appeared to consider his proposition.

'Again, I am sorry, but that would mean breaking my clients' right to their privacy.'

'Your *clients*?' This threw Sam off balance for a moment. Surely she did not mean the women whose clothes she pretended to mend? Sam sighed heavily. 'I'm afraid you leave me no alternative.'

'Where are you going?'

'To find a constable!'

She walked slowly in his direction, shaking her head left and right, as if she were deeply saddened by something, or as if she were his governess and he a little errant child.

'Then you leave me no alternative either,' she said, and before Sam could react, the infuriating young woman had delivered a blow to the lower part of his neck that rendered him expertly unconscious.

It was all over the papers: the third under-manager of the Waterloo Variety had been operating a white-slavery operation from the theatre, serving rich men, and preying on the young female entertainers. Definitive proof had been unearthed, in the form of a couple of coded notebooks detailing the grim transactions, and the man and his accomplice were now behind bars, awaiting trial.

The atmosphere backstage at the Waterloo was ecstatic, with many bottles of authentic champagne opened and consumed. The mysterious seamstress, however, was nowhere to be seen, and had not been seen since the night of their peculiar encounter. Sam had not cared to share with anyone how he had really come to be unconscious. The others had put it down to alcoholic excess, and he had let them think exactly that. He had woken up in the corridor, under the worried gaze of some of the girls fussing over him. What he couldn't see anywhere was his attacker.

The vanishing of the woman shouldn't have been so remarkable; people were coming and going from the place all the time. But Sam's curiosity had been piqued after their unexpected exchange. And if he was already curious, he was much more so when none of the girls admitted to ever having met her. A seamstress? Here? They explained how they did all their mending themselves. But Sam had seen them talking to her—why were they lying? The more he asked, the more he confronted a combination of shrugged shoulders, looks askance, and the notion that people were trying to avoid the issue. And, as so often happens, the more rebuffs that came his way, the more compelled he felt to find out the truth. Surely he had not invented her.

Or had he?

Was she another vivid dream? Was he going mad, perhaps?

Freddy proposed his own theory one evening over pints of cloudy ale:

'Do you think she might have been a ghost? You know, the ghost of a seamstress who used to work here, or in the Alhambra? But there are too many ghosts in the Alhambra,

13

everyone knows that! So maybe there was no place for her, and she *had* to come down here instead.'

'Lord, Freddy, I've no idea.'

But his friend had made him curious. What if he were indeed sensitive to these oddities of nature, as his uncle had mildly suggested after his arrival in London? He decided to explain the situation to Charles; the old man was, when it came down to it, the expert on unexplained presences. According to his uncle, nothing made one more prone to pick up on these hidden currents than closeness to death, or the sudden loss of someone beloved. Sam had tried to drop the subject; he could not think of anything more ghastly than coming into contact with a deathly version of his former beloved: Viola pointing a skeleton finger in his direction.

Sam quickly summarised the story of the vanishing young woman whom apparently only he had seen one morning, over his kippers and buttered toast.

'My suggestion, Samuel, would be to attend a séance.'

'A séance?'

'We can try to make contact with this mysterious creature, or else ask guidance from an all-seeing spirit.'

Charles got up, rummaged through his recent correspondence, and put a piece of paper in front of Sam. It was a playbill, and it read as follows:

MADAME FLORENCE WAYFARER,
the Californian Psychic, has returned from America,
and will be in London for another season.

SÉANCES HELD ON
Thursday evenings, 7.30 for 8, at 135 Gower Street, W.C.

'An American medium?'

'The Fox sisters were American!' Charles beamed, choosing to ignore, as always, the scandal on his religion that Margaret Fox's confession had brought. But then he frowned, and grumbled: 'In any case, this new science originated in the New World!'

Perhaps Charles had been right all along; perhaps Viola's death had heightened his sensibility somehow. He could not remember clearly what had happened on the river. He just had a persistent feeling of dread; he felt as if he was chewing death all the time. He also dreamt of the house every night, and woke up not knowing where he was, or who he was. Something needed to be done.

Two weeks later, on one of those cloudy evenings when it looked like the sky was deciding whether to rain or not, Sam set aside his book, and started getting ready to attend his first séance. At the agreed time he came down to find Charles even more nervous than usual. The older man kept looking through one of the little windows to the side of the main door, adjusting and readjusting his cravat with shaking fingers. Sam peeped out discreetly.

An odd-looking beggar was standing on the other side of the pavement, leaning against the street lamp. He was big as a bear, clad in strange old-fashioned robes, with a long mat of grey hair covering his shoulders. The amber light of the lamp projected his long, amorphous shadow.

They left the house. The street was completely empty by then, and the redbrick buildings around them shone, wet with the light evening drizzle that had decided to fall. Charles kept looking left and right, and Sam sensed that the older man would be grateful for any topic to discuss.

'Have you ever been to one of this American's séances before?'

Charles turned to face him, and fixed his eyes on Sam's.

'You are so young, Samuel. So young and full of life.'

This took Sam by surprise. If only his uncle knew how he felt when someone mentioned youth and life in the same sentence. A few months earlier, Sam would have smiled with the true detachment of youth, not really feeling any pain, any loss, any fear. Now all he could think of was Viola.

They climbed into Sam's car in silence and set off. The machine vibrated like a consumptive in a coughing fit, as if ready to die at any moment.

'Sam, I have been meaning to talk to you.'

'Yes?'

'I am most impressed at your recovery. Health and occupation are the main purveyors of a happy mind! Have you had any inkling of what you might want to do next?'

Sam had feared this conversation, but he was prepared for it.

'Mind you, you are welcome to stay as long as you want!'

'I had the notion of preparing myself to climb some mountain,' Sam cut in, in the face of Charles's embarrassed look.

'Very good! Train the body and the spirit will look after itself. The most important thing is to be able to control the dark impulses—'

Sam had a private, interior laugh. Was his uncle serious? Was he preaching against dark and fanciful notions, while taking him to a séance, of all things?

'Let the work of the day tire you so that you fall into a black well when you go to sleep,' continued the older man. A cloud passed over Sam's mind; what did his uncle know about his nightmares? Perhaps he shouted in his dreams. Did he shout about the ruined house, about Viola, about the ghostly seamstress?

Charles imparted some more of this kind of vague, Spiritualist-magazine advice during their drive to Gower Street, while Sam nodded and uttered agreements in all the right places. They reached their destination shortly after half past seven. A maid opened the door for them, and they were shown into a parlour. The room was in half-darkness, and what light there was twisted the aspidistras at the other end into fantastical shapes. Sam weighed up his surroundings, an old habit from a time when he used to pick fights in taverns. Entrances and exits.

Two members of the Gower Street Circle were greeting the guests: serious Miss Clare Collins, a poised young black woman with a shocking streak of white in her hair, and a Scot, Thomas Bunthorne, whom Sam had met previously. Charles greeted both of them, and introduced Miss Collins to Sam:

'My dear boy, here you have the most faithful group of devotees in the whole of London!' he announced, and Miss Collins laughed heartily, as though Charles had said something truly amusing. Sam felt as if he had missed a trick.

'How do you do, Miss Collins?' he offered.

'Sam, Miss Collins here will direct the séance,' Charles explained.

'But I thought—'

Charles and Miss Collins smiled at Sam's confusion.

'Don't worry, Mr Moncrieff. Madame Florence is the one you have come to see tonight, and you will see her. She will lock herself in that cabinet,' Miss Collins explained, signalling an imposing piece of black mahogany furniture at the other end of the room. Sam was unpleasantly reminded of an oversized coffin. 'From there she will summon the spirits, but *I* will direct the questions from the table.'

The rest of the small gathering was completed by a little plump woman in a worn-out gown who kept wringing her hands, and a distinguished-looking lady dressed in heavy mourning regalia, sitting on a chair with the aloof air of not needing to talk to anyone. Sam noted that Charles greeted her coldly, in a manner suggesting that he must have known her in passing, but he did not offer an introduction. Mr Woodbury, an elderly bookseller whom Sam had seen sometimes in Charles's house, arrived shortly before the proceedings began.

He had not expected to see the medium before the séance, but Madame Florence appeared in the dimly lit room. She moved like a graceful hostess, talking to everyone, quite as if she were about to announce dinner instead of a meeting with the dead. She was not at all as Sam had expected: he had pictured a plump spinster, an earthly matron surrounded by a group of admiring fools.

'Madame Florence,' said Charles, 'may I introduce Mr Samuel Moncrieff?'

She extended a heavily bejewelled hand in his direction, and Sam bent down to kiss it. He had the impression that she was sizing him up, and that she was happy with what she saw. Madame Florence seemed to be a woman who made sure her partialities were understood. She had deep, intense green eyes, which seemed to pierce through his skull and communicate hidden meanings.

'Are you a believer, Mr Moncrieff? Or will I have a problem with you?'

Her directness disarmed him for a second. She must have

noticed the slight bewilderment in his eyes, for she added:

'I'm only joking! Please excuse me. It's just that I can smell a non-believer from miles away.'

'Madame Florence, if I may—' he started. 'I am new to Spiritualism, and there are still certain things that perplex me. One question, for example. If mediumship is a service, as the members of your religion proclaim, pray inform me on one point. I do not quite understand why these people have to pay to be here.'

'Sam!' Charles looked horrified.

'Don't worry, Mr Bale. Nothing gives me more pleasure than dispelling these little malicious and unfounded myths about my profession. Let's put your assertion to the test, Mr Moncrieff. Do you see that lady?' She pointed at the woman in the worn-out dress. 'She came to see me days ago. She needed help, solace. I could not turn her down. Of course, she could not afford to pay for my services, but she needed them nonetheless. People have their pride, Mr Moncrieff, even the less fortunate among us.' She fixed him with an icy stare, as if daring him to take up the issue with her. 'She is a very talented milliner, and has promised to make me a new summer hat in lieu of payment. I have accepted. It is more than fair, and I only fear that I shall be benefiting much more than her in the exchange.'

Her honesty was refreshing, he thought. Sam noticed that his uncle had moved away, with a wounded look.

'That is very generous of you,' he said.

'And that man over there…' To Sam's surprise she pointed to Mr Woodbury, who was conducting what looked like an agitated exchange with Thomas Bunthorne. 'As well as being a celebrated vegetarian, and a significant figure in the temperance movement, he happens to want to study my psychic powers. Perhaps even to shame me as a fraud!' She suppressed a little laugh. 'Anyway, I cannot charge him for attending this gathering in his pursuit of scientific knowledge! You are in safe hands, Mr Moncrieff. I assure you he will scrutinise everything that happens here this evening.'

To her amusement, he didn't know what else to say.

'Pray, excuse me, I had better prepare myself,' Madame Florence cut off. 'A psychic expert and a non-believer!' she laughed. 'I have to offer an *excellent* performance tonight, don't you think?' and she walked away from him.

The séance would turn out to be rather a theatrical affair. There was an argument that there had been a particular design in mind to be extrapolated from each affectation, as if a stage manager from the Waterloo Variety had been in attendance in Gower Street that night. Sam's recent exposure to the bright lights and painted faces of the theatre did to a degree recall what had transpired in the candlelit parlour, even though the effect had been the exact opposite: if the chorus girls and comic singers and magicians tried to please and enchant, then

Madame Florence's purpose was none other than to introduce a sense of the uncanny into the lives of her sitters.

The first thing that he had learnt from the experience was that raising the dead seemed to be a tedious business. He couldn't tell how long ago Madame Florence had entered the dark mahogany cabinet, where she had allowed Mr Bunthorne to tie her up and lock her away. She had been left unable to move, but had been smiling faintly, like a heroine accepting her sacrifice. So far there had been no sign of Kitty, Madame Florence's spirit-guide, and the sitters avoided looking at each other as much as possible. Sam's concentration faltered, and he tried to focus on anything, but found nothing.

And then it appeared, all of a sudden, clarifying itself in his mind's eye as the one thing he truly feared: the ruined little manor house, with the capricious moss in its walls, so wrong and so abundant, as if it had a will of its own; the decayed abandoned structure left to rot as if it hid a horrible secret.

Sam shook the image away, and his hand left the circle momentarily to readjust his cravat, an unwitting gesture. Miss Collins directed a furious look in his direction. His hand darted back to the table, and he responded to the woman's disapproving look with an apologetic nod.

The reality was that not much was happening. How many in that parlour were starting to feel cheated? From what Charles had explained, guaranteed hand or face materialisation was assured with this medium. The group was not even breathing in unison, and whatever concentration they had managed at the beginning, there was no sign of it now. The milliner was trying to muffle her uneven gasps; she seemed frankly agitated and on the verge of tears. The old lady, a Mrs Ashby, looked frankly cross, as if she were being made to lose a perfectly good evening among a group of fools.

It suddenly struck him what a hideous business was now being conducted in that candlelit room. He saw the 'parlour game' for what it really was: they were inviting the dreadful shadows of the dead to join them; unknown presences that, he feared, would be anything but angelic if they were truly to show themselves, even though he did not believe such apparitions possible. He wondered vaguely about Madame Florence's safety inside the cabinet.

He tried to recall the exact lyrics of the hymn they had sung at the beginning of the séance; ghastly, horrid words, made all the more horrid for they sounded like a children's rhyme:

> *Hand in hand with angels; some are out of sight,*
> *Leading us unknowing into paths of light;*
> *Some soft hands are covered from our mortal grasp,*
> *Soul in soul to hold us with a firmer clasp.*

And then it happened, three knocks.
That was what Miss Collins had told them to wait for.
One. Two. Three.

Next to him, Mrs Ashby swallowed a scream.

Sam saw all eyes turn towards the cabinet where Madame Florence sat alone inside, arms and legs tied, inducing her trance.

Without a word Miss Collins got up, and moved towards the heavy piece of furniture. She turned the key, and the door of the cabinet creaked slowly open. The mahogany interior was as black as a deep cave. That could not be; they had all seen Madame Florence sitting on a little stool placed inside the diminutive interior, no hidden depths. Miss Collins resumed her seat at the table, and for a moment nothing else happened.

Something moved inside the cabinet. And then they all saw her.

The figure revealed itself, little by little, as they heard the rustle of a dress, distinguished a face. Or was it a trick of the light? Madame Florence was completely still. The light condensed around her, changed shape, and this pale and flat whiteness shone a little, reflecting her sombre features.

Each and every one of the sitters had encountered death, witnessed how it subtly changes the features of loved ones, turning them into wrong versions of their living selves. Putrefaction settles at once on a corpse, and hollowness imposes itself on the face, altering it almost at once, shockingly definitive. Madame Florence's face was changed in such a manner. It was the same face they had all seen thirteen minutes earlier, entering the cabinet. But it was also a corrupted version of it.

And then Sam realised. Surely the medium was—*dead*?

He got up with a jerk, his chair falling behind him with a loud clatter. Miss Collins flared up.

'You can't break the circle! What do you think you are doing, young man?'

He resented her calling him that—surely she was barely older than he was!

'Mr Moncrieff! If you do not sit down now I will have to ask you to leave!' she insisted.

'Miss Collins, for goodness' sake! Madame Florence is in obvious distress!'

Madame Florence shifted, as if on cue.

'You see? Madame is fine. Now, sit!' Miss Collins indicated, as if talking to a poodle. Sam found his chair, and sat down. He felt his cheeks burning.

'Dear one? Is Kitty here?' asked Miss Collins, closing her eyes and rolling her head. Sam was no longer sure what he was witnessing. His detachment from the proceedings was faltering at an alarming speed.

'Kitty, dear one! Are you *here*?' insisted the woman.

Then something took place, of which there would be several accounts later on: contradictory, embellished, truthful. Impossible.

In plain view of all those present, Madame Florence shrank.

The woman's body lost its gravitas, as a child's balloon loses air; her small hands disappeared up her frilly sleeves, freeing themselves from the ropes as they did so, and the skin of her deathly face sank further into her cheeks, transforming her into a veritable skeleton. Unexpectedly, this uncanny vision started to levitate, and moved, hands free of the ropes, slowly manoeuvring itself out of the cabinet. The medium's old-fashioned dress, the full black skirt, the sleeves, hung loosely around her, a shell; her face had changed beyond recognition, impossibly wrinkled, as white as paper among the expensive black frills.

Charles gagged as the floating figure approached the table. The stench it spread was overpowering and sweet and incoherent. It put one in mind of wet, freshly turned earth. It put one in mind of the metallic smells of a hunt, when the powder and the blood and the fear mix together.

Miss Collins grabbed the hands of the two people next to her, and pressed them hard, instructing the others to do the same. Sam could sense the alarm in her voice when she spoke next.

'Who are you? Who is here with us? Are you friend or foe?'

The medium, levitating a few feet from the floor, her arms extended and her head lopsided, opened her eyes, and they were dark and deep as a well, as a cave, as the waters of the Isis.

'Speak! Friend or foe?' Miss Collins insisted bravely.

The figure was sweating what looked like a muddy liquid. She opened her mouth to reveal an engorged tongue.

'*Fff—*' came the dark black voice.

'Foe…?'

'Of course she is! What a stupid question!' exploded an indignant Mr Woodbury.

'What do you want with us? Why are you here? Tell us!'

The medium's ghastly doppelgänger turned to stare at Sam, and spoke again.

'*Fffff*—'

'Foe, yes, foe, *what do you want to tell us*—?' interrupted Miss Collins, to which Madame Florence, or whatever had taken possession of her, exploded:

'*FLORA!*'

After uttering that word she fell heavily onto the floor. Sam and the milliner got up, and both rushed to her. When Sam knelt by her side Madame looked normal again, her old self miraculously restored; but a faint green mist, like fairy dust, seemed to be leaving her mouth. Hell-breath.

All the sitters were now getting up with trembling movements.

'Is Flora someone you have lost?' ventured Miss Collins in Sam's direction, trying to salvage whatever she could from such an unexpected turn of events.

But Sam wasn't listening; that farce had gone too far. All his attention was directed at Madame Florence.

'Water, now, please,' he ordered.

'I was told not to attend a séance in Lent. I should have listened…' murmured the milliner, the longest sentence she had uttered all night.

'Mr Moncrieff!' Miss Collins insisted. 'Do you *know* anyone called Flora? Is she someone you *lost*? Pray tell us, I beg you! This is a circle of trust!'

'What are all these theatrics?' protested Mr Woodbury. 'Is this everything? No flutes and ghostly hands playing levitating violins? No Kitty and her flowers?'

'For goodness' sake, Mr Woodbury!' cried an offended Thomas Bunthorne. 'We have seen a full-figure levitation here tonight! Perhaps for the first time in British Spiritualist history! What on earth more do you want, my good man?'

Sam found himself agreeing with Mr Bunthorne. Did that mean he was a believer now? He was only sure of one thing: Woodbury was a fool.

Mrs Ashby got up unexpectedly, and headed resolutely for the door. Sam noticed that she exchanged a look with Charles, who also looked yellowish, as if he were about to vomit.

'Mrs Ashby! Please, wait!' said Miss Collins. 'We ought to sing another hymn, to thank the spirits for the successful deliverance of our friend.'

'Excuse me, but my business here is done,' answered the old lady with an unexpected American twang. 'I'm sure you can sing without me.'

'But—'

'I'm sorry, Miss Collins, but I have seen enough of—*this*.' The woman waved her hand vaguely. 'I will personally see that your circle is amply compensated, and will give you the necessary funds to settle Madame Florence in England with immediate effect.'

Miss Collins lost her tongue for a second, but quickly composed a professional smile.

'That is most generous, madam.'

Mrs Ashby opened the door, and was gone in a second.

No one said anything for a few moments. As soon as propriety allowed, Mr Woodbury rushed to inspect the cabinet, frantically looking for some hidden mechanism, levers and ropes, which of course he didn't find, except the ones used to tie up Madame. Slowly, one by one, all the participants in the evening's pastime started to gather themselves, each of them wondering in silence what had happened, what dark magic they had just witnessed.

CHAPTER TWO

The doll was abandoned in the garden. She wondered how it had got there; she hadn't played with dolls in twenty years at least. And she didn't think Mrs Hobbs even noticed the things, except for dusting them, which didn't happen very often. Still, she was slightly put out: it was a valuable object, like all the others. They were all that remained of her mother in this godforsaken place.

The garden was empty of sounds, looked after by the housekeeper's husband, with the heavier tasks undertaken by a man who came from the village once a week. And those were all the people she ever saw, from Sunday to Sunday. Church offered more variety of faces, although they all looked so similar somehow. There was Peter, of course, her elder cousin, now a serious village doctor. When she looked at him she still saw the same little child she used to climb trees with, play with next to the canals. His was the only presence that prevented her loneliness. She had always felt so lonely in this place.

At least she would have the garden from now on. For the past two weeks of rain it had been a dead, messy thing.

She looked through the window at the abandoned doll, so like an abandoned boat after a flood. The glass gave her back her own reflection, paler than usual, the untamed wheat-blonde hair, the tiny curls stuck in an unmanageable tangle. She hadn't taken care of herself properly in weeks, and didn't plan to do so. Who cared? She looked no better than the doll, she thought. Secretly, she felt happy about the doll's fate. She despised them. The French Jumeau, with its sad porcelain face, long eyelashes drawn on its forehead, and its real, dead hair. The mechanical baby from the Steiner house, the most valuable thing in that cottage, although none of its occupants was aware of the fact. The distracted grimace of the little blonde doll, bought in Paris in another lifetime.

Each morning, Eliza wrote. She put down her observations of the mysterious disappearances in nature in her notebook, and she worked on her monograph, the book that would bring back Eunice Foote to everyone's attention. After a while, she opened another, secret drawer, and took out another, secret notebook, a second one. Other things went in it.

It had started as a pastime, many years ago. It was abandoned while she and Mina were together. She had taken it up again, not knowing why; perhaps because she craved simpler times:

write line upon line of your own name on a piece of paper. An old incantation, for dreaming the name of her future companion. A useless, inanimate list of Elizas conquered the white day by day, no single space left for indeterminacy. It was difficult to believe there would be a companion. She dreamed of Mina's soft curls falling like sand between her fingers every night. And of them both, falling together. The silliness helped pass the time, nonetheless; it was like automatic writing, and it brought ideas, associations, to her inquisitive mind. It was also vaguely comforting, like eating marmalade sandwiches, laughing with Mina in front of the fire, playing with dolls when she was little. But she was a woman now, and she was alone. Perhaps it was an exercise in reaffirmation: *I exist! I am here!*

The housekeeper had caught her at this exercise in repetition. Mrs Hobbs probably did not know the reasons why Eliza had set up house by herself, why she had insisted on making habitable again the old family carstone cottage. She did not know, obviously, that Eliza had lost her life companion to a quarrel; she did not know, for she had got it into her head that Eliza was invoking the face of her future husband of all things.

'You are still young, miss, if you don't mind me saying so,' she would point out. 'And there are other things that a woman can do to find out.'

'What other things?'

'If what you want is to see his face, if you take my meaning, miss.'

Poor woman. She was quite insistent on this husband business. It was only a game, after all. And so Eliza let Mrs Hobbs impart her wisdom; who knew what she might learn? It was only an experiment, an exercise in opening up the realms of the possible. Wasn't that what scientists were meant to do?

Take new wax, and the powder of a dead man, make an image with the face downward and in the likeness of the person you wish to have; make it in the new moon; under the left arm place a swallow's heart, and its liver; you must use a new needle and a new thread; you need to say *his* name, confess *his* sins, speak *his* character.

Eliza felt strangely guilty. Deep down, she despised all that nonsense: mediums, clairvoyants, magicians and their tricks; but there could be something in rural notions, she thought, some dark knowledge of preterite times, some strange form of science, or at least of harnessing the powers of nature. She wanted to learn it all, and so she listened to Mrs Hobbs. But this? *Nonsense.* Where to find a dead man? How to give shape to powder? How could someone wait until the new moon? And a *swallow*? Absolutely useless.

The dolls observed her from the wooden shelves. In the daguerreotype she still kept, her mother looked like another doll, one among many, sitting among the crates and chests and boxes of her luggage. She was going to China, Eliza thought, Mongolia afterwards.

Each morning Eliza had breakfast, and then went back to

her room to write. And each morning she would add to that other, secret knowledge. *What would Eunice think?* The notebook she kept hidden in a little drawer, locked with a little key. It was mere chance that she had the key, for there had never been closed doors in the little carstone cottage, secrets. As if she had any. Everyone, she thought, would have heard about Mina by now, everyone from here to China; everyone, except poor Mrs Hobbs. But everyone thought that this particular drawer had been locked forever, and the key lost. There had never been any secrets here. They would come for holidays when she was little, and she would always hear it at the back, the grumbling, shaky noise that her parents' fights used to carry, her mother shaken around like a doll, thrown against the walls, hitting the wooden doors. It would invariably happen at dusk, her father's change of mood. She had never known why this precise moment, out of all the possible moments. And her mother pretending afterwards, a set, manic smile on her beautiful, doll-like face.

A woman must take an orange, prick it all over in the pits of the skin with a needle, and sleep with it in her armpit. The next day she must see the man she loves eat it.

When she was four, Eliza's game was that a baby doll killed a mammy doll when it was born, although she didn't understand the mechanisms that put that death in motion. At six she understood better, and the game was abandoned. What she wanted was to find a game in which the father died, not the mammy. She never knew how to make this happen.

Now, each morning, Eliza wore one of her mother's old dresses, so similar to the ones the dolls were wearing. Money was tight, and she had finally fully grown into them. They came from a box in the attic, smelling of damp and naphthalene patches. It was possible that her father had expected her mother to be preserved like a doll, to behave like a doll. Moved from here to there and back again, uncomplaining. It was possible that she herself was one more doll in the doll's room, but she hadn't noticed because Mr and Mrs Hobbs were keeping the secret from her. Eliza opened the locked drawer, hoping to see Mina's face; Mina, who would come to rescue her, who would forgive her for what she had done. And she daydreamed that she was a doll and that someone, thinking her dead, had abandoned her outside.

This dismal place wasn't a new landscape. Eliza's father was from around here, from a place called Waltraud Water; and so she had spent a few years of her childhood coming down from Lincoln to the cottage for little holidays, all year round and in all kinds of weather. She knew of young college men skating in winter or sailing in summer all the way up to Ely, usually to find some girl or another. The short sailing boats with two cabins, climbing up the Little Ouse. Those were the memories of youth, she thought now, kinder than a summer's breeze. Her father had recounted it with pride, that long-gone world of fishing, fowling, of common wetland that was self-sufficient, well managed, cared for. Of the domestic geese that supplied the whole country with quill pens, those long feathers she marvelled at when she was little. Wildfowling season, from May to September, 'fen slodgers' carrying their decoys, and their tame ducks. The overabundance of pasture. The dykes dug up among the reeds, practically unseen when covered by snow or grass. And the moments when the snow started to melt, with those spring tides in motion. And the lost children, and the children that died in the eerie floods, and the children who were lost even before being born. For of course, there was no fairy tale here, and those were treacherous roads, deadly if misunderstood.

Crumbled churches like the one at Wicken Far End were a reminder that nature *would* reconquer, eventually. Or would she?

The Matthews' abbey was nearby, and Eliza sometimes walked there in her morning stroll. As soon as she left behind the tamed landscape of its grounds, still holding some shape even after years of neglect, the view of the world changed immensely. From time immemorial, that countryside had been composed of those same fields of faded green, all of them covered by marshy reeds, unkempt patches scattered here and there, surrounding little islands of sturdier land. It was difficult to imagine all that expanse submerged, but that is how it had been. The fenmen had reigned over the water, conquering it. As the land had been drained, all that had changed forever. When the land was dried and cut and divided into those disorientating fields, traversed by thin unmoving rivers, what had happened to it? It had gone to men like Sir Malcolm Matthews's ancestors. Eliza thought she understood that this countryside was haunted, by the bitterness, by the sorrow, by the suffering that went into its making. The same men who were forced to drain it lost their way of life while they did it. They had not benefited from the change. No one had given them a piece of land to grow crops and feed their families. Was it possible that the land itself was furious, as those men might have been?

The scientist in her was recounting the missing birds, the spring that didn't want to come. It had begun by mere chance, this exercise in vanishings. She had failed to find the tern, at a time when it *should* be here. There were other oddities: lack of some insects, strange pulpy grass, and, worst of all, some places where you could hear no birds at all. Something was going on. She had seen an eerie green light moving over the marshes as well. It seemed that all living creatures were making themselves scarce, getting away from its path; as if they knew that it was an uncanny thing, something that had no business being here… But of course, she insisted to herself, these were only fancies. There must be a scientific explanation, cause and effect, a reason behind those absences, removed from those strange green shades that seemed intent on advancing inland, intent on devouring it all.

Following it, she had got to what she thought was its source, a ruined Tudor manor house by the North Sea. It wasn't very imposing, but almost cosy and small; nonetheless, Eliza had felt a creeping unhappiness there, as if her life had no meaning somehow, as if she had founded all her beliefs on lies until that moment. There was a white sticky substance floating around the ruin, posing on places where multicoloured fungi sprouted; she did not have a lot of mycological knowledge, and thought of Peter. She would have to ask him. If she ever were to return to the place; for what she had felt, more than anything, was as though an invisible boundary between two places was slowly lifting, and was going to trap her at the wrong side.

She needed to breathe, and had walked around the odd structure, looking for the flat sea. The marshes, the reed swamp, the open water at the end. In a moment, a wrong vista had revealed itself.

The tide had freakishly receded, and the water, distant in a flat, eerily never-ending expanse, was nowhere to be seen. At the end of her vision, the same soft greenish mist, but no clear line where the water and the land touched. The ground itself also seemed to have been taken back by the water, to have sucked itself up and out of place—and then she saw it. Enormous, shining black and green, traversed by unexpected orange streaks, the largest seam of umber green rhyolite, the stone that, she knew, was found in Madagascar, Oceania, the Pyrenees, Germany, Iceland, and in this particular stretch of the coast of East Anglia. A black and green sea of hardened stone, as hard indeed as a witch's heart.

CHAPTER THREE

B arely a fortnight after Madame Florence's séance, Charles's entire household was thrown into a flurry of activity. The new frantic atmosphere was a response to the demands of The New Occultist Defence League's brand-new publication. The gazette was going to be called *The Open Door*, and was funded by Charles and his friend Mr Woodbury. There was much to do for everyone, dealing with illustrators, typesetters, printers, and so on. Managing authors, a brooding and fragile bunch. Charles was going to direct the publication, and a select committee, which included Mr Woodbury and some others, would act as the board. The bulk of the production fell on a group of pale youngsters under Charles's command, the kind who are simultaneously occupied with hiding their pimples and growing implausibly thin moustaches.

Until suitable premises were found, Charles's library acted

as headquarters, and Sam welcomed the general hubbub. The séance at Madame Florence's had stirred something within him. He continued being a sceptic on Spiritualist matters; nonetheless, something *had* happened. Mr Woodbury graced them often with his presence to discuss matters concerning the publication, or simply to gossip. Sam didn't mind Woodbury's company as long as he abstained from preaching the many virtues of vegetarianism. The three men dined together often, and the sumptuous smells of plum tart and guinea fowl, roast parsnips and clotted cream were replaced, in Mr Woodbury's case, by those of stewed lentils, barley soup and buckwheat pudding. Once the dishes were retired, and the decanter of brandy and the cigars brought forward, along with a glass of hot water with a slice of lemon for Mr Woodbury, the topic would invariably turn to the evening at Madame Florence's, which had been highly praised in *Two Worlds*, in an article written by none other than Thomas Bunthorne.

'A most suspicious practice, if you ask me: a member of the medium's own circle reviewing her accomplishments, and without having the decency to mention his connection to her as a part of her entourage! Outrageous!' Woodbury complained. The older man was a bookseller, dealing particularly in records of unusual phenomena. But his principal activity was as chairman of the Society for Psychical Research. Woodbury was an expert in Spiritualist fraud. He made it his personal fight to unmask false Spiritualists, who were, according to him, a plague on their religion far worse than unbelievers. Woodbury confided in Charles and Sam that he had so far been quite unable to ascertain any fraud in Madame Florence's case.

'However, it is most suspicious that she has refused point blank the Society's proposal to conduct a séance under test conditions.'

'You want her to undergo a test séance?'

'That's right, Bale. Every medium should do it, at least once!'

'Perhaps, Woodbury. But she happens to be one of the most gifted clairvoyants and mesmerists of her or any generation!' Charles protested. 'Why are you so intent on unmasking her? What we saw the other night was extraordinary!'

'Exactly. Too extraordinary, if you take my meaning.' Woodbury winked at Sam.

'What do you mean, a test séance?' he asked.

'Oh, it's a very simple affair, Sam; you simply place the medium under some restrictions and vigilance. Let me ask you why Kitty only appears to guide Madame on the nights when paying customers have crossed her threshold? Mediums these days, my friend, and for some time now, have insisted on "appropriate environments" that are suspicious at best...'

And so forth. Listening to the older men discussing these matters, a picture emerged. Madame Florence, and others like her, were thought of as representatives of a rather fastidious type of Spiritualist woman, accused by Woodbury of 'sprouting everywhere'. In the early days of Spiritualism, mediumship had been a revolutionary activity for women. They were considered natural vessels of communication with the spirits, and often took control of the rituals. This was problematic for their male counterparts, so much so that Sam suspected people like Woodbury had been thankful for Spiritualism's decline, as it had meant the disappearance of many prominent female mediums. Now there was a risk that, after Victoria's passing, the renewed fashion for séances would mean people like Woodbury were pushed aside once again—by people like Madame Florence. Sam could see what the problem was: the old man had fought fiercely for his own corner of the Spiritualist world, and he would protect it to the death.

'Women have no role to play in the public sphere; their nature is not suited to open the way for the social reforms that Spiritualism should lead!' he was fond of saying, letting his anxiety show.

'And what are these reforms, Mr Woodbury?'

'Vegetarianism, of course!'

'Let me see if I understand you well,' Charles would reply gently. 'You do not trust Madame Florence because she is a woman, and eats meat?'

'Precisely!' the vegetarian would reply with conviction. 'What you have to ask yourselves is this: what is Madame Florence *really* trying to achieve by carefully composing a scene such as the one we witnessed?'

'Is she trying to earn a living?' suggested Sam.

'Ah, my friend! Would that it were so simple!'

The issue for Woodbury, Sam thought, was not if Madame's powers were real, but rather what use was made of this reality, the ends to which it was deployed, how it was presented, manipulated and used. In other words, on which side she positioned herself among the many factions and doctrines floating around London, all messily colliding with each other. Sam could not help but be reminded of the childish scuffles in his college common room. It was clear that Madame Florence was respected, although men seemed to stand a little at odds with the notion of a Goddess, or Gaia cult, which she was trying to resurrect. Apparently, the American medium was waiting for the arrival of a female Messiah, of all things. Among her many ardent detractors there stood out the rival mediumistic circle of The True Dawn, led by the mysterious Count Bévcar. Mr Woodbury was a strong advocate of the gentleman, although Sam wondered how he could reconcile his ardent admiration with the Count's apparently ravenous carnivorous appetites. Very little was known about him, although two notions had caught the London Spiritualist community's imagination: the fact that the Count was a Hungarian aristocrat, and his family's strange coat of arms—a wolf devouring a deer, overgrown reeds, the moon and a star.

There was a boy who used to sit in the twilight and listen to his great-aunt's stories.

Sam was sitting by the library fire. He had rummaged Charles's library for some light reading, only to find, to his surprise, Viola's favourite book amongst the shelves, almost hidden on top of another one. His heart had missed a beat.

After the evening at Gower Street Sam's dreams had been strangely vivid, even more so than usual, as if his experiences had awoken another layer of dream-reality. He now voyaged to the ruined manor every night in his dreams. He had started seeing Viola there, smiling at him. She looked so much at peace, it made him almost relieved. By now the fog was lifting, no doubt; but the pain still came and went, like waves on the sea, telling him he was not yet ready to forget her. Sometimes he found himself thinking of Viola performing some concrete action, like reading, writing a letter, or playing the piano. But he couldn't tell any longer if these were memories, or scenes his mind had created.

As time passed, other snippets and bits of information returned as well: somewhere, in the recesses of his former college room, there should be some photographs of Viola by the river. He thought he could look at them now in spite of his guilt, and resolved to make enquiries about where his uncollected belongings had ended up. There had been another toy, a phonograph recording machine, onto whose cylinders Viola had read passages from the very book he now held in his hands. Those were probably lost, he thought with sudden agony.

For some time, he had felt as if a thread was finally being severed, and that perhaps Viola could start being something more akin to a fond memory, a presence he could recall and banish at will instead of a constant shadow. He had decided to remove the black ribbon from his arm, thinking the pain would subside and be no more than a thin shade.

How wrong he had been. If anything, he ached for her now more than ever.

Finding the book had opened a wound, fresh as if it had been made yesterday. He silently mourned the loss of the cylinders into which this very sentence had been read, what seemed like aeons ago. He tried to no avail to recall the exact pitch of her voice.

She told him that if he could reach the place where the end of the rainbow stands he would find there a golden key.

A light knock on the door startled them both, as Mrs Brown, the housekeeper, stepped in.

'Mr Bale, sir. Lady Matthews is here to see you.'

Charles didn't look surprised at the announcement, although he had failed to mention the visit to Sam.

'Please show her into my study. And bring us some tea and sandwiches, if you would be so kind.'

'Very good, sir.'

'And I trust we have a bit of cake somewhere—'

While this exchange was going on, there was a rustle at the library door, and Mrs Brown was forced to move, giving way to an old lady, expensively dressed in garments that would have been fashionable years back, and who irrupted into the room uninvited.

Charles didn't seem put off by the *faux pas*; after all, lords and ladies could behave however they pleased, could shape and reshape the rules of civility.

'Lady Matthews—'

There was no other way to put it: Lady Matthews was glaring at Sam. Momentarily at a loss, the young man started to get up.

'Pray, do not trouble yourself, Mr Moncrieff. It looks as if you need your rest.' What on earth could she possibly mean? 'I trust I find you in good health?'

'I am perfectly well, thank you.'

'Sam, Lady Matthews is one of our neighbours up in Norfolk,' explained Charles. 'You probably do not remember her, but when you were little—' Charles's voice faltered.

'You used to play in our grounds, Mr Moncrieff. You have become a fine young man.'

The words were perfectly civil, but Sam had the impression that they meant exactly their opposite. Lady Matthews continued fixing him with her odd stare, in a manner that Sam could only interpret as unwholesome curiosity. Her expression was bewildered at best, with a faint whiff of badly concealed disgust.

Sam felt he ought to say something. Thankfully, Charles led her out of the room at that moment, leaving the younger man alone to reflect on this odd meeting.

Their business, whatever it was, lasted no longer than half an hour. When Charles came back into the library, he clearly felt the need to address the peculiar incident.

'You must excuse Lady Matthews—she has suffered a great deal.'

'I've never seen her here before. Is she a regular visitor?'

Charles seemed to find this amusing. His smile was wide, slightly manic, as he took up his pipe and newspaper.

'She hardly ever leaves her old pile. One of those eccentric women, you know. But she is very fond of Norfolk folklore, and even more so of everything connected with the story of her estate. Not that there is much of that, mind you. I had the chance to procure a little set of photographs from the early eighties made by a talented pioneer of the art. Some of them, I know for a fact, were taken on her land.'

Photographs were important to Charles, as empirical proofs of the spiritual world.

'Are they what you call "*images of phenomena*"?' asked Sam, demonstrating his newly acquired vocabulary.

'After a fashion. The photographer in question certainly recorded many unusual occurrences. But he didn't limit himself to images of the weird, mind you. He also photographed the usual subjects: peasants, mudflats, and pretty little boats.'

Each of them resumed reading in companionable silence.

But that wasn't the end of the matter, or, indeed, the last visit from the supposedly reclusive lady.

The following week, over breakfast, Charles announced, to Sam's bafflement, 'Lady Matthews is coming to tea this afternoon. She has asked particularly after your health, and whether she may be able to see you.'

Sam frowned. He remembered the woman's quizzical stare.

'There will be another friend coming to see us, to see Lady Matthews in fact: Miss Helena Walton.'

'Helena Walton?'

'Helena Walton-Cisneros, to be precise. You should enjoy her company; she is quite a well-versed Spiritualist, growing steadily in reputation. However, she is closer in age to you. You may find her interesting to talk to. She is a young woman of singular talent.'

Shortly before teatime, Lady Matthews was shown into the afternoon parlour. It was a comfortable room, looking over Charles Bale's private garden, and lavishly furnished. Lady Matthews, however, sat perched very straight on the Morris chair. *Noblesse oblige*, thought Sam, considering the old lady's peculiar set of mannerisms. It amused him to think of these characters wandering about in the brand-new twentieth century. This time, however, Lady Matthews had not deviated one millimetre from etiquette, aside perhaps from avoiding looking at Sam altogether.

A few minutes later, as the clock struck four, Mrs Brown announced Miss Helena Walton.

'Miss Walton! A very good afternoon to you! May I introduce Lady Matthews?'

'How do you do?'

The old woman acknowledged her with a curt nod.

'And this is my godson, Mr Samuel Moncrieff.'

'Welcome,' Sam said, and he bowed. The young medium curtsied flawlessly, but on getting up she seemed to tremble slightly, a little trifle no one apart from Sam appeared to notice. The young woman sat, tea was served, and a charming conversation about the benefits of country air filled the unavoidable first few minutes of awkwardness.

It happened in the course of this exchange, as Miss Walton rolled her eyes prettily after announcing that she was never happier than in a pair of strong boots with a long expanse of open land ahead of her. Something about that gesture was strangely familiar to Sam—

It couldn't be!

Sam looked at Miss Walton with renewed interest, transforming in his head the charming white muslin dress and the ostrich-feathered hat into a humble cotton blouse and strong dark blue linen skirt. And there she was: the same green-honey eyes whose exact colour he had spent weeks trying to recall, the rosy cheeks in an oval face of a slightly darker complexion, the little dimple below the left eye that he had found himself, to his dismay, admiring.

The woman sipping tea in their house was the Waterloo seamstress.

Either that, or Miss Walton and the seamstress were twins. He now realised that she had recognised him too, hence the lapsed curtsy. And the fact that she hardly looked in his direction.

'Miss Walton,' he started. 'I feel as if I know you, as if I have seen you before—'

'I have no idea where we might have met, Mr Moncrieff. I meet a great deal of people through my profession.'

'And what is that, exactly?'

'I specialise in palmistry. But I have other powers of sight. My great-grandmother on my mother's side was a talented Romany seer.'

'Indeed!' Sam's tone was not open to misinterpretation: he did not believe a word. Charles looked at him confusedly. 'I must admit I find it hard to believe that my future is set up in the lines of my hand,' he continued. Miss Walton smiled that patient smile he remembered so well, and looked directly at him, apparently amused. 'It is a question of common sense, I fear,' he concluded.

'Well, Mr Moncrieff, I can understand how it may seem so to a layman like yourself. But, you see, not only the lines are involved. The shape and form of the hand, indeed many other markers visible and invisible, latent as it were, also act as an indication of character. It is true that someone truly perceptive would make a lot of the external signs. And yet, isn't phrenology based upon similar principles? And it is now accepted not only by science, but also by the great powers—I know for a fact that the police at Scotland Yard take the shape and form of the skull as believable indicators not only of present character, but even of future predictions of criminal behaviour.'

Sam felt defeated.

'I'm sure you are right, Miss Walton.'

'Samuel, would you mind fetching something from my study?' Charles cut in.

'Of course, uncle.'

'You will find it on my secretary desk, a red leather case. If you would be so kind as to get it.'

He obediently left the room.

Who was this woman? What was she doing here?

On the commode in the hall he saw a little square of paper on the silver card tray. He picked it up. It said simply: 'Miss Helena Walton-Cisneros. Medium. Palmistry. By Appointment Only' followed by an address. He put it in his pocket and entered the study. On the secretary desk he found the red leather case. Sam felt a burning desire to see what was going on; he hated to break Charles's confidence, but he was unable to resist.

There were a few items inside: a handwritten copy of a family tree; a couple of cuttings from the *Norfolk Daily Standard*, yellow and frail; a few old photographs. The photographs were beautiful and dark; they captured to perfection the eerie, haunting loneliness that always made him think of the flatlands, of the Broads, as home.

He inspected the cuttings. They reported the disappearance of three sisters twenty years before, in 1881. He was little surprised to read their name: Matthews. Curiosity flared in him with renewed intensity.

He came out into the hall, his heart thumping, and almost collided with Charles.

'Sorry. Was I too long?'

'Not at all! Look, I hope you don't mind, but Lady Matthews and Miss Walton would prefer to continue their business in private. I will drop this off with them, and will join you in the library in due course.'

'I'll ring for some coffee.'

'An excellent idea.'

Charles joined him almost at once, but didn't talk, preferring to busy himself with the weekly copy of *Light*. This gave Sam time to reflect on what was going on. After some time had passed, Mrs Brown entered to announce that Miss Walton was leaving. Lady Matthews, apparently, had just done so, asking Mrs Brown to convey her regards to Mr Bale. Charles didn't look hurt.

'She is a very strange woman, Sam, a very strange woman indeed. Let us see Miss Walton out.'

They went into the hall and found Miss Walton putting on her gloves. Sam wasn't surprised to see that the red leather case had been intended for her.

'Thank you very much, Mr Bale. Most generous of you.'

'Not at all, not at all. Miss Walton, if you would be so kind as to wait for a minute, I would like to give you some of our reading material.'

'What a charming offer.'

Sam thought he detected a hint of mockery in her voice, but Charles went into the library beaming. It was now or never.

'I don't know what you're doing here, Miss Walton, if that is your name. But I should advise you to be careful: I don't know Lady Matthews very well, but I won't allow anyone to harm my uncle in any way.'

She smiled her dark, knowing smile.

'As usual, you are missing the plot wildly, Mr Moncrieff. Perhaps you have a natural gift for doing that.'

Confused by the answer, he did not have time to formulate any reply: Charles was coming out of the library.

'Please allow me to express once again our interest in your joining the Holborn Circle.'

Miss Walton laughed heartily.

'I am sorry, Mr Bale, but as I explained in my letter, it is out of the question. I prefer to make my own way.'

'But a young and talented woman, without the protection of a Spiritualist circle! It is unheard of!' Charles protested, half in jest. Miss Walton smiled.

'Many unheard-of things are already happening, Mr Bale. The twentieth century will belong to us, I'm sure of it.'

'You mean to Spiritualism, my dear?'

'Oh yes, that too. Spiritualism will be relevant, in my opinion, as long as it continues to find a common interest with the political reforms that this country needs.' Sam wondered if the young woman was a suffragette, and hoped not: Charles could not abide them. 'But I mean women, Mr Bale. The twentieth century will belong to women.'

Yes, a suffragette!

Evidently wishing to change the topic, Charles blurted out, 'Sam, listen: Lady Matthews has invited Miss Walton to her country house in a month's time, and she has been kind enough to extend the invitation to us.'

Sam murmured how nice that would be; Miss Walton, already at the door, looked particularly vexed at the idea of his going. Civil farewells were at last exchanged, and she was gone. At last he had solved the young woman's riddle: Helena Walton was almost surely a thief, and quite probably a confidence artist.

Sam put his hand to his pocket, to her card. He had the intuition that he and Miss Walton would meet again before the month was up.

Some days passed. Charles was sitting by his desk writing a letter. Its purpose was that of distinguishing The New Occultist Defence League from the London Spiritualist Alliance, with which they had a minor feud involving the virtues and follies of Mesmerism. The London Spiritualist Alliance swore by the practice; The New Occultist Defence League, following a more modern approach, insisted that, in the long decades in which the so-called science had been active, there had not been real scientific proof of any kind as to its benefits, and therefore the label of 'science' ought to be removed from it once and for all. Unfortunately, the Manchester newspaper he was writing to, *Two Worlds*, seemed to have busied itself with muddying this issue, on occasion attributing the sayings and doctrines of one group to the other. The matter was a serious one, not to be taken lightly. A number of important clarifications needed to be made.

Sam was trying to read, but wasn't in the mood. Eventually he spoke:

'Charles, I'm curious: Helena Walton.'

'Yes? What?' Charles seemed a little too vague when he looked up from the angry letter he was penning.

'The young woman you introduced to Lady Matthews. What kind of business brought them together? I was just wondering, why did they meet *here*?'

'It is no mystery: I simply acted as mediator, knowing both parties. You know me, Sam: I like to lend a hand wherever possible.'

'That's to your credit, of course.'

It was clear he would not get more information from Charles. Should he press his uncle? Sam could sense that there was more to the connection with Lady Matthews, a story of some sort. He had the vague recollection of his uncle collaborating with some titled lady in some enterprise years back. He did not recollect the particulars and, in any case, the notion was odd, even fanciful—their part of the world was farming country. But he had remembered visiting a place, a kind of factory by the coast, with a large arm pumping in and out of the North Sea. He had a distinct recollection of his tiny hand engulfed in Charles's, a small chubby child with short pantaloons standing next to the older man. His uncle's partner had been a lady of great wealth; could it have been their reclusive neighbour? The adventure, whatever it was, probably connected with the new fashion for steam power, had not prospered, and Sam had not been back at that spot in decades.

But, far from the old lady, it was the younger woman who intrigued him and, he eventually came to realise, who could provide him with the information he craved.

That afternoon Sam went to visit John Woodbury, paying a long-overdue visit to the old man's newly refurbished establishment in Cecil Court. *The Little Haunted Bookshop* specialised in books on Spiritualism, psychic research and its related sciences, as well as bewildering phenomena in all their possible manifestations. It also boasted a little printing press in the back, from which some small pamphlets condemning Spiritualist fraud had been published.

Sam found Mr Woodbury writing notes in a thick dusty ledger.

'My friend! What a welcome sight!'

Woodbury insisted in giving him a tour of the cramped

premises. Once Theosophy, Magnetism, Clairvoyance, Psychology, Mesmerism, Phrenology, Psychical Research, Astrology, Spiritism, Spirit Communication, Phonography, Agnosticism and the inevitable Vegetarianism had been dealt with, Woodbury insisted on showing him the latest book arrivals, among them *Towards a Science of Immortality: Heat-Death of the Sun, and a New Dawn for Mankind*, the lengthily titled monograph by none other than Count Maximilian Justus von Daniken Bévcar. Sam found himself compelled to buy a copy.

Mr Woodbury intrigued him. He was a genuinely zealous prosecutor of tricksters and fakes, who seemed to have many other interests outside of his work for the SPR. Once the business was done of admiring and interesting himself—as much as he was capable—in everything he was shown, Sam asked Woodbury if he knew the mysterious Miss Walton. Woodbury smiled oddly, a gesture Sam refused to read much into as he drank the cup of tea that the older man had prepared for him. Nonetheless, he seemed happy to respond:

'She has gained the reputation of being a "respectable vessel" for communicating with the shadows. She is a serious young woman, the granddaughter of Ovid Walton.'

'The classical scholar?'

'Exactly. Miss Walton is educated—the last thing one would expect in a medium, if you ask me.' Or in a *woman*, Sam thought he meant.

'I see.'

'She studied at Girton, by all accounts with the full support of her grandfather. Afterwards she trained briefly in one of the London hospitals, I think.'

'She trained as a nurse? Nothing odd in that!'

Woodbury smiled his crooked smile again, full of square teeth.

'Oh no, my friend. The *woman* trained to be a *doctor*, of all things!'

'Is she a doctor, then?' Sam refused to be scandalised by the notion; this was the twentieth century.

'She was expelled from her studies. A little bit of a scandal, if you ask me, although I can't remember the particulars right now…'

That was all the old man was prepared to share, it seemed.

That night Sam was feeling particularly restless, and he decided to go out for a drive around the city to clear his thoughts. His new motorcar had proved an adequate distraction, as the delicate machine seemed to need a lot of care even to perform its minimal duties. Charles, of course, did not approve of cars, feeling that the hubbub they created was distasteful to the spirits.

Before Sam knew what he was doing he found himself crossing the Western Bridge in the direction of the Waterloo Variety, where he sat in the empty bar while a performance was taking place, listening to the cackling laughter. A well-known voice sounded at his back.

'Sam!' Frederick Edgington had appeared out of nowhere. His presence was not particularly desired at that moment. However, Sam had to admit that the friendly face calmed him a little. 'What are you doing here, tonight of all nights? Look, it's not a good day to be seen here... There's been some bad business at the back!'

That was exactly what he didn't need: the gossip; all the rottenness of illicit relations between cabinet members and second-rate actresses.

'I'm collecting all the chaps together quietly, and we'll remove ourselves to the Advancement for the Century Society dinner in Pall Mall. A bunch of us were going anyway, hence the tails,' Frederick explained, showing off his impeccably stylish outfit.

'Do you want me to come?' Sam was feeling rather pathetic. He resented himself; he resented Helena Walton: the woman didn't seem to have any intention of vacating his head. Jim was, as usual, hovering behind Freddy, and Sam had the notion, not for the first time, that Viola's cousin was keeping an eye on him. What on earth was Jim doing in London, anyway? He was getting quite bored of the young man's presence. At some point, the tacit agreement not to mention the river incident would be abandoned, and they were going to have a fight. Sam almost wished it would be tonight. At Oxford, Sam had been something of a boxing hero; he still boasted a scar over his left eye that some women found darkly attractive. Out of all his opponents, one stood out, a strong Hungarian, the son of a baron, who had possessed a particularly devilish right arm. He had almost knocked him senseless once, the fiend.

'Sam? The dinner? You may find it interesting—it is in honour of the man of the moment, Count Bévcar!'

Of course, the ubiquitous Bévcar. Sam now had a copy of the Count's book by his bed, although he had made no attempt to start reading it.

He finished his glass of champagne, the fifth—or was it the sixth?—at a gulp.

'Why is he such a popular fellow?' he asked.

'Wouldn't you be if you promised eternal life, resurrection, putting your soul into some younger, more able body?'

Sam's interest was suddenly piqued.

'And how on earth can he do that?'

'Ancient shamanistic techniques. Transmutation! What would you say of having the late Queen's soul transplanted into another body? Or perhaps bringing Albert back?'

Sam had read about shamanism in college, and knew of its dark pursuits. Freddy was starting to look impatient. And Jim kept looking intently at him.

'Look, my friend, I was trying to avoid telling you, but… the truth is that the police will be here any minute, old man! This place is about to explode! Someone has been attacked, one of the theatre workers! He might not survive, the poor fellow… No one has said anything yet—they do not want to provoke a stampede—but the police are on their way.' Freddy's tone while he explained all this was conspiratorial, not devoid of excitement. He grabbed Sam firmly by the shoulder and ushered him into the foyer, where a group of young men clad in expensive dinner jackets was headed for the main entrance, leaving those less in the know to deal with the forthcoming upheaval. By now Sam felt too drunk to drive, but Jim sat obligingly in the driver's seat. A couple of police vans were arriving at that moment, and there was a bit of a commotion by the door of the Waterloo. But they were safe. Men like them usually were, Sam mused, hating the thought. Someone put a flask into his hand and he drank a gulp of warm liquid that tasted like watery rum.

They drove through the winding streets, which kept twisting and twisting, until they reached the club. The bronze plaque on the doorjamb showed a star surrounded by a circle, a sign that with a burst of alcoholic lucidity Sam recognised as the sun. The plaque read: THE TRUE DAWN. Where had he heard that name before? He remembered: it was one of London's many Spiritualist circles, one that had adopted Bévcar as their leader and guide.

He entered the building with the others and followed them towards a set of dining rooms at the back of the first floor. Everyone was huddled in the vast rectangular ballroom, decorated with fake Egyptian idols and elaborate charms, exaggerated symbols of fertility and rebirth. Someone put yet another drink into his hand. The sickly-sweet taste brought him back to his senses a little, and he recognised several people of consequence partaking in the frivolities: politicians, famous physicians, even a poet he had once admired, generals, businessmen, aristocrats... It seemed that the whole of London was in attendance. What were these men doing, surrounding themselves with these false symbols of power? He knew that some of them had barely a month ago accompanied the Queen's coffin through the London streets. These men already possessed everything, but they still wanted more: more power, more influence, more champagne, more women. It made him sick.

The room was decorated with banners depicting a coat of arms, and Sam moved to inspect it in more detail: a wolf standing over a deer, overgrown reeds, a fungus emerging from it in the shape of a star. The wolf was licking the puddle of blood rather than eating its prey, which seemed significant somehow. Sam knew that in some cultures drinking blood was the equivalent to ingesting the heart or the brain, two practices connected with the consumption of the vital impulse, of the energy that animates the creature.

Some faint clapping filled the room, and everyone turned in its direction. The clash of a gong invited those present to silence.

'And now, the festivities start,' someone in passing, Freddy, whispered wetly into his ear.

The butler saluted the peers, generals and majors, the chief superintendent of Scotland Yard, and the rest of the gentlemen present, inviting them to gather around. The men started to move noiselessly, and only then did Sam notice it: a huge circle carved on the wooden floor, with a maze pattern inside it. Once everyone was disposed around it, two servants entered carrying a rug, which they put on the floor and unrolled. It was also circular, and white. The new electric lights were dimmed. A servant in Cossack dress came in, and carefully placed a cushion at the centre of the circle. He also brought out a cage with a sparrow in it, and then a cat, asleep in his arms, or so Sam thought. It took him a few seconds to realise the animal was dead.

Another clash of the gong preceded the arrival of a man. To the dismay of those present, it was not Bévcar. He was wearing a red Eastern coat, and a necklace of bright yellow daisies. He sat cross-legged on the white pillow, rolled his eyes back, and began his chant. All of a sudden the previously dead cat stood clumsily on his two back legs, utterly terrified. Sam didn't understand what had happened, until he noticed the sparrow unmoving.

Some minutes later the man began the chant anew, and this time it was a far more complex sound. The cat fell down once again, and the bird resurrected, as if on cue, convulsing dementedly, hitting itself against the little metal bars, leaving a thread of blood and a flurry of brown feathers.

Sam would later think that he had witnessed a trick, some collective hallucination, a well-orchestrated illusion. Those poor animals had been used as puppets for their fun. The greenish light that had emanated from the two creatures had brought something to mind; he could not remember exactly what. But he had seen that strange glow before.

One thing he wondered: if the force they had just witnessed was real, who could have access to it, and to what ends? And what was Bévcar's role in all this?

The unnerving demonstration over, Sam left without saying goodbye to Jim, or Freddy, whom he had lost long ago among the many groups of conspirators. He made his way back through empty corridors, shoes clicking against the marble floor, and got out into the frosty night still hearing the clamour behind him, the loud cheers and the standing ovation.

Outside, Sam was shaking with fear. What had just happened? Exhausted, he bent down and vomited copiously on the pavement. He climbed back into his car, and sat for a moment, holding his arms against the cold. After a few seconds he drove off, allowing the streets to guide him.

The machine took him into a shadowy London he barely recognised. It was a landscape where the shapes of the buildings and their soft corners seemed to be composed of the fog itself, with narrow gaps between the dimly lit labyrinthine alleys; the city a treacherous and intricate map of little rows put together like spider webs. Streets and avenues were full of people getting in and out of horse-drawn omnibuses that stopped where they pleased, men pushing carts after the day of business, people getting into the Underground. Unbearable. Sam manoeuvred without stopping until he reached emptier areas away from the madding crowd, even if they seemed to him imbued with that same dismal aura of decay and darkness.

He was still shivering after the events of the evening. The buildings blurred into one another, formless shadows, strangely unreal. Through the fog they looked as if they belonged to another plane of existence, and he was only getting an unfocused vision of them through distant ages and times. Dung and brick and mortar mixed with the sweat and blood of men and women to compose those thoroughfares, and Sam had the strange fancy that he had entered onto some kind of stage set, put together by the men from the dinner he had just abandoned. He was aware of the contradictory energies that floated around him: the siren chants of the nightclubs, the obscure little alleyways, the secret taverns; the city as an enormous living god-like animal deciding the fate of each one of its subjects.

He passed street lamp after street lamp, sometimes

glimpsing a figure standing in the cones of light, and thought he saw him again, creeping amongst the shadows: the huge beggar that Charles had been scared of all those weeks back. But it probably wasn't him; all those poor souls who descended upon the capital looked very much the same, Sam thought. The little lights from the lamps soon gave way to vast dark areas where street fires multiplied. These only illuminated a small circle around them, next to which sat the dark. They might give a little warmth to the men who stood next to them, but those fires didn't give any protection against the shadows. London possessed its own darkness, a darkness it was impossible to pierce. Sam shivered as his motorcar advanced much too slowly through this forgotten landscape which pretended to be a city.

Finally back home, a light supper awaited him on the stove, and some dry sherry had been decanted, which he drank avidly. He tried to read a little, but wasn't in the mood.

London was like a labyrinth, Sam thought, because it had been built by men with secrets, double lives, unspeakable desires. Sam, and others like him, would change all that, making sure the future was bright, void of duplicity. They would transform the world into a lighter place, crisp and clean. Those men were doing the opposite, refusing to give way, trying to cling to an outmoded way of life. He expected the twentieth century to dispel their long shadows once and for all, to be the century of Light.

Bring back Victoria, or Albert? He couldn't think of a more ghastly notion. They belonged to the past, and they had to remain there. Sam preferred to look into the future.

CHAPTER FOUR

Downstairs, the sumptuous smells of a country breakfast awaited: sausages, pork pie, bread, ham, pickles. The Gibbet Inn had been built, as its name indicated, to host the crowds who came all the way to see the corpses of criminals, left to rot inside the iron cages at the crossroads just a bit further from the house.

The journey into Norfolk had been tiring. Helena was trying to cover as much ground as possible before the visit to Lady Matthews's estate later in the month. That part of the county had proved further away than she had expected, and she had been forced to stop for the night. It had been a sensible decision, both to allow herself some hours of much-needed rest, but also to think and process her findings before going back to town, where her other cases awaited.

The previous night the landlady had shown her to her room,

a little place with a window overlooking a never-ending field, a bed too big for the space available but with a pretty if faded eiderdown, an all-purpose table with its chair, and a washstand.

Helena was still shaken by the experiences of the day. She wrote for a while, and eventually climbed into the bed to rest. But as soon as she was under the blankets, she found that she could not sleep, and kept turning right and left instead. She found herself thinking about the Tudor ruins, and the strange impression they had given her, a kind of morbid feeling, of darkness descending. She started shivering. Some instinct told her that the place possessed some hidden danger. The idea of the children playing there was ghastly; but children did play in ruins all the time.

Where was this coming from? She was not a squeamish person, and she had seen her fair number of ruined places. But these ruins were different. It was as if some cloud had descended over the building, conquering it all; a nothingness that had swallowed it up, transporting it to a realm of sadness and decay.

She tried to fix her mind on happier memories. Helena hadn't been to Norfolk for a while, but she remembered how they used to come all the way up here sometimes, noisy groups of friends renting a pony and cart to go skating in the flooded fens, an occupation Girton girls were fond of whenever there had been a week-long frost. She was always amazed at the local boys, the way they gathered speed over those flat mirrors. The fenmen also came down to town in their skates sometimes, following the frozen river, their long hair reaching their shoulders. Once, a fenman was brought down to teach the girls from Newnham how to skate, and some of the Girton girls also went over. Suddenly, they found themselves surrounded by vicars, reverends, even a couple of bishops. She soon cleared the little mystery up; it was one of her first successes: it turned out that priests were the only men allowed to skate alongside the girls on that stretch of the river, and that the costume shop in Sidney Street had run out of religious attire that same week.

Of course, she had seen them, all those same fields, covered by tons of water, ghostly and deadly. For the swollen floods carried with them anything they could find in their way: stems, timber, mud, small dead animals, cattle, the remains of lump thatched cottages. Men, women, children. When the snow flood came down the river, it overflowed a little, its brownish waters lurking like marshland mist. The breaking of the ice was much more terrible. For the men, used to those great frozen expanses, could cover so many miles skating much faster than they could keep an eye on them.

She remembered that early case well, the missing child—how could she ever forget it?—and how the father had tried to make them all believe that the little one had been drowned in this manner. The village where it happened had been close to Huntingdon, just where the Ouse turns abruptly eastwards, and the father had no doubt got inspiration for his long tale out of the local ghost story. The ghost in question was that of a soldier stationed in Huntingdon in Napoleonic times, who fell in love with a girl who lived upstream. He went to visit her, skating over the river, as that year the frosts stayed longer. When the temperature rose he didn't notice. It was still bitterly cold. He was close to her house when the ice cracked and he fell into the water. It was said you could still see him sometimes, recognisable by his old-fashioned cassock, speeding over the river.

Soon after leaving Cambridge, the world had become open fields of tired green, and farming lands of darker soil, traversed by oily ditches. A solitary church, shooting up; a long dyke; fields of wheat, potato fields, busy in planting season. A plough led by a pair of horses in the distance, almost at the edge of her vision, a man labouring with difficulty behind it.

An artificial landscape this was, with its unmoving rivers, all those silent masses of water, like quiet pools covering dark secrets. She was always surprised that the coachmen knew the direction to take. For it all looked the same to her, north, south, east, west, with the horizon so flat, so deceptively clear. Even on light days the Fens never ceased to be a landscape of uncertainties. Would it be possible to get lost here? The answer was yes. For three bodies never to be recovered—that was certainly a much harder proposition.

As they left Cambridgeshire behind, the mist of the early morning rose above the ankle, much higher, and the spires of the churches started to appear and disappear as if in a dream, looking as ethereal as if they were made of the mist itself. She was heading towards the east coast, to a part of the county put together by villages founded in Saxon or Danish times, a heavily invaded part of the world, and therefore wary of strangers. That part of the county also prided themselves on their punts, and there was still duck, goose and plover catching. One of the pictures Lady Matthews had passed to her in London showed one of those primitive vessels.

The previous days it had taken her only a few hours to reach that haunted realm: the man-made inland lakes of the Broads, surrounded by reeds and thin lines of trees; the tall, elegant church towers, ruins at the mercy of the tides and the advancing seas, so many of them finally claimed, with so many ghostly bells that chimed because they had forgotten they did not exist any longer. There, the thatched roofs of the huts changed from the saw sedge to the common Norfolk reed, with its final ornamentation a pattern indicating the particular thatcher who had employed his artisanship. She had never seen that done anywhere but here.

Further away, she knew, the edge of the sea was hardly an edge, as both land and water refused to give way to one another. It was a space unsure of itself, a mixture of marshes and mudflats, and a capricious tideline. This was where it all started, where the three little girls had vanished, and Samuel Moncrieff had appeared. This was where she was heading.

*

Helena had found the little copse of ash trees, not much bigger than a miniature forest where children might play hide-and-seek and find each other after two seconds. She had been told that behind it was the meadow where the Tudor ruins stood; it had been clearly pointed out to her from a distance; the driver would not go anywhere near it.

She was sure that anyone, even the least perceptive person, would have noticed the light. Before she entered the copse it had possessed its normal fluidity. It wasn't a particularly pleasant or sunny day, but perfectly adequate for an afternoon stroll, with a breeze that now and then brought traces of sea air. The birds were chirping, and the copse was alive with that vibrating soul of the countryside, clearly present although discreetly and unobtrusively, the way nature tends to be. There but not there.

And then she came to the other end of the copse and out into the meadow.

Before she did so, Helena noticed something odd: the ash-like substance. It was similar to the black sticky residue that floats in the air after a fire; but it was pallid, white, and she had no idea where it came from, how to account for it. She noticed it gradually, and when she came out the other end she realised that the whole meadow was covered in it; though, to tell the truth, it was not exactly covered, for the way it floated around her made her think for a moment that she had stepped into a snow bubble.

Helena asked herself a simple question: was it possible to be *scared* of *light*?

For the light had changed its quality somehow; it had become denser, less fluid, more leaden with white, less transparent. The best comparison she could think of was doing a watercolour sketch, that moment when the sky is worked and, by mistake, you dip your brush in the white paint and add it to the light and fluid water-and-blue mixture. It suddenly acquires density, weight, becomes opaque. Later on, when the moment came to put all of it in writing, that was how she came to explain it. Imagine, she would write, that happening to light. Imbued in this odd substance, bathed by a *wrong* kind of light, the meadow felt a little claustrophobic, for lack of a better word.

And now, the ruins.

It was a Tudor manor, or what remained of it, built and abandoned a long time ago. It had all happened many years before, all that history which could be read in those remaining walls: the rapid ascent of the family fortunes, the impressive building in the Norfolk countryside. The rise and fall of everything, the lost luck. And afterwards, last of all, the fire: licking those walls, eating up the tapestries, blackening the Great Hall forever. She could imagine it all. As well as the collapsed ceiling, most of the eastern wing was gone. She slowly made her way into the ruin.

Despite the blackened walls in the Great Hall she could inspect the carvings. Three sirens, one playing the flute, one playing the lute, the third one holding something in her hands, a rock, perhaps. It was an odd image to have put in there. In the old days people preferred to decorate their lavish rooms with scenes from the Bible, in this part of the country perhaps with some discreet Marian concession. But there they were anyway, three sirens, presumably beckoning men to die in the dark embrace of the North Sea.

Most of the structure remained, but the ceiling was mostly gone. Instead, the visitor got a canopy of overgrown tree branches, and the leaden sky of the region. Dirt and stones covered the floor, and the remaining walls and panels, even the odd remaining door, were incredibly mouldy. Helena put her hand to one, and she found it warm and soft to the touch; it felt to her like a living thing, for it seemed that it was probably always warm, as if time had somehow stopped here. Perhaps the floating white-like ash substance was designed to do exactly that: stop time, condense it. As if time itself had infused the fungi with an energy that the prodigious decay could not abate.

But it was in no way a positive energy; it was negative, dark, *wicked*.

She noticed the silence, for no bird could be heard. And where had the breeze gone that should have moved the canopy above her head? The branches she saw, forming a substitute, withering ceiling, were oddly still. And yet she knew that, were she to come out the other side of the copse and move away from the house, she would feel the wind again, freshening up her face.

Helena thought she had seen jackdaws as well—why were they so silent? Why were they acting as if they were mere shadows of their brothers and sisters on the other side of the copse? *Were they shadows of their brothers and sisters?*

The only audible sound was a faint murmur of water, waves splashing and breaking in foaming splendour. Where did it come from? Completely disorientated for a second, something that didn't happen to her often, she could not figure out which direction the sea was, or how far away. She had thought that she had come farther from it, not closer, when leaving the village. To say that she was confused would be to understate the obvious: Helena knew where she was; but then, she was lost also. Or rather she *felt* lost.

As soon as she realised this, a sense of dread took hold of her, as if her being lost were not a temporary state, but one that threatened to carry on forever.

Then she thought of them, those three little girls, lost the same year that Samuel Moncrieff had appeared, seemingly out of nowhere. And she tried to imagine them in that horrid place, in those ruins where, according to the records, they had been so fond of playing.

The story ran as follows: In 1881 the three Matthews sisters, Maud, Alice and Flora, mysteriously vanished during a hunting weekend at their father's newly built manor house in east Norfolk. The search that followed the disappearance centred on this new building, with its peculiarities of construction (the eccentric architect had later jumped from a tower), and also took in the members of the hunting party, the Broads' quicksands and marshy beaches. Downham Market Horse Fair had just taken place—true, it was on the other side of the county, but nonetheless it had brought in gypsies from all over the land, crisscrossing the Fens, raising fears that the girls had been kidnapped.

Helena had flinched when she had read this, wondered what her great-grandmother, a proud and beautiful Andalusian Roma who married an aristocratic landowner, would have made of reading something so daringly expressed by a reckless newspaper.

Whatever had happened to Maud, Alice and Flora, the truth of the matter was that nothing was ever found. The girls were never seen again. Lord Matthews died shortly after. Their stepmother, the new Lady Matthews, became a recluse. A distant cousin from an impoverished line of the family, much younger than Lord Matthews, and going from being the children's governess to being their stepmother, some malicious minds had seen foul play at work, and she had been a suspect for some time. In the end they could not charge her with anything, so the matter was dropped. But it did not surprise Helena to find out that her line of the family, although as poor as a church mouse, in fact used to own the estate before losing it to an entail.

That was the tale.

Once upon a time, three little girls, gone.

Helena always did this before taking on any case: making sure that everything matched the version of events that she had been given, not taking any story at face value. Putting the story together took her the best part of a morning in the Round Reading Room, working piecemeal from twenty-year-old tomes of bound county newspapers, a copy of Debrett's, Lord Matthews's obituary in *The Times*, and a couple of the county parish gazettes. Accessing Scotland Yard's records office had been harder to achieve, but eventually she had got there as well. According to the official investigation, Lady Matthews had been romantically involved with one of Sir Malcolm's friends. None other than the architect of the new abbey.

The tale Helena had put together had left her strangely unhappy. It had the odd flavour of a story already known, the feeling of a nightmarish fairy tale she had heard long back. Something told her that there would be no happy ending here.

In a few weeks, Lady Matthews and her companion, Mrs Ashby, would open their house to some practitioners of the Spiritualist religion in order to conduct a number of séances. And, before that, some meetings would take place in London, where mediums, clairvoyants, the Matthews family and their friends, would get together in the pursuit of the truth.

During her brief encounter with Lady Matthews in Charles Bale's house, Helena had made sure that the old lady understood everything about her, and which kind of answers she would bring to the table.

'May I ask a question, Miss Walton? How did you come to do what you do?' the old lady had asked.

'A child disappeared.'

Lady Matthews frowned.

'May I ask what happened, exactly?'

'A child lost in the Fens.'

'I see; that disorientating, flat place. Easier to get lost there than in the labyrinth of this wretched city, I'm sure.'

'Then I'm sure that you understand exactly what the problem was, Lady Matthews. But he hadn't just got lost, mind you. I can assure you the fairies didn't spirit him away.'

The older woman did not reply, although she sat upright with a jolt. 'I have to be honest: the reason why I found him before the police did utterly escapes me,' Helena continued. 'His father's rage was all too obvious, as was the jealousy with which the man hovered around his wife, as were the little, mean, creative ways in which he punished her. To me, it was painfully obvious that he would use the most defenceless creature to get back at her.'

'Did you find the boy? Was he alive?'

'Yes, I found the child alive. Quite nearby, in fact, on the outskirts of Newmarket, hidden in a derelict hut where horses had been stabled, badly. That little building had seen a lot of suffering.'

'And the mediumship?'

She looked at Lady Matthews intently. She did not usually share this kind of information with her clients. But something told her that Lady Matthews was not just any client, and that she would not be placated by a rebuff. Eventually, she said:

'You must understand that this is strictly confidential. The situation complicated itself. The county papers got involved, and I was forced to pretend that I possessed occult mediumistic powers. It seemed easier for people to believe that I had found the child with some hocus-pocus or other, rather than imagining that a woman was capable of using her brains. It was entirely unavoidable, and if there is a God somewhere, he can attest that it wasn't my intention to mislead anyone. It all happened in the most natural manner: the mother of the missing child presented the solution of the case to the police as the result of some young lady having a "dream", or a "vision", that led her to the hut where the poor child had been hidden by his own father. And I saw it then: the policemen's glances at one another. Where previously there had been suspicion, disbelief, demands for an explanation, now everything fitted into its place in their poor little overworked brains. Let it be so, I thought; I would have them believe anything they wanted to believe, if only the child could be found, the mystery solved, the father sent to jail, the mother and her son reunited before something more dreadful happened.'

'I see.'

'It did cost me my studies. I was summarily expelled.'

Silence hung in the air.

'Psychology, Lady Matthews, the study of the mind. I constantly deal with the same human traits—deceit, fabrication, duplicitousness—and their obvious result: the suffering of the most innocent of creatures for other people's selfish purposes.'

'That is a very sad way of looking at the world,' the older woman ventured.

'It is also frighteningly accurate.'

Lady Matthews didn't reply. She simply allowed Helena to carry on talking.

'Afterwards, I could not deny the usefulness of what had happened. And now, tell me: do you despise me for pretending to have supernatural powers? I assure you I hardly ever request that people come to see me and have their palm read, and I absolutely refuse to "do" séances. In fact, I cannot help you, Lady Matthews, in the way that Mrs Ashby, and perhaps even Mr Bale, assume I would. No, I cannot communicate with ghosts; I don't have a "spirit guide" at my command. However, I can assure you people get results from my efforts, albeit through methods different from those they are expecting. They get to know the truth.'

'So you don't believe in ghosts?'

'I believe in physical proof, and as far as the supernatural is concerned, no one has been able to provide me with that, at least not yet.'

'We were fully aware of the situation, Miss Walton. And you may know that we have tried many... unusual means to get to the bottom of this over the years. However, your particular... double sensibility on the affair is precisely what we are looking for. This sad business requires more open-mindedness than usual...'

'I understand.'

'Correct me if I am wrong,' the old lady continued, 'but the main purpose of what you do is to demonstrate that our daily interactions are more determined by what people hide and don't say, or even what they don't know about themselves, than by what gently simmers on the surface—as if every one of us was in possession of a parallel existence that has somehow to be unmasked.'

'Yes... I believe so. I would have never put it in those words, but I guess that is right. Finding the truth beneath the surface.'

'But then, it is not *that* simple, is it? What *is* the truth?'

'What do you mean? The truth is the truth.'

'Really? What we count as reality might simply not be there in the first place. Different people tell stories in different ways; family stories are usually reshaped to conform to the rules of society—and the stories we tell our children.' Lady Matthews laughed sadly. 'How can we feed them all that rubbish, fairyland and all that?'

'You think there is more to the children's disappearance than foul play?'

'I know that there is more to the children's disappearance than foul play, yes.'

For a fleeting moment, alone in the Round Reading Room days after their conversation, Helena had believed her. But there was something else, she thought. It happened to her often, as soon as she immersed herself in a story; some instinct flourished, a missing piece she could almost see hanging in mid-air, a part of the puzzle that she knew would shed light over some dark corner. She was sure there was something else and, whatever it was, it was letting Lady Matthews's guilt show.

She found it, eventually, perusing records and deeds of ownership. Lady Matthews and her neighbour Charles Bale had been partners in a failed business, a kind of extraction agreement on the Norfolk coast. It wasn't exactly clear what they were extracting and it seemed void of connection to the case at hand. It gave Helena a further perspective, nonetheless, of the kind of trusting relationship between Bale and the old dame, if after failing at a business together they were still good friends. Of course, they could have been complicit in keeping quiet about something related to the issue, some misdeed. One thing was true: she had asked Lady Matthews for as much background as possible, and she had failed to mention the extraction business altogether. In Helena's experience, that kind of behaviour pointed at one thing only: guilt.

She also unearthed some oddities connected to the case at hand: Samuel Moncrieff had been born in the year of the girl's vanishings, or at least 'found'. For Helena had not been able to find any record of his birth. True, perhaps his birth certificate was still waiting to be discovered somewhere or other. She suspected he might have been abandoned somewhere in the estate, and wondered where it could have been. Perhaps in the ruins of the Tudor house?

During her inspection of the ruins, she had tried to imagine those three little girls playing there. She wondered if the dirt had stained their silk slippers, the hems of their skirts. They obviously had to be very clever children, as a certain amount of care needed to be exercised if they were to avoid being caught. Going to the ruined manor was strictly forbidden, or so Lady Matthews had insisted. They probably had needed to learn to keep clear of the broken panelled windows as well, the ruined glass sharp as carving knives. They had to learn it all again, how to walk, how to move quietly through those rooms, like silent ghosts, those children. They had to learn to pretend and to lie; perhaps learn to disappear.

On the left-hand side of the fireplace a few steps led down into a back garden. A broken door hung open, allowing a bit of light to enter. It smelled different there, of recently cut grass, of woodsmoke, of life; or perhaps the intense smells of the deepest forests, three times magnified.

Three is a magical number, and they were three.

Helena felt observed. It was the quiet secrecy, and the light, as if the house itself was looking back at her.

And then she entered the room, whose walls would later be revealed to have witnessed such portents.

There she could feel the haunting of the place at its fullest. The room looked like an image in a daguerreotype, and it felt like a *wrong* room, a mirror image of another. She was reminded of the frozen fens, of skating over those colossal mirrors the fields turned into after a few days of frost. One of her Cambridge friends had said something to her that now she felt was truly perceptive: that it looked sometimes as if the skaters, speeding in that manner so typical of the fenland, were doing so followed at all times by their head-down doubles, an inverted mirror realm. That room was like an image as well. Here, it was as if the real room in the real house in the real world had been left behind, and she had crossed some kind of boundary. The sudden burst of unmoving time was off-putting; it revealed something oddly untrue about the place.

Helena swallowed a gasp when she saw that she was not alone.

The woman, for it was obviously a woman, although she was wearing trousers, was standing with her back to her, her face deep in one of the corners, as if she were a child chastised by a stern teacher. The unnatural stance sent shivers through Helena's spine, for she had the idea that the woman was looking into the wall in such an odd manner as a way to avoid looking at the room.

Her clothes were in shreds and covered in dirt; her grey hair was uncombed and interlaced with everything imaginable—leaves, feathers, little sticks—as often happens when you sleep rough for a long time; there was an indeterminate greyness around her, around her clothes and her hair and her skin and her eyes. She must have sensed Helena's presence, as she started slowly turning, and she looked at her eventually, with such longing and sadness that Helena felt for the first time the enormity of the task ahead of her.

'Good afternoon,' Helena said.

The old woman didn't reply, but extended her arms and slowly stumbled in her direction. She noticed then a further oddity, for it was odd for an old woman to be holding a little rag doll, tattered and dirty.

'Do you live here?' she continued, for once she saw her fully it was obvious she was a beggar. The woman still did not reply, but Helena felt that might be the case, and mumbled an apology for disturbing her.

Then the woman opened her mouth.

She babbled for what seemed a long time, gesticulating and trying to explain something about the wall, from the way she insistently pointed at it. But Helena could make nothing of her strange sounds; she sounded exactly as if someone had cut out her tongue, although she had a tongue inside her mouth. She looked like a grown woman who had once known how to communicate, but had lost the ability to do so.

Helena was carrying an apple and a bit of bread and cheese, and this little bounty she offered. The old woman gathered it all and, with strange elegance, didn't put it into her mouth coarsely, like those less fortunate usually do when offered something. She found pockets somehow, crevices in her dirty clothes, put the food inside them, passed next to her, and was gone. Helena thought that the woman might despise her, the way she could not understand what she was trying to tell her, and that she was right to do so.

CHAPTER FIVE

The missing tern, the birdsong, all those vanishings had brought to her mind *other* vanishings.

Eliza had stumbled upon Eunice's article in a library in Manchester, which miraculously held a complete set of *The American Journal of Science and Arts*—libraries; losing access to them was one of the things that made her heart ache   and she had at once noticed the similarities with a much better-known experiment, performed three years later. By a man.

Coincidence, bad luck?

This made her curious—though a woman should never be curious, as everyone was fond of repeating. But it was too late for her, for she *was* curious; she had always been. *Curiouser and curiouser*. And so, she continued digging, meddling, learning, finding out... She discovered that Eunice Foote, the celebrated American female scientist, had not been able to present her paper on the circumstances affecting the heat of the sun's rays and carbonic acid at the 1856 meeting of the American Association for the Advancement of Science. A male colleague had done it for her. It hadn't been easy, but Eliza had managed to find a contemporary account of the occasion, from which she had copied some passages: *'Professor Henry then read a paper by Mrs Eunice Foote, prefacing it with a few words, to the effect that science was of no country and of no sex. The sphere of woman embraces not only the beautiful and the useful, but the true.'*

Eliza did not know if women *held* the truth; and who did, really? Did *the true* even exist? But she was incensed nonetheless, furious. And so, Eunice had become her new subject. Meanwhile there were other things to look forward to, of course; for very soon it would be spring, and she might catch a few dragonflies from the region, the *Aeshna isosceles*, which she had never before had the pleasure of seeing—if the elusive tern did not appear, they would have to do instead.

What really, truly infuriated her were the stories that these men of science insisted upon, bending certainties into whichever narrative they wanted to impose on the rest. Surely *they* had a duty not to be fanciful; what could they be thinking? The gentleman to whom Eunice's results were attributed—he seemed to have reached exactly the same conclusions, made exactly the same observations as the American, in another country and years after she published her paper—had insisted on a preternatural, almost mystical explanation for this energy that men so voraciously were consuming, sending the wrong message, as if announcing the arrival of a fake God, claiming that it was infinite, that it would never end, and that there would be no time of reckoning.

The sun digs the ore from our mines, he rolls the iron; he rivets the plates, he boils the water; he draws the train. He not only grows the cotton, but he spins the fibre and weaves the web. There is not a hammer raised, a wheel turned, or a shuttle thrown that is not raised, and turned, and thrown by the sun. His energy is poured freely into space, but our world is a halting place where this energy is conditioned. Here the Proteus works his spells.

Proteus? Spells? How *dared* this man of science imbue the Empire's ravenous need for consumption with such cosmic, fanciful notions? Worst of all, the passage conveniently forgot about all those men and women, all those children, who were the *real* force behind the building and rebuilding, which started each day with each new dawn. This man's 'metaphors', for lack of a better word, were deliberately forcing them into oblivion, conveniently rendering invisible all those who, with their hard toil, generated the energy that progress needed, demanded. In a way, Eliza thought, these stories were hiding the fact that, in order for voracious growth to continue, the rest of us were, in effect, sucking the energy out of them... their vital impulse. Their lives were mere particle of dust, needed to propel those of others. London, she knew, was consuming as much as 13,000,000 cubic feet of gas every night; and, in order to be lighted and heated, required the burning of 3,000,000 tons of coal per year. The results were all too well known: blackened skies, soot-covered buildings, filthy waterways and streets, and respiratory disease. And most of it falling on those poor souls who made it possible, who ended up chewing the toxic atmosphere with their daily bread. The Earth itself would soon be rendered uninhabitable for mankind—and all these men did was to look the other way, and pretend they were special, somehow predestined for progress.

How were they different from the charlatans, the penny-theatre magicians, the palm readers who traversed the roads of this forsaken county, disturbing true observations with the promise of a new dawn? Fake idols, all of them. It was clear that these 'scientists' were as versed in storytelling techniques as Mr Dickens had been, and too fond at times of creating fancies rather than presenting facts. Equally, she had also encountered many literary men who seemed well-versed in the scientific and mechanical branch of natures that most interested Eliza, and at times these men of letters were those who saw the metropolises of the Empire for what they really were: big-mouthed monsters intent on devouring it all, vomiting in return a sad melange of noxious gases, effluvia, soot, smoke and ash. One only had to read Dickens or Ruskin to see that these men understood the root of the problem all too well: the consumption of everything nature offered, and the damage done to agriculture and the landscape of places like the one she had retreated to, creating a never-ending cycle of chaos and an altered order that could have no good end.

But, was *that* what was happening here?

By now, Eliza had collected and compiled enough evidence: the measurable data, as well as the dreams of eerie greenish light that tainted the morning mist. And she knew, or at least suspected, that whatever was happening here needed the two strands of knowledge. But where to gift her findings? Who to share them with?

She had her own reasons to allow her curiosity to be courted by the two strands of knowledge: she needed to gather as much information as possible if she was going to be successful in her quest. It was an exercise in dispelling the shadows, no more and no less than that.

She might have been ten or twelve when it happened, on a morning that started like any other. She woke up, too early to jump out of bed, to the electricity of a summer storm. She remembered clearly that odd feeling. As if she weren't alone, and, at the same time, as if she were the most alone she would ever be.

So Eliza sat up in bed. And there it was, the oddity, a silhouette moving in the anteroom she used as a classroom, a strange clinking noise, like a delicate china tea set on a trolley;

or bells, perhaps, like those woven into the manes of funeral horses, black horses, ominous horses; little chinking noises that are deceptive in their childish simplicity—deep down you know they announce something terrible.

It was curious how, after all these years, the memory was as clear as a summer morning, as disturbing as *that* summer morning; shadows revealing themselves in plain daylight. She could hear the woodpigeons outside, endlessly chatting. That world belonged to them, that world of white, heavy light, in that indeterminate hour where dream and reality collide.

But she was a child, a curious one. So she got up and went in search of that sickly-sweet sound, and it revealed itself to be none other than she; she, *she!* The person Eliza most longed to see in the world—the woman she loved, mourned. And she looked like a porcelain doll, so beautiful she was.

And when she moved her head, the little bells sounded, here and there; and the distant memory of something else chiming rushed to her, something lost in the depths, a bracelet she thought, with silver amulets hanging from it— she remembered it then, her mother's bracelet, with its little charms, memories of her voyages. Her father had taken that bracelet, and it should go to her, and Eliza knew right there and then that she wanted it.

Was she gone now? She was. Eliza remembered not feeling scared, not exactly; she remembered thinking that if she could see the living, why not the dead? The logic of that early hour was the logic of dreams. She went back to bed, closed her eyes, tried to get back to sleep. When she woke up again to full morning, 'normal' light, it all felt like a distant scene, something that had happened aeons ago. For a long time Eliza did not know if she had dreamed it. The longing was so unbearable.

Did she think that her mother wanted to give her a 'warning', like ghosts traditionally were known to do? Almost immediately, her practical childhood mind rejected the idea. She was more comfortable thinking that there could be no explanation or reason for the presence of a dead woman in her anteroom, and perhaps the best strategy was not to adopt any strategy, not to look for explanations, omens. Accepting this was simple.

But she had started crying, still in bed. She remembered that. Shocked by the vision, she had not 'used' the chance offered to be with her mother. She should *not* have turned round, she should *not* have moved a single muscle, she should *not* have dismissed the portent and gone back to her sleepy bed. Eliza had the intuitive sense that she had made her mother disappear. And so, she would reflect years later, a knowledge, deep within her: the dead could not be summoned to perform parlour games on any given evening between nine and ten o'clock. They could not materialise, de-materialise, show themselves, sing, do tricks, do anything at our earthly command. The only means of communication was as Eliza experienced it then, that childhood morning, in a house in Lincoln. Then and there with no reason, no intention, no plan. Then and there, uninvited.

She was a strange child, for the next thing she did was to check that she was not feverish—she knew how to do that from very early on—and she knew that she did not feel bad, so there was no possible excuse, no physical reason that might explain this encounter, and if there were then it would be inside herself. Perhaps something was wrong with her brain. An error in the blood, hereditary and endemic. Chronic and incurable.

The rest of the day Eliza spent numb and unresponsive. She started to be aware little by little of the unnaturalness of the occurrence itself, of doubting her place in this plane of existence, a place to truly call her own in that darkened mirror, the real, grim world that she was condemned to inhabit without her mother. By dusk she had worked herself into a fever and she was anxious and terrified to go to bed— pure terror it was. The coldness of the many rooms that were closed to her at her guardian's home; the absence of her infamous father; her mother under the earth. She felt terribly alone. As people did when they knew a secret and there was no one to share it with. The most lonely she had ever felt.

Eliza did not tell anyone; would never tell anyone. What instincts she had: to act 'normal', even when feeling that she had failed and kept failing at doing so. What an instinct she had to survive!

The memory was still as fresh as a summer breeze. It had probably been that late summer storm, gathering electric currents around everything, making her see visions...

She did remember one thing, quite clearly, an image that had not abandoned her all these long years: how much the ghost of her mother had shivered. She must have been very cold.

The new morning brought a red sky laced with dark foreboding: wreck to the sailor, trouble to the land-dweller. The crimson would have been more welcome once the dusk had settled, with its nightly promise of shepherd's delight. At this early hour, however, it didn't foretell anything good. As soon as she set out for her pre-breakfast stroll, she had noticed it: a change in the weather. The east wind crashed against her face, and the light carried an unexpected winter gloom, just when the birds were already thinking about spring.

Walking on an ancient marsh causeway, carved here in the time of the Saxons, was a favourite pastime, the wet soil and unkempt reeds thriving with little winged creatures. It was reached through a holloway, a path settled into the earth long before the Saxons came, proof that rural folk had always been attracted to this bit of marshy land, even before it was safe to cross. At low tide the path was more felt than visible, all the way to Wicken Far End, the little island where the stones of the old church lay scattered. Further away was the fortress, a disused factory where steam engines had been manufactured decades back, a futile and doomed attempt to bring the region into the industrial age.

The wind had frightened away the mist. But still, that particular stretch of coast seemed always to possess a foggy quality. She never failed to notice how the light changed here, conferring gravity to everything. It felt more oppressive than usual today, and the expected birds all looked alien: the harriers, the snipe, the redshank. But where, she thought, where was the tern hiding?

The causeway seemed to be connecting her to something more than mere land: life itself, perhaps, for its existence afforded safe crossing.

A goshawk passed above her head. She remembered how hawks were granted free movement between this world and the next, and wondered which message the bird was taking to the beyond.

Then she saw it ahead of her: a formless shadow.

No, there was nothing. It had come and gone in a flash, and it seemed for a second that it had a human shape; but there was no one there, and she resumed her walking.

But someone had moved right ahead, she was sure now. Eliza advanced slowly, hardly making any noise. Yes, someone was moving capriciously among the reeds, stumbling in and out of her vision. The rustling of a skirt on the overgrown reeds.

Had a stranger fallen in the reed bed, perhaps? She ought to go and see.

The reverend had recently given a sermon about Guthlac, the Saxon saint who travelled deep into this land to found Crowland Abbey, and all the demons he had encountered in that expansive wilderness.

He had gone but a very little way when he saw a foul fiend coming over the field to meet him.

Eliza shivered. So many fanciful notions recently, she scolded herself. Better to keep her curiosity on this side of reality, forget her second notebook once and for all.

It was impossible. Her mother had found her. She always did. Could it be…?

The tide would turn soon enough, and all those faded greens and hard browns and marshy, reedy patches would get completely covered by the eerie, unmoving laden sea. Wicken Far End would be the only thing visible in the distance, surrounded by this deadly pool.

To tell the truth she was not even sure what she had seen, if the peculiar shape had been a trick of the light. She froze for a second. It could be, for it was definitely a woman. And she was trying to cross over. She thought she was looking in her direction, even if the vagueness of the light and the hour had made it difficult to know if she was seeing a face or a nape. Coming here, then, not going there.

She had to get to her, or she would drown. The thought snapped Eliza into action.

She stumbled over the reeds, crashing through the peaceful nature she had been seeking, and advanced in the general direction of where she thought she had seen her.

At last she got to the girl, for it was no more than a girl, much younger than her, fifteen or sixteen years old, lying face down on the ground, with flaxen hair and good enough clothes but no shoes, dirty and wet with mud and bits of weeds, as if she had come swimming all the way from Holland.

'And how am I supposed to get you home now?' Eliza asked, as much to herself as to the sleeping girl. She turned her over with an effort, and then saw that her eyes were open, although she was indeed unconscious. Or partially unconscious, as she responded at last, but slowly, hardly there, to Eliza's worried imprecations. It took some time, too much time, to sit her up, but then she swung her round somehow and the girl helped a little as she pushed her to her feet. The girl, in spite of her catatonic state, was capable of moving one foot after the other as she clung to her saviour.

Eliza's dress was filthy now, and creased. She wondered about the Hobbses, what they would say. But she couldn't have left the girl there, for she would surely have perished.

It was exhausting work, stumbling rather than walking

with her fortuitous cargo. When they reached the shore, the tide was gaining force, and lapping oily water already covered the place where the girl had been lying. They continued towards the little carstone cottage, and so worried was Eliza that she failed to see the peculiar greenish light that glowed heavily from the old church stones lying scattered in Wicken Far End, heaving like a beating heart.

AUTOMATIC WRITING DEMONSTRATION

LONDON, FEBRUARY 1901

MEDIUM: WILLIMINA LAWRENCE

Brief initial statement: Willimina Lawrence has arrived as Madame Florence's protégée from America. She is a young woman of singular talents. She offered this demonstration under the supervision of impartial witnesses. She claims that the spirit she was in contact with was that of the celebrated traveller Mrs Charlotte Waltraud. Mrs Waltraud disappeared under unexplained circumstances, while accompanying her husband Mr Tobias Waltraud on an expedition. This account contains details which Miss Lawrence could not in all conscience have known, and it has offered further clues as to the possible true nature of this most mysterious case.

His new bride will come in now, and will realise that the silence of the house is a false silence, now that her eyes are accustomed to the dust and the dark, to the rounded shadows, the nooks and corners, and can make out the abandoned spider webs, can see the stains on the dark wine carpet—chosen precisely for its ability to hide them.

I know about her uncontrollable emotions, the terror that flows and ebbs, as if her heart were skipping beats. I do not know how I know it. It is the same kind of certainty that I have about everything these days.

I know what he will do to her first. And what he will do to her eventually.

If she had made it this far, she would have seen the shadows, those uneven corners of blood and suffering. They are tainted, each and every one of them. It is a shame that she cannot feel them. Or perhaps, perhaps… What if she can see, feel? Then maybe she will leave. Before she makes it as far as this alcove. There is no escape from here. I have seen them all, coming in here tentatively, their hands, aged by housework, by suffering, uncertainly running over the wallpaper, some of them with their eyes shut, listening to the irregular beats of their unruly hearts. Here, it's already too late. Here is where death lives. Their deaths, my deaths.

They miss him; they don't feel him coming upon them, his eyes bulging and bloodshot, the poker held miraculously high over his head in those arms which will one day suffer from arthritis, the sweat and the saliva that he spits out with the effort mingling with that liquid which is brownish in this light instead of red, and which marks the end of the act and the curtain falling.

Run away, disappear! Don't become another heap of turned earth in our garden.

What are they doing now? Darkness in the library, the champagne pinching your tongue, the dull smell of the sempervivum.

Life.

They are living.

How can I see it? Why can I see it?

We were sitting in the kitchen, it seemed yesterday. Or like yesterday. Perhaps it was a decade back. Perhaps, perhaps… it was sometime in the future. No, Eliza was there, she was little. But I, I see it clearly as if it were yesterday. Married, and Eliza in my arms. In front of me, in front of her, this man from my new life, this man I don't really know smiles at me, at her, slightly lifting the corners of his mouth.

For the first time I understand what it is that annoys me about this house: I have never before lived among oil paintings, dark and gloomy, transmitting their lack of light to everything that surrounds them. I was not born for this, whereas he moves through his existence with the certainty of a snake charmer.

He was, or is, or will be, writing a book about our voyages. The Book. Capital 't', capital 'b'. Our future depends on it. When he finishes It—or has it happened already?—everything will be sorted out.

But what if it is not like that? What if nothing happens that we are expecting to happen? Maybe we will have to stay trapped here forever, between these walls, walking down the same corridors, climbing the same staircases covered in hairs, up and down, up and down, meeting your desiccated relatives in all the corners, in all the darkened oil paintings. What will we do then? What will you...? What will I...?

Everything will turn into ashes, is turning into ashes...

I can see how I am in your way. I can see how women get in the way.

The stench of the flowers, the champagne in the library.

I thought there were ghosts that followed me, and there were none.

I was destined to become the only shadow here.

I would like oh so much to talk to you, about the anger that follows me, and the books, those inanimate objects, that steal your affection from me.

Perhaps this is not a memory, but something that happened—to me? To her?

This is my gift. I have touched with the tips of my fingers the impossible veil; I am trapped here. I cannot move, I cannot talk, but I know, I see these things, things that have happened and that are happening and that will come to pass.

He calls me my love.

I move more frantically. Something pricking in my arm, something to calm me.

I want her to understand it all, I want her to come no further. Because this chamber is the end of the road. And I am kept here by the ogre.

I ought to do something about it, I know that. I should protect Eliza.

I ought to stop it all.

Stop the eternal cycle of fathers, uncles, guardians, brothers, stepfathers, priests, doctors, all selling their daughters and nieces and wards in marriages most advantageous to demons in the disguise of gentlemen.

Where am I now?

Where is he?

Darkness in the library, the champagne pinching my tongue, the dull smell of the flowers. Those are not my memories. I am gone.

But she, Eliza, lives.

CHAPTER SIX

The next morning Sam woke to a hangover, and general upheaval. The police had made some surprise night raids on a few palmists and Charles was at sixes and sevens, organising an urgent meeting of the League to tackle the issue, and despatching a large number of telegrams. The name of Count Bévcar resonated in all the little cliques of incensed Spiritualists: his was the kind of leadership that their movement needed. Standing in the doorway, Sam made his excuses: it was the appointed day for a palm reading he wasn't planning on missing.

Miss Helena Walton lived in a retired suburb where city and country could almost touch. The neighbourhood in question proved to be much further than Sam had anticipated, and he was a little bit late. From the outside her building looked like all the other ones around it: a redbrick detached house that could have belonged to a successful businessman or to someone in trade, each of the dwellings surrounded by the same expansive private garden, with a view of the distant city at the back and the river floating behind them.

Sam rang the bell, and the door opened to a modern vestibule full of winter light. The maid showed him into a back parlour overlooking an extensive garden, which he expected to be decorated with gypsy shawls, aspidistras and tasteful reproductions of Venus, Aphrodite, Galatea.

Instead he found himself in a room lined from floor to ceiling with groaning bookcases. His uncle's library was well equipped with the classics and some poetry, though most of Charles's books were dedicated to Spiritualist matters. This was different: what Sam had in front of him was a substantial collection gathered with patience and love over many years. A cursory glance showed him that Miss Walton possessed an eclectic taste. Most of the leading Spiritualist journals were present, but also police reports and many newspapers, which Miss Walton seemed to receive from every corner of the country. A headline shouted at him from the chaise longue: one such paper had been recently abandoned there.

STRANGE OCCURRENCES IN BOLTON'S ASYLUM FOR WOMEN.

MASS FEMALE HYSTERIA AND
CONTAGIOUS SLEEP-DEATH!

Between two of the book-covered walls sat a huge writing desk, and to one side stood an odd dark cabinet, similar to the one that had been used in Madame Florence's performance, but more severe-looking. It was painted black, and its only decoration was the drawing of a funeral wreath on each side of its double doors. It was scratched and ridged, and some of the paint on the bottom had lost its lustre. But the most impressive piece of decoration by far was the library's northern wall, covered in its entirety by the biggest map of London he had ever seen, the river twisting around the city like a snake.

'Mr Moncrieff. I have kept you waiting, and I ought to apologise.'

'Not at all.'

Miss Walton closed the door behind her. She was wearing a long kimono-style yellow dress that hung loosely around her, and her dark brown hair was pinned with two tortoise-shell combs. She wasn't exactly a pretty woman, but she had deep, beautiful eyes, and a curious mouth that could change swiftly from smirk to smile. Her expression metamorphosed very quickly, as sometimes happened with trained actors.

'I'm afraid I got lost on the way here,' Sam started. 'You have chosen to shun civilisation, if I may say so.'

'It has its advantages. People like your friends from the

Society for Psychical Research do not think it worth their while to come all the way out here to expose me.'

Did she mean Mr Woodbury? He was hardly a 'friend', Sam thought.

Miss Walton moved briskly around the room. At a little side table under a window she lit a cigarette, the sun sending orange reflections around her.

'The idea of the SPR coming here frightens you?' Sam offered.

'On the contrary, Mr Moncrieff. I'm only afraid they would be very disappointed indeed. They'd find the trek here a waste of time.'

'Trek. The word is apt.'

'As I said, I value my privacy,' she gave another brief smile.

'Quite an impressive book collection,' he said, turning round admiringly. He had thought she would be pleased with his comment, but to his surprise she rolled her eyes in that way he knew well by now.

'What is it that you want, Mr Moncrieff?'

'I've come to have my palm read, of course.'

She ignored his attempt at a smile.

'Very well. Sit at that round table. There's tea coming up.'

'Tea? That is very kind of you, Miss Walton.'

'It's Walton-Cisneros, Mr Moncrieff.'

'Of course, I beg your pardon,' Sam said, although he could not help noticing that she had not corrected Charles or Lady Matthews.

'I just need to do a couple of things while you have your tea, if you would be so kind as to humour me. Afterwards, I'll do the reading. Is that agreeable?'

'That would be perfect, and thank you very much for your hospitality.'

'Also, to be fair, I owe you an apology,' she said, lowering her voice and letting her eyes travel to the place where she, in her guise as a theatre seamstress, had delivered her expert blow.

'It is of no consequence; do not trouble yourself. Although I must confess I do not very much like being hit on the head,' he said good-humouredly.

'It was the back of your neck, to be precise.'

'If I may say so, that is a colossal map of the city,' he said, feeling that a change of topic would be welcome. He was rewarded with another of those smirk-smiles.

'It is, is it not? It came with the house, and I have grown extremely fond of it. It helps me imagine my dear spirit friends in their free wanderings through our mighty capital.'

Tea arrived, and she asked him whether he would mind terribly pouring it himself. Sam did as he was told. The young woman busied herself with a tattered copy of the *Library Map of London and its Suburbs*, penned a note, rang the bell, and gave it to the maid.

'Would you be so kind as to pour me some tea as well, Mr Moncrieff? I'll join you momentarily.'

'It would be my pleasure.'

Again, he complied.

'Thank you for your patience, and for pouring the tea. It's so charming to see a man doing it for a change,' she said, sitting down at last. 'I could, of course, read your tea dregs, Romany style.'

'It is also the customary way of reading the future where I come from, in Norfolk.'

She looked up directly at his eyes for the first time, and he said nothing more, enjoying her puzzlement. It appeared that possessing this kind of knowledge did not tally in her head with the idea she had formed of him. A second later she was regaining control of the conversation.

'Perhaps you would prefer the cards.'

'I had no idea there were so many alternatives.'

'It rather depends on what you are interested in finding out. Is it fortune or health, or might it even be love?'

A sudden pang, but he could control it. For a moment Sam was at a loss what to say. He hadn't had the sense to prepare the scene in advance.

'Perhaps a little of everything,' he offered.

'I see. The Tarot cards are better for these kinds of vague, imprecise questions.'

'That is a peculiar cabinet,' he said. 'It rather reminds me of another one I've seen recently.'

'Indeed? May I ask where?'

'At Madame Florence's.'

'Of course. Madame Florence happens to own the twin.'

'Really? What a coincidence.'

'Not at all. This is a very particular mediumistic cabinet, connected with Madame's family history, as it happens. It was recovered from the wreckage of a passenger ship lost at sea near the coast of Essex. It all happened many decades ago, before I was born.'

'How did it come into your possession?'

'By the simplest method of all: money. I acquired it a few years ago at a public auction. It belonged to Sophia Wayfarer, the celebrated American Spiritualist, who died on that ship when she was coming for her first tour of England. It is the very cabinet from which she performed some of her more celebrated séances, the ones reproduced in exquisite detail in *The Medium and Daybreak* and *Two Worlds*.'

'*Medium and Daybreak*?' Sam was momentarily lost.

'An old Spiritualist publication. It doesn't run anymore.'

'I see.'

'From inside it she succeeded in producing one of the first spirit materialisations in history—after the Fox sisters, of course,' she added. 'If you believe in that kind of thing, that is.' She looked intently at Sam.

'And why does Madame Florence own the twin? Did she buy it too?'

Miss Walton laughed.

'Madame Florence's name is Florence Wayfarer; she was

Sophia Wayfarer's twin sister. They fell out and went their separate ways. They say Sophia was the more talented one, and that Florence only came into her own after her sister's death.'

Of course, Sam thought. He now remembered Madame Florence's full name from the bill announcing her séance. Something did not add up, something that brought darkness into the room all of a sudden: exactly how old was the youthful and charming Madame Florence?

'Shall we proceed? I shall read the Tarot. Or, I could of course simply give you what you want, and then we both will save some time.'

'I am afraid I do not follow.'

'Mr Moncrieff, it is obvious that you are here because, somehow, you have decided to mistrust my abilities. I will not claim to be an expert at either card reading or palmistry; however, things tend to be less simple than we give them credit for.'

'What do you mean?'

'I will assure you, sir, that my reading of the cards will be—*real*. However, I will not deny there is more to it than a supernatural gift.'

'May I ask what do you mean, exactly?'

'There are theories, methods. One can study the basics. There's no need for deception, if one were to simply apply oneself, and follow what one learns. But, of course, at the end it is mostly psychology that matters.'

'Psychology?' He seemed to consider this. 'I am afraid I'm not very sure what you can mean.'

'I mean that I *can* read the cards because I've studied them, but, ultimately, one doesn't need them to know.'

'To know what?'

'Everything one needs to know, desires to know. Besides, Mr Moncrieff, I will not give you a true portrait of yourself, I will only tell you two or three things of no consequence you will not mind hearing from a total stranger.'

'I see. Nonetheless, I have come all the way here.'

'Would you really like me to show you?'

'Please; but, in that case, may I ask for the honest version?'

'Honest version? My dear Mr Moncrieff, it is I who doesn't follow you now.'

'Very simply put, if you are going to demonstrate your psychological knowledge, could you at least please spare me the little trifles, and attempt a true character portrait? That would be far more impressive,' he said, punctuating his talk with a long sip of his tea.

'I see. Very well. But please, do not be alarmed.'

'Alarmed?' he chuckled.

'And please remember that it was *you* who asked *me*.'

He half-smiled, pretending to be amused at her reaction, but inwardly he was wondering what he had volunteered for.

'Very well. I'll start.' Miss Walton looked at him intently; and, eventually, she spoke. 'You have never truly felt that you belong anywhere, and have problems relating to one place. Your life has been a succession of forward movements, always so as to not have to ask deep questions about what you left behind. You have always felt like an outsider, and indeed feel that you are looking at life as if through a window, as if you are considering someone else's existence. From that we can ascertain that you suffer serious problems in engaging with reality. Am I wrong?'

Sam didn't say anything. He found it hard to swallow the tea. She continued shuffling the cards in her hands, but she wasn't drawing any, she didn't need to do so to speak. 'You don't remember, or know, much from your childhood. In fact, you avoid thinking about your childhood altogether; this means you confuse things sometimes. I was struck by your reference to Charles as your "uncle", when you two are not related, are you? Charles is your *guardian*, and you are his *godson*, his charge. Let me see, what else—'

It was on hearing this that the young man obviously wanted her to stop talking; although it seemed that a part of him wanted to listen as well. She was observing him intently while she gathered speed; it was almost possible to see one idea leading into another as she threaded her argument. Miss Walton drew three more cards, completing a circle on the table.

'Which leads me to believe that something—something happened to you, at some point. Probably very early on. Something that has made you mistrustful, something that weighs a great deal—'

'Please, stop.' He was standing now, and had moved close to the window.

She could not refrain from a little smile as she collected the cards together.

'Please, accept my apologies, Mr Moncrieff. I should know better.'

He turned round to look at her, and their eyes met for a few seconds before he spoke:

'You are quite right,' he conceded. 'Charles and I are not related.'

'It is of no consequence,' she said. 'It only struck me as peculiar. What does it say about you, as it were?'

'Does it need to mean something, Miss Walton?' Sam tried to sound lighter than he felt.

'*You* tell *me*, Mr Moncrieff.'

CHAPTER SEVEN

Helena's previous experiences of the supernatural had been so disappointing as to be considered fraudulent. Even now, so many years later, remembering it all made her feel so sad, so angry.

The mediums had come all the way from Leeds on a southern tour, and agreed to stop by in Cambridge for a few days as her grandfather's guests. She knew very well what Grandfather wanted, for didn't she want the same thing? He wasn't a believer; it wasn't like that. He was a practical man, and he was simply checking a possibility. He invited those two famous Northern mediums as a kind of scientific experiment.

'What we will be testing, my dear, are the rationalist, humanist and Cartesian ideas that underlie the Spiritualist faith; its claims to being an empirical religion, continuously tested and retested by its zealous members.'

All that was very well, but they both wanted it to work: to see her again, to hear her laughter, to smell her perfume.

Alas, that proved to be all that they could grant them, to fill the parlour with Grandmother's Andalusian smell of warm oranges and cinnamon and the acid twang of lemons in the nostrils—until it all smelled of rotten lemons, and Grandfather left the room to walk into the garden angry and talking loudly, and the two mediums retired into their room with the promise of a more successful séance the next day. And Helena—

Something was wrong in that carefully curated scene. *Cinnamon?*

She treasured a very precise memory of that patio in Seville. Overbearing heat, looking for shade amongst the plants, the delicate murmur of the little fountain. It had two cherubim, looking intently into the little lemon trees in their massive terracotta pots. She liked to see the women splashing the fresh water on the *loza* floor to clean it, and, with scientific curiosity, she would kneel down and see it evaporate almost at once in the intense heat before her very eyes. Helena was amazed by everything she was seeing, although it probably didn't happen like she remembered it. The colours, the yellow light of the sun, the smell of dung from the horse-drawn carts, the courtesy of the people. Coming from London, where they had been briefly living before the trip, a despicable human haunt, a veritable jungle of bad manners and humans crashing on top of one another, this courtesy shocked her deeply. Until then, she had thought that the adult world was about pushing aside the person before you in the queue, about eating or being eaten.

But she remembered the smells well. Oranges and lemons. A strange flower called *dama de noche*, lady of the night, that only opened at dusk, pouring its pungent aroma into the world. The kitchen she secretly haunted. The fresh smell of the animals in the heat. The sweet fumes of the nearby river. It was called the Guadalquivir.

But *cinnamon*? She didn't recall any cinnamon. Of course, she could have simply been wrong; the visit had happened many years back, when she was five or six years old. And Helena knew all too well that her mind had started forming its own version of her grandmother's Seville. But still.

Helena had never accepted that she possessed a particularly acute intuition, but she had always been a good observer. Of people, of places. She seemed to possess some manner of grasping a situation; it is almost as if she had strategically assessed in her brain the many possible outcomes in a few seconds; and so, she could perhaps anticipate a fight in an inn, a passing moment of danger. These little trifles did not mean she 'foresaw', of course; they could not do so, she explained to herself, for foresight, as such, did not exist. But observation, careful and meditated, common sense, rationality, having the patience and the inclination to gather the different fractured pieces of a puzzle and put them together… these traits she did possess. And they sometimes conjured up a frighteningly accurate reading of a particular situation.

And her reading of their guests was as follows: it felt as if the two mediums had put together a version of what they imagined a Seville townhouse to smell like; that is, without ever having been to the actual place, but rather gathering their ideas from books and third-hand testimonials; therefore they had got a thing or two wrong. Nothing terrible, of course. Mere trifles. Deep inside, their business was not about actual communication with the shadows, but about giving solace to those left behind. Grandfather and herself.

Of course, she had not been allowed to attend, but she had found a way of seeing it all, smelling it all. She was good at that kind of thing, as she imagined most children were.

The next session was more successful, but all the mediums had been able to materialise was a pair of ghostly hands, too pale to belong to Grandmother. And so on and so on.

They had not seen her, alas! She had not come. And the two mediums departed for London, to start on the last leg of their journey.

A sad, disappointing moment from her life, one that was better left forgotten.

Helena had been following James Woodhouse for a whole week. She knew he was keeping an eye on Samuel Moncrieff, but didn't know the reason for his interest. Mr Woodhouse was a college friend of Sam's—and Helena suspected that there was more to Sam's recent past than even someone as sharp-eyed as herself could have seen. She needed to talk to this young man. What she didn't realise was that she had been caught, that her pursuit was not as invisible as she had fancied. She turned a corner, and was disappointed to find the young man waiting to confront her. She seemed to be losing her touch.

'May I ask why you are following me, miss?'

Helena sighed, put out by having been caught so easily. Eventually she spoke.

'My name is Helena Walton. We both are investigating the same person. And I wasn't following you, exactly; we both have, in fact, been following the same person for days.'

It was obviously the last thing that the young man in front of her had expected. He looked confused.

'Mr Woodhouse, I have been investigating Samuel Moncrieff, and I know you are doing the same,' she explained. 'It is clear that we need to talk.'

He looked at her with a curious, odd expression, more sad than angry, she could see. He gave her the impression of being exhausted, as if he had just completed some superhuman task. She could now see the deep black shadows underneath his eyes.

'Talk?' he seemed amused at the notion. 'What about? I cannot help you. I cannot help anyone. You should go back to your nice new house.'

She had not expected this. So he knew who Helena was, and where she lived. He turned away from her and started walking, and only when he was about to disappear again round the corner and into the crowd did she say:

'Mr Woodhouse! Please, at least listen to what I've got to say.'

He stopped, but didn't turn to face her.

'How do you know I am investigating Sam?' he asked.

'I've got my methods.'

'Who else knows?'

'No one. Just me.'

He pondered on this.

'I suggest a truce, Mr Woodhouse. Let me buy you lunch at my club, and we can talk. Afterwards, if still you do not believe that we can help each other, I will leave you in peace.'

Reluctant, but also curious, he accepted. Helena hailed a hansom, and told the driver to take them the short ride to Maddox Street. They got out at the entrance of a severe-looking building. Once inside Helena talked to someone at reception, and they were immediately shown into a small and cosy private room on the first floor. It had a panelled double window overlooking a small garden with fruit trees, desolate in their winter guise. The walls displayed books and paintings, and the room itself was furnished with chaise longues covered with cushions and drapes, side tables with vases, and little lamps that gave out a warm and pleasant light. In the grate fluttered a welcoming fire, and, next to it, a small round table was laid for a private lunch. The young man confessed he's never been in a woman's club before, and he looked favourably impressed.

'Mr Woodhouse.'

'Jim, please.'

'Jim. I ought to thank you—knowing that someone else is keeping an eye on our common friend, Mr Moncrieff, lets me rest more soundly at night.'

'Our friend…' He could not contain a chuckle. 'Not at all. It is my pleasure to be of some use,' he said, mockingly.

None of them said anything for a brief moment, during which time two servers entered the room with lunch. The young man was obviously thankful for the opportunity the meal offered not to interrogate his unexpected nervousness. They took their seats at the little table, and he looked for something to drink. He was served some excellent wine.

They both busied themselves with the warm rolls and the celery soup.

'I'm curious, how did you become a detective?'

She smiled. 'So, you do know what I do?'

'I also have my methods.'

'Is that how you describe my work?'

'How else could it be described?'

'Let's just say I like helping people. And I happen to be good at it, if I may say so.'

'I see. But you *do* work for the police—'

'On occasion. The police have used female investigators for

decades, not that it is generally known to the public. It is very simple, really. I discovered early on that I had an ability for finding lost people and objects, for "clearing up" little matters.'

Helena saw him considering her with curiosity. She hated this part; she hated being 'perceived' or 'assessed' in a particular manner just because of her accent, her looks, her age, her gender. But she knew quite well what the general public thought: everyone admired how policemen, or anyone who worked for the safety of the public, endured the brutal streets, their chaos and smells, the fetid humidity that simmered up from the river. How could they imagine those activities as woman's work? Surely no one in their sane mind imagined that someone 'like' her—again, assumptions—could cope with bone-chills and uncomfortable waits in the cold and the rain and the snow. She knew that he was curious, that he was wondering whether she had to do all those things.

'Can you tell me what happened in Oxford?' she asked. 'Why are you investigating Sam?'

In short order, Jim detailed the main elements of his cousin's fate, how an outing in the river with Sam had led to tragedy. She had only cheated death by inches, it seemed; Sam, who had got lost briefly after the accident, had emerged apparently convinced that Viola was dead. This had rung alarm bells with the young woman's family, who had not set him right; in fact, they had allowed him to believe in her demise, in an effort to put as much space as possible between the two.

'I see.'

Helena shared the Matthews case, and was surprised to discover that Jim had stumbled upon the incident when looking at Sam's past.

'I have my own ideas about it.'

Helena's eyebrows shot up.

'Mr Woodhouse,' she said, trying to smile, 'I admit it has been very perceptive of you to connect whatever you are investigating with the Matthews case. It is obvious that Samuel is a... person of interest in it. But I would please ask you not to pry much into it. The Matthews case is decidedly complex. To be perfectly honest, I'm not sure if the external interference of an amateur could help or hinder my investigation. The first steps one takes in a case are fundamentally important, you see. They have to be worked out properly, methodically. A good many things could be lost otherwise.'

'I apologise. It wasn't my intention to— I was hoping to be helpful.'

'Besides, I am sure you will not tell me anything I didn't know already.'

She could see her words had stung him a little more than she had intended.

'Is Sam a suspect? He was...'

'A baby, I know. But, as you yourself have noticed, two... unexplainable events have happened, occurrences that seem to fall outside of a rational explanation. And they both involved

Samuel somehow. Or at least, he was present in both.' She stopped talking, seemed to weigh her next words. 'Our common friend, Samuel Moncrieff,' she explained at last, 'is a complete mystery. I have found no records of his being born, in Norfolk or elsewhere. I have no idea where he comes from. It is as if he materialised out of thin air.'

'Perhaps he did.'

'Yes, perhaps he did.'

They both sipped their wine, and a silence fell on the table. 'And Charles Bale?'

'Lady Matthews seems to trust him implicitly, even to the extent of sharing her affairs and plans with him. They both belonged to a very close circle of friends who tried to bring the Industrial Revolution to the Norfolk coast. They were partners in setting up a factory manufacturing steam engines. A failed enterprise, I'm afraid,' she explained. And then she added: 'Still, I should not rule anyone out just yet. And it is obvious that he, and perhaps Lady Matthews as well, both know more about Sam than they care to share with the rest of the world.'

At this point one of the servers re-entered the room. She bent her head low to murmur something in Helena's ear.

'I see. Well, I'll have to see him, of course. Can you show him in here, please?'

Jim was curious at this new development. Helena explained:

'Someone has requested to see me. It is, in fact, in connection to the Matthews case. I put out an advert looking for a man who used to work in Lady Matthews's stables in 1881. One of his co-workers was killed in strange circumstances. It seems that the police did not have the time or the inclination to occupy themselves with this, in the middle of the girls' disappearances.'

'Indeed.'

Helena seemed to weigh up what to do about him. Eventually, she said:

'This is the moment to decide, Mr Woodhouse. If you truly wish to make yourself useful, you are very welcome to stay. Otherwise, and I do not intend to be rude, but I shall have to ask you to leave this moment.'

He had not yet replied when there was a knock at the door, and the same server came in, this time leading a man. He was dressed in coarse working clothes, with a blanket wrapped around his shoulders against the cold, and he held his cap in his gloved hands. He greeted them awkwardly, looking left and right.

'Please have a seat, Mr Friars.' Helena indicated one of the cushioned chaise longues closer to the fire, but Mr Friars perched himself awkwardly on the edge of the one closest to the door. 'I am Helena Walton, and this is Mr James Woodhouse. How did you know to find me here?'

'Your housekeeper was kind enough as to inform me of where you usually take your lunch, miss.'

'My housekeeper? You went all the way out to my house today? That is a long way, both there and back.'

'Once the missus and I decided I had to see you, better get it done with, miss.'

'Did you walk, Mr Friars?'

'I'm used to walking, miss.'

Miss Walton rung the bell, and asked the server who responded to bring refreshments for Mr Friars.

'You must have remembered something very awful if you decided to cross the city in this weather looking for me, Mr Friars.'

'I'm sorry.'

'Whatever for?' Miss Walton asked, lighting a cigarette. She offered one to Mr Friars. 'You worked on Lady Matthews's estate at the time of the disappearances, and saw something odd at the time, perhaps connected with your friend's death, if I'm not mistaken.'

'That is right, miss; I'm sorry if—'

'Excuse me for interrupting you, sir, but I take it that you need to tell me something, so please stop apologising. Better out with it, at once. You are shaking, Mr Friars. You are white as a piece of paper. And you look as if you've seen a ghost.' As she spoke, Helena walked over to a cabinet in the corner of the room whose panelled double doors opened to reveal a number of bottles. 'I often find it is better to leave that to the professionals.'

'To leave what to the professionals?'

'Seeing ghosts, Mr Friars.'

The server entered the room with a tray, and the comforting

smells of coffee and eggs filled the room. Helena poured three large brandies.

'Sorry. I am not a drinking man, Miss Walton.'

'I apologise, Mr Friars. Why don't you try the eggs? And let's get to the point, shall we? On the weekend of the events in question, did you see something alarming, unexpected, unusual?'

'Yes, miss, all of that.'

'Why don't you try to explain it to me, in your own words?'

'Well, miss, I thought for a long time if this would be a useful thing to say or not. It was the dreams, miss.'

'The dreams, Mr Friars?'

'I've contracted a dream illness, and was in quite a bad way. At first I thought there was nothing the matter with me, but then the dreams came, and he was in them, and so was Mr Chapman, and—!'

'Very well, Mr Friars,' Miss Walton interrupted. 'Let's start at the beginning. You were telling us that you saw something unusual the night Mr Chapman died. How did this happen?'

'Not something, miss. Someone.'

'Can you remember the circumstances of your friend's death?'

'He had an apoplexy.'

'Well, nothing odd in that!' put in Jim. Helena shot a look at him.

'He was barely twenty-two, Mr Woodhouse. And by all accounts in excellent health,' she explained.

'That's right, miss! He looked strangely old somehow, as if he had rotted… Oh, poor lad. That is when I started seeing the creature around, all the time.'

The creature, as Mr Friars insisted on calling him, seemed to be followed by his own secret pool of darkness, so dark that the street lamps, the light pouring from a distant window, even the moon, made hardly any impression on the obscurity he carried within him, turning his surroundings into some black abyss. That he was accompanied by his own dusk was what Mr Friars had noticed first. And then the shapeless mass of robes and bags, which seemed to possess the quality of moving of their own accord, no matter which way the wind blew, as though they heaved with their own dark life.

The apparition had been there that night, when Mr Friars went out to the back of the stables. He had seen it before; something told him that it was there waiting.

'I saw him in other places around the estate, miss. He seemed to follow me around! As if he knew that I knew what he had done!'

No matter where he went, he had the notion that the accursed thing would not lose sight of him. As if he could fly, or materialise anywhere he wanted. As if the creature were able to perform some kind of magic, to follow him all the way to his grave.

'I realise this sounds silly, miss. Then one day I didn't see him anymore. But things didn't get better.'

It was then that the dreams came. They were vivid and strange and confusing. In them, Mr Friars seemed to be inside the cunning-man's head.

'Cunning-man?' Jim interrupted.

'Yes, sir. He is a cunning-man, one of the last few that remain in England. The dreams told me.'

'A cunning-man is a kind of rural wizard, Mr Woodhouse,' said Miss Walton. 'I'll explain later. If you would be so kind, Mr Friars, please continue.'

'He was in some sort of ruined place, imagining it all, replaying it in his head, once and again. It gave him pleasure to do so.'

'Replaying what exactly, Mr Friars?'

'Why, Mr Chapman's death, miss! I woke up feverish each morning, my blanket soaked through! I could not take it! It was as if each night I went into this creature's head! I could not take it, miss! I am not mad! I know I was inside his head! You don't think I'm mad, do you?'

'Calm down, Mr Friars, I beg you. I assure you I do not think you are mad, and I have to thank you for answering my advert. May I ask, why didn't you tell the police?'

'I would prefer not to deal with the police, miss. They'll send me to Bedlam, likely as not.'

'You have done the correct thing, and I am grateful to you.' Jim noticed how her voice was soft, understanding. The man shook himself, mumbled his thanks, and got up to leave, not before Miss Walton had coerced him into accepting some money, ostensibly for a cab fare.

Before going out he turned and said:

'There is something else, miss.'

'Yes, Mr Friars?'

It seemed that the places where he had seen the creature standing appeared to oddly change shape after he was standing there.

'*Change shape?* I'm afraid I do not follow, sir. Could you please try to be more precise?'

The old man sighed.

'Well, miss. It was as if those corners had—rotted. Everywhere he passed through, ruin and decay came after him.'

'Rotted?'

'It was all dirty, and old and… there was fungus everywhere—' the man noted her eyebrows shooting up and stopped talking. 'I'm sorry. I don't know if I dreamt it all—'

'Not at all, Mr Friars. I truly thank you for coming today.'

Mr Friars nodded, and left. Miss Walton sat down with a worried expression.

'This is acquiring layers of meaning that escape me… I need to sort out my ideas properly before travelling to Norfolk. Can I ask something of you?'

'Please.'

'Samuel—I trust that you will keep an eye on him?'

'That was my intention.'

She was considering something else. Eventually she said:

'I am wondering, have you ever considered what would happen if you facilitated a meeting between young Samuel and your cousin?'

'My God! To what purpose?'

'The particulars we are dealing with require... alternative methods. I am positive we will learn something.'

'But Sam thinks Viola died!'

'Then maybe he ought to be told the truth, don't you think?' Jim didn't reply. 'Think about it, please. Good day.'

Helena went back home and changed quickly, for she had an important task ahead of her that night. Her informants had finally given her an address. This was a still open case, one she had been working on for months, the abduction of children all over the capital.

She arrived with her coachman, a reliable ally in similar situations. What a horrid place that church was. How imposing its tower, how desolate its setting. No one had been able to give her its accurate history, when all she wanted to understand was why it had been made so big and self-important, so out of place in a borough like this, distant and to the south of the city, where the dung of the cows and the overpowering stench of the nearby marshes thickened the air. At the end of her vision, the estuary. Ahead of her, a brief square. The only lamp to be seen poured its sad yellow light over the pavement. It did not perform a good job, and some of the corners sat in darkness. They inspected the building. It was a square thing, deceptively solid, with a tower lifting up from the middle of it, half destroyed by fire. To the right there was a graveyard, filled to bursting, to judge from the sickly-sweet smell. The other buildings were a brief row of small cottages, a barber-and-dentistry shop, a baker, all of them seemingly abandoned. A stray dog crossed their path, unsure where to turn.

Doors and windows were inaccessible, with planks of wood nailed over them. A sign read condemned for demolition. As they circled the building, they saw a derelict hut set at the back of the churchyard. She indicated by gestures that they should approach the little structure. Her coachman followed. They found a small space between the planks covering the window. A small boy was chained to the wall, lying on a heap of straw in a corner. He was not moving. There was a man asleep next to the door, with the remains of a pie at his feet, alongside several empty bottles of ale.

Once they were inside, Helena lost no time in approaching the child, and tried gently to wake him up. He was either very small or dangerously thin. As carefully as he could, her coachman took the keys from the drunk man, who was far enough lost in his alcoholic dream to do no more than move one hand a little, as if he was pushing away a fly. He soon resumed his drugged sleep. They opened the cuff on the boy's ankle, and the child softly mumbled something in his dream. There was a strong stench of urine, of wet straw, of fear.

'Come on, we have to go,' Helena said gently in the boy's ear. He opened his eyes as wide as they would go. Beaten to submission by his captors, he knew better than to argue. He simply did what he was told. With sleepy eyes he got up and let himself be lifted by her embrace, and the little group headed for the door.

But it wasn't going to be that easy.

There was a disturbance in the air. Someone, a man, appeared out of nowhere. He was tall and broad-shouldered, wearing a very old overcoat, stained and falling to pieces. The child wriggled in her arms, intent on advancing towards him.

Helena made a sign to her companion to hold him back, while she took out her revolver.

'Hey!' she shouted in the direction of the man. 'You! Leave him!'

'Miss! Look!'

In the dim, flat, early morning light, she could not see the man's eyes. He began jerking around, describing circles. Then he stopped, and turned to look at them, extending his huge hands in the group's direction. The child moved more wildly, as if a powerful grip was pulling him.

'No!'

They both grabbed him at once, two adults almost incapable to contain the will of a small and weak child, holding him with all the strength that they were capable of summoning.

'I will *not* let you take him!' Helena shouted.

The man smiled through pointy teeth and crossed through green light. On the other side, he transformed into a bearded gentleman, holding a cane and with an expensive suit. But the same horrible smirk. Helena wished that they had been spared that gesture. Then the weak morning light exploded into an unnatural whiteness that filled the world.

The boy fell dead on the floor.

Helena was shaken, uncomprehending. Scotland Yard took charge of the situation. There would be an autopsy, reports to compose, ideas to thread, more places to look into.

She woke up the next day to a realisation: there was still another angle to pursue. The thugs in charge of the boy were known to her; they were members of The True Dawn. She didn't need to make any enquiries to know that it was the group that had recently accepted the leadership of the mysterious Count Bévcar, author of the new Spiritualist bestseller *Towards a Science of Immortality*. All of London seemed to have fallen under the spell of the gentleman who promised eternal life by an as yet unknown method.

She penned a preliminary report to Scotland Yard, and made her way to the club in Pall Mall that had been put by its members at the disposal of the Count's circle. She was wearing a plain black dress with a subtle white frill, with the idea of passing for a maid if needed. When she arrived, she found the tradesmen's door open, and a great deal of comings and goings, which allowed her to make her way through the kitchen and pantry area into the building undetected. She found herself among the considerable hubbub of a large place preparing itself for a big party. What could they be celebrating? On a table there were a group of trays ready for transporting champagne glasses into one of the dining rooms. She took one of those, and grabbed also a plain white apron that she tied over her dress. Head down, walking with the resolution of those who know what they are doing, she exited the kitchen into the main area of the building, part of a flow of servers. As soon as she was able to she took a turn and separated herself from the group.

She found herself in an emptier part of the building, long corridors of marble floor surrounded by portraits of imposing-looking men. There was some odd music coming from another corridor. Following the sound took her back to the landing of the main staircase, where both wings of the building united; she had to be more careful here, she was more in the open. And there it was, clear as the air, dark and still as the night. Somewhere on the right corridor there was a melody, and someone sobbing freely, two sounds mixing irrevocably together. She peeped in: another corridor, going down into the depths. A cursory look helped her ascertain which room the noises were coming from, behind a heavy-looking door of dark wood. The whining was more intense here, and she had no doubt that whoever was crying at that eerie music was doing so on the other side. Helena moved towards the next chamber, to find it locked. She took out a long hairpin from her hair that she tended to carry for such an eventuality. Picking locks was something Helena had learnt to do in Cambridge a long time ago, for her grandfather kept his library closed—due to a minor feud with the housekeeper, who showed no respect when cleaning and re-shelving the books—and that wasn't going to keep her away from Melville, Shelley or Brewster. The familiar click told her that the job was finished, and she turned the handle slowly. Once inside, she sighed with relief: the two rooms had been connected, as she had expected on a building made up mostly of offices and meeting rooms. She went to the communicatory door, and put her eye to the keyhole, revealing the inside of the next room. That could only mean one thing: the key was not in the other side of the door. Congratulating herself on her good luck, she peeped through the hole.

There was a child of no more than sixteen years, hanging in the air. Perhaps this wasn't an accurate description, as his feet were touching the ground. But his posture was all wrong, as if an invisible rope was hanging from his shoulders. She moved to get a better look: his feet were touching the ground, but only by the points of his toes. He certainly could not have had that posture without supporting himself on anything, so it appeared as if he was levitating. He looked unresponsive now, his eyes all white.

Next to him, on a chair, an elderly gentleman also looked unresponsive, his eyes white too. Unfortunately, she could not see the source of the music from her position, but she could hear it, a haunting melody, coming from some kind of flute.

During the few seconds she had been concentrating on the task, the sobbing had changed, and now someone was humming a tune. And now it was the old gentleman who started a quiet sobbing.

She got up, an odd feeling shooting up her spine as she attempted to interpret the horrid scene, but she had to double back quickly: two men were coming her way. She retreated once more into the empty room. She could now hear them clearly; they must be getting close.

'You must know that I am doing all within my power—you absolutely should assure Madame Florence of this. Bévcar is not an easy man to keep happy—'

From her hidden position inside the room, Helena could see the two men: one was unknown to her, perhaps part of Bévcar's inner circle. But the second man she knew well: Thomas Bunthorne.

'Oh, Bévcar, Bévcar... The man is a bore, and I haven't even met him yet.'

'And you probably won't!'

'Yes, well. Look here, what I am saying is that you cannot

keep using Bévcar as an excuse for not doing what we're paying you to do. Surely you must see that.' Bunthorne's tone was conciliatory, if with a trace of impatience.

'I know, I know—but surely you must see that I am risking my neck! If I don't succeed, you won't get what you want; but I won't get to live another day!'

'Very well, I see…'

'What exactly do you see?'

'You want more money. That's the whole point, isn't it?'

'My dear sir!'

'It's time; the new vessel is ready. The longer we take, the greater the risk. We need to act, and act now, my good man!'

Helena retreated further into her room. Vessel? What was Madame Florence involving herself in? And what had Helena stumbled upon?

Back home, Helena sat at her desk, a pen in her hand, her head trying to order the pieces at her disposal. She had never liked this bit. She imagined enjoying it, for a change, to sit in a private compartment, perhaps, with only the moon for company, scribbling in her personal notebook while contemplating a beautiful landscape floating behind a train window. Or perhaps resting on a bench in the middle of the cheerful hubbub of a public park. Humanity going around on its important business of leisure, while she recounted her odd adventures. But this exercise in self-narration had never come easy to her. Helena had never been able to keep a diary, perhaps because her grandfather insisted on instilling the habit in her. But she knew that now it would be impossible to avoid it, that the many complications of the most mundane of lives might demand perhaps that act of retelling, of generating some order out of chaos, reaffirming existences as more than mortal creatures. The soft, cream-coloured pages of a journal giving the writer the wrong impression that they were like an explorer, charting some terra incognita. But the mundane does not allow itself to be tamed that easily. She could never gather the required energy to sit down every night like a dutiful girl, and recount her exploits. And now, even less. Curiously, the more interesting her days had become, the less Helena wanted to record them. There was darkness all around her. Even if the outcome was a happy one, the getting there was always messy; she had no desire to archive those abominations.

And now she had to put in writing not one, but two strands of separate investigations that she was following: the Matthews case, and the children's vanishings from London's poorer streets. With mounting dread, she found herself questioning why she had picked her chosen profession, only to give herself the same answer as always: *it* had chosen *her*.

*

At the time the Matthews children liked playing in ruins. Samuel Moncrieff 'appears', out of thin air, it seems, on that same fateful week—

She stopped—Samuel. What to write? How to write it?

Samuel Moncrieff is twenty years old, about to turn twenty-one. Therefore, he arrived at Mr Bale's door the same year that the children went missing as a newborn. That is a fact.

Samuel Moncrieff was not a missing/stolen child, since no baby disappeared in the area (that I know of).

So far, no records of his being born that my associates have been able to find.

He has been raised by Mr Bale. Fact.

Helena did not believe in mediumistic writing; however, this exercise of letting her mind go, of scribbling as if some force directed her pen, had some similarities with the mystical science.

Mr Bale is good friends with Lady Matthews, so much so that she trusts him with her most intimate affairs. They were also partners in a business venture, a failed steam factory, up the coast, now an abandoned building—check this place. Is the factory really abandoned? Could it now be used for some criminal activity?

Samuel Moncrieff does not remember much about his family. Some hidden stain instinctively means that he would rather not ask. Is Samuel Moncrieff the illegitimate son of Lady Matthews and the house's architect, Mr Williams? According to Scotland Yard's records, the architect threw himself out of a tower shortly after the girls' disappearance. Was he connected to the events? If Samuel Moncrieff is their illegitimate son, how is his sudden appearance twenty years ago connected to the girls vanishing?

Could Lady Matthews have made the girls disappear so Samuel could inherit the estate? And after everything went awry, or perhaps out of guilt, she gave the child to Mr Bale to raise?

Helena wrote a thick question mark at the end of these last lines: they didn't ring true. And she was getting side-tracked from the facts by questions she could not yet answer.

Everything ought to have a rational explanation; she could not, however, take out of her mind Lady Matthews's words on the afternoon they met.

'*I know that there is more to the children's disappearance than foul play.*'
She sighed and started another page.

Possible connection with the case of the children's disappearance: Madame Florence's partner, Thomas Bunthorne, seems to be in cahoots with Bévcar and The True Dawn, even though they present themselves to the world as enemies. Why? Bunthorne mentions a 'vessel'. Are children taken for this purpose? She stopped to think for a second. She resumed her writing.

However, how old is Madame Florence? Several accounts describe her as blonde; she is dark. It is possible that there is an innocent explanation for this. But why this word, 'vessel'?

Bévcar is famous for his supposed 'transmutation' powers. Even if these powers are not real, is it possible that some people 'believe' in them, and hurt children in their quest for immortality?

She underlined heavily her last sentence.

*

It was curious, she thought, how science and spiritualism had always gone hand in hand with her. One of the things that Helena decided on the very moment the two Northern mediums left her grandfather's house was to study medicine. Her grandfather had come to believe that the mediums were a fraud, and that they had tried to fool him. Indeed, she was able to ascertain that the pale apparition, the hand hovering over the table, had been nothing but a trick; and she could have proved it to him. But she and her grandfather did not always see eye to eye.

No one had told Helena, but the unconscious current of knowledge in the house had made sure she knew it: he was the one responsible for sending her mother away. Helena hated him for it, with passion. And if she hated something else passionately, it was agreeing with him.

And so it was that Helena kept the mediums' little secret.

Somehow, it had been an early attempt at detection. And she had succeeded in unveiling the truth. She didn't despise the mediums for it; on the contrary, she found herself admiring their ingenuity, how cleverly they made their living in a world populated and dominated by men like her grandfather. She rapidly took their side; after all, she wasn't going to give him the satisfaction of corroborating his opinions.

The only time they seemed to have agreed on anything was on her going to Girton. Her grandfather thought her a lost cause by then, and was very happy to see that she valued learning, and had the disposition. But the college saddened her a little: it welcomed her with its air of an abandoned asylum, and it was located miles from town, in order to discourage male visitors. Grandfather insisted on a classical education, and Helena could not escape this little compromise. She was already interested in what perception could achieve, in exploring the inner recesses of the mind, in knowing why people saw the world as they did. As soon as it was possible to do so, she started attending other kinds of lectures, other kinds of settings. Cabinets of curiosities, laboratories, experiments. She remembered well her thirst for knowing things, the endless nights of study by candlelight, how she couldn't let something lie if it didn't add up in her head, or if she didn't understand it.

It was different now, so different. How much she would give never to have known, never to have learned certain things.

She knew it, she had always known. Even if no one had told her directly. That her mother had not died of a consumptive disease. That she had been sent away, by Grandfather, to a madhouse, where, alone and scared, she had committed a horrible sin, the most horrible of all; and she should rot in unconsecrated ground, and in the deepest circle of hell.

CHAPTER EIGHT

The child that Eliza had found catatonic in the marshes was now being looked after in her cousin's house. As soon as he had seen her, Peter had commented on the similarities to another local case, someone connected with the big house. This had made Eliza curious.

'They are looking for help, in fact. Mrs Burroughs, who looks after Dot, is getting on in years.'

This had spurred Eliza's interest, and she had immediately volunteered.

'I will put in a good word with Mrs Ashby. I am sure that they will be grateful for your help. Your scientific knowledge will come in handy.'

'Thank you, Peter.'

Eliza considered her cousin the cleverest man around. She had confided in him her findings, both about the disappearing nature, and about the strange, sticky fungi substances, pale grey or green, that seemed to emerge from the fetid north coast.

At Eliza's insistence, they had gone on a little expedition. This time they were prepared. They were both carrying old rags to tie around their mouths, to protect themselves against the putrid fungi in the ruined manor. They came to the other end of the little wall that surrounded the property, and descended in the direction of the sea. Eliza was trying to remain rational, to compose a map of the terrain she had covered in her head, perhaps. Measurable data. Certainties.

The road wound down to the marshes. A line of trees, forming a little shady avenue, also twisted its way down to the sea. So she went to find the marshes, the reed swamp, the open sea at the end. With the tide down, she could see the rhyolite. At the end, the midst resolved itself, and the old abandoned fortress appeared. And what was that? With the water so far out, so far back, they could make out a long steam-like arm, a metal contraction, ready to dig deep into the sea base. Eliza advanced a little to focus on the image, and her boots touched something soft and meaty. She looked down. It was a tern, dead on the floor. She held it in her hands; it was real, she was touching it. But, at the same time, she feared the tern ought not to be there of all places.

'We have to continue, we have to get to the factory,' she had said, although she was scared.

'I am not sure that's a good idea.' Peter was collecting

samples of all the fungi-like stickiness that he could get his hands on: white, grey, green, orange. 'I am getting an awful headache; something here is not right.'

Once back, Mrs Hobbs served them tea by the fire. The day had turned strangely dark, but they were both thankful to have escaped the ruins.

'*The plague-wind, and the plague-clouds,*' Peter had said, quoting Ruskin.

'You are absolutely right: men's greed will never abate. It is obvious that something has been unsettled out there.'

'Why *men* in particular?'

'You are always quick at exploiting nature.'

Peter chuckled.

'Well, why don't you tell that to the women who wear plumage on their hats, or cover themselves with dead animals? And we all slaughter animals for meat!'

She knew he was right. Peter got up, rummaged in the bookshelf, found what he was looking for, and, rocking the little book in his hands like a naughty schoolboy, read:

'*It looks partly as if it were made of poisonous smoke; very possibly it may be: there are at least two hundred furnace chimneys in a square of two miles on every side of me. But mere smoke would not blow to and fro in that wild way. It looks more to me as if it were made of dead men's souls—such of them as are not gone yet where they have to go, and may be flitting hither and thither, doubting, themselves, of the fittest place for them.*'

'I find it very hard to believe that Ruskin believed in ghosts…'

He laughed. Eliza quoted, from memory:

'*An atmosphere of that gas would give to our Earth a high temperature; and if as some suppose, at one period of its history the air had mixed with it a larger proportion than at present an increased temperature from its own action as well as from increased weight must have necessarily resulted.*'

'Who?'

She rolled her eyes.

'Eunice Foote.'

'Ah! The very lady…'

'I wonder if she meant, you know, *there are more things in heaven and Earth…* Ah! This is silly. Do you think that the factory disturbed some kind of pollutant in the seabed?' asked Eliza.

'It is possible. But what I don't understand is why this is happening now: the factory hasn't been functioning in years.'

There was no answer for that.

Peter was as good as his word, and the next week Eliza received a letter from Mrs Ashby asking her to come to the cottage on the grounds of the estate where her charge was kept on that very night. Eliza got there on the appointed evening. No one answered her knocking, so she let herself in. Someone was crying softly, and she followed the noise to a little room, lit by the sad glow of a few candles. There was a bed, unused despite the late hour, a big wooden wardrobe, a chair and a table underneath the only round window, and an imposing dressing table with a huge mirror. In front of the mirror sat a young woman. Eliza calculated that she was probably in her early thirties, a few years older than her, with dark hair traversed by grey streaks. She was combing it with a repetitive gesture, almost mechanically, and her eyes were large and unseeing: although Eliza's reflection covered the huge mirror as she advanced behind her, appearing in fantastical proportions over the reflective surface, she didn't make any sign that she saw her, or cared about her presence. On each side of the dresser sat two huge vases filled with meadow flowers.

She moved with strange docility, like an old-fashioned doll.

'Hello,' Eliza ventured. The woman didn't react. 'My name is Eliza. Eliza Waltraud. I am here to help look after you.' Nothing. But, what reaction had she expected? It did look as if the woman could *not* see her. She kept repeating the same languid gesture with her arms, combing her hair down. Eliza approached her, and saw the grey threads that sprouted here and there. She kneeled down next to her and tried to make her stop; she was cold to the touch, a coldness that disgusted Eliza for some reason. A little line of spittle was falling from one corner of her lips. Her eyes were too dark, as if her pupils were continuously dilated. Suddenly Eliza felt afraid of looking into that blackness. There was something odd in the scene, as if she were existing in a space and time different, and only her physical body remained in that room. As if she were beyond good, evil.

Eliza thought it remarkable, the similarities with the girl she had found in the marshes.

As she couldn't get any reaction from the young woman, Eliza decided to inspect the room. In a corner there was a little shelf. Nothing amiss, nothing unwholesome. The fresh flowers in vases on her dresser, books, drawings of flowery and furry things pinned to the walls, an expensive tortoiseshell set of brushes and combs, and a dusty pile of large sketch notebooks lying on a chest.

The drawings in the sketchbooks. They were old and yellowish and she immediately saw why: one had the inscription 'Maud Matthews, 1878'. Eliza started passing the pages slowly, finding it difficult to describe what she was seeing, and wondered what uncanny spirit could have taken hold of a little girl's imagination to invent the scenes depicted in the ordered, cream-coloured paper.

They mostly showed the ruin of some kind of city, with twisted spires, turrets and domes, all placed under an ominous moon and covered in a dark mist. A mighty citadel of standing stones surrounded the buildings, as if they were soldiers protecting them with their long shadows. The fantastic edifices, the pillars, the gargoyle tops, all spoke of wrong angles, twisted symmetries, uncanny architectural rules; as if a set of demons had been entrusted with the compass, the square, and the building materials.

'She adores those drawings. Lord Matthews made sure his daughters learnt how to draw properly; he thought it the mark of a lady. She seems to be very fond of those.' Eliza looked up and saw an elderly woman with a face that was furrowed and worried.

'But you should not be here. I would have liked to show you tomorrow morning. She gets very excitable at this time of the night.'

'I'm sorry. I thought Mrs Ashby's letter said to come tonight. To tell you the truth, I could hear her crying all the way from the main road.'

'Well, then I haven't been doing my job properly,' the woman simply said, and walked towards the mirror. 'Come along, Dot. Let's go to bed.'

She tried to cajole the young woman to get up, and they had a little scuffle. Eliza moved to help her, but the woman indicated that she didn't need her assistance.

Eventually, Dot got up docilely and, like a doll, let herself be guided to bed.

'I am Mrs Burroughs.'

'Miss Eliza Waltraud,' she said, extending her own hand, and they greeted one another properly. Despite the late hour, Mrs Burroughs was dressed in the usual attire of a governess rather than a nightgown: her duties must be plentiful, Eliza thought.

Once in bed, Dot started whining again.

'Reading to her always has a sobering effect,' Mrs Burroughs said. Trying to make herself useful, and being closer than her, Eliza turned in the direction of the little shelf, and took down a copy of *Alice's Adventures in Wonderland*, which she brought over to the bed.

'Will this do?' she asked. From the bed, Dot caught a glimpse of the book cover, and her eyes went wide and manic, and she crunched herself against the wall, trying to put as much distance as possible between herself and the book. Her eyes were shouting; a silent, contained interior cry that chilled Eliza's soul.

'Whatever is the matter?' she asked, as Mrs Burroughs deftly took the book from her hand and, from the threshold, threw it into the other room.

'She doesn't like the surreal musings of Reverend Dodgson,' she offered, moving to the wardrobe.

'I can quite see that,' Eliza replied.

Mrs Burroughs took a key from her pocket, unlocked the furniture piece, and opened it to reveal some clothes hanging and, on the shelves, a collection of little bottles and jars, a convalescent's expected assortment of medicines. She started mixing a drop of something in water.

'Miss Waltraud.'

'Eliza, please.'

'I must ask one favour from you,' she said, while she moved to the bed, and deftly made Dot swallow whatever she had concocted, which had a sobering and soporific effect.

'What is it?'

She looked directly at Eliza's eyes.

'To remain discreet about Dot at all times.'

'Mrs Burroughs, you can rest assured of my discretion. I have been hired to help by Mrs Ashby, and I do not make a habit of exposing my employer's secrets to anyone.' Eliza could detect a sigh of relief. 'Nonetheless, may I ask who Dot is, how she came to be here?'

'Oh, she's Dorothea Jenkins, the butler's daughter.'

'Was she born—?'

'Idiotic? I don't like that word very much. But no, not in the least. She was a very promising student, or so I'm told.' The sadness in her voice made Eliza realise how fond she was of her charge.

'Has any doctor seen her?' was her next question.

Mrs Burroughs laughed.

'Many doctors have been to see her these past twenty years...' She didn't see the need to finish the sentence. Her silence stated the obvious.

'What happened to her?'

'Nobody knows. She was good friends with the missing

children, used to play with them sometimes; mind you, only when she could. Even a schooled butler's daughter sometimes has duties to perform in a big house like this.'

'The children? Do you mean the three little girls?' Eliza had heard the story many years ago, when she was a little child. The woman's age seemed right. Mrs Burroughs's words sent a shiver up her spine. 'Are you saying she was present the day the children disappeared?'

For the second time, Mrs Burroughs turned to look directly into Eliza's eyes. She stopped rearranging the books, drawings and the little objects on the shelf.

'She was found like this the day the girls disappeared, Miss Waltraud.'

Eliza could not help noticing that Mrs Burroughs's eyes kept firmly concentrating on every single book and object available to her busy hands, but that she deliberately didn't look at the drawings, almost as if she didn't see them; or, rather, as if she didn't want to look in their direction.

The next morning Mrs Burroughs took Eliza to Dot's daytime retreat. They met at the bottom of the winter garden, and from there they took a little path she indicated, a shortcut of sorts. At some point she stopped, turned round to look at the back of the weird house, pale as a ghost, and beckoned Eliza to do the same.

'Do you see that window, the second one on the right-hand side, top floor? That's where the architect jumped from.' She smiled a knowing smile.

Curiouser and curiouser, Eliza thought.

'I'm sorry, Mrs Burroughs, you've lost me.'

And so the older woman explained: the famous architect who had built the abbey had committed suicide shortly afterwards, while staying as a house guest.

'May I ask,' Eliza started, 'why is Dot scared of *Alice in Wonderland*?'

Mrs Burroughs shrugged.

'No idea. It seems it was one of the Matthews girls' favourite books. No one has told me that, but everything Dot uses comes from the girls' things, and you could not find another book more dog-eared.'

Eliza did not reply.

'Do you want to know something else?'

'By all means.'

'It was the nursery window,' insisted the old woman, intent on keeping conversation within certain subjects.

They resumed walking and, by a low vine-covered wall, Mrs Burroughs vanished. Eliza followed: among the greenery a space was revealed, only visible when you approached it from a certain angle. A hidden yellow path. It led towards a further garden, a back kitchen garden much neglected. At the end sat a dilapidated glasshouse, with a half-ruined pavilion in the French style. Once they got closer Eliza realised that it was an orangery. She could see there was someone inside.

'Is that—?'

'Yes. It calms her a lot to work with her flowers.'

A light drizzle started to drip from the sky. They reached the orangery, overrun by plants, pots with seeds in different stages of growth; at the back, test tubes and glass jars on a wooden table: the tools of an amateur botanist. Small bouquets hung upside down from the walls. It took Eliza a few seconds to notice that all the plants were sempervivums, or *immortalis*, which she had seen distributed all over the cottage in vases, chipped china cups filled with petals, covering dressers and tables and every possible surface. And this was presumably where they came from.

The butler's daughter sat by a discarded old-fashioned oak desk covered in worn-out leather. Dot was cutting the dainty petals, purple and white and yellow, into a kind of potpourri that she collected on used scraps of paper scattered here and there, some intention dictating her methodical procedure. She seemed to be making pouches with them. Eliza took one sempervivum by its stem and rolled it between her fingers; it pricked her. She had thought them fresh; they were dry, utterly rigid. The rain fell softly over the glass structure, slowly ticking.

'Dot,' Eliza said, 'I'm glad to see you are feeling better this morning.'

Everything was odd about that moment. It felt as if she was speaking with a ghost, but there she was, distant and indifferent and alive, entirely unaware of her presence.

'Mrs Burroughs, excuse my bluntness, but why was Dot not sent away, put in an institution?' Eliza asked. The governess replied that she didn't know, but Eliza had the impression that she understood the reason: Lady Matthews. Whatever had happened to the child, Lady Matthews felt guilty about it.

'Dot, do you remember your friends, Alice, Maud and Flora?' asked Eliza.

Mrs Burroughs shook her head softly.

'She has been questioned many times, and has never spoken.'

Dot started violently shaking the flowers, and crushing them on the table.

'That's it, calm down!' Mrs Burroughs tried to hold her arms before she could hurt herself, and shouted in Eliza's direction: 'There! That green vial!'

She handed it over, and Mrs Burroughs deftly made her drink a couple of drops, which instantly calmed her.

'That's the most reaction anyone has got from her this past decade!' She tried to smile, but Eliza was feeling unnerved by the proceedings: she liked Mrs Burroughs, and no doubt her task of looking after the young woman was daunting, but she had misgivings about the idea of keeping her drugged as the only means to manage her.

'What's in the vial?'

'A herbal mixture with laudanum. I will teach you to prepare it.'

Eliza dropped the bud she had been handling on the desk, now crushed, amongst the disorder of scissors, canisters, bits of rope and dirty mugs. Calm, unmoving, and suddenly pale after her brief moment of passion, Dot reminded Eliza of a living corpse. She shuddered. Eventually she got up from the table covered in papers, fountain pens and little pots with crimson liquid inside, all needed for whatever Dot was doing with those flowers, and she left. She crossed the overgrown kitchen garden without once turning to look at the crumbling building. It was better that way, in case she caught sight of a ghost smiling at her from one of the broken windows. You never knew where they lurked at that deceptive daytime hour.

Once Mrs Hobbs had exhausted her local wisdom—all the black horses, Old Shucks, Tiddy Muns, and giants that roamed the Broads, which did not really amount to much, to tell the truth—she had suggested visiting Old John. Eliza had found a labourer happy to take her there on his pony and cart.

It was far away, on the other side of Lady Matthews's estate. He had dropped her at the edge of a field she happened to know from her wanderings; had she really been so far out? He explained he would go and visit a friend, and told her how to get to Old John's house. He set off, and soon was a black dot in the distance.

The field extended evenly into a distant horizon. From what she knew, there should be a meadow at one end, Lady Matthews's estate on the other, a brief copse, not consequent enough to be considered a forest, mud, some cows, old wooden fences to keep the cattle, kissing gates to climb over. What she couldn't see was the end of the field, or her way out of it, nor could she hear the nearby sea.

She looked for the sun to orient herself, and then she noticed that the light had changed all of a sudden, that the very air seemed to be gathering darkness around itself. All was tainted a dull colour, opaque and unwelcoming. She found herself in a meadow. Ahead, the little house, with animals running around, clothes hanging in the breeze, and children playing, running, singing.

Give a thing, take a thing, to wear the Devil's old ring.

She started advancing in its direction; she felt tired. Then she saw him, an old man resting against a tree. In the distance the poplars of the uncanny meadow were oddly still. Old John.

'Hello there?'

He didn't turn. He didn't stir.

'Hello, I'm Eliza Waltraud. I have come to see you.'

Still nothing.

'I wrote you a letter, and your daughter replied that I should come today.'

Nothing.

And then she felt it: a contraction in her stomach that told her that she was looking at someone dead.

Slowly, she started going round the tree to face the old man. His mouth and his jaw were strangely greenish and mouldy, as if someone had poured an acidic substance over his lower face. His tongue was green and swollen.

In the cottage, the old man's family were occupying themselves with their many daily chores. One of the children saw her there, and started advancing in her direction, and by some instinct must have reacted to Eliza's expression, for the child stopped, turned round and ran towards the house. Shortly after she reached the house a woman came out running.

'They must not see him!' Eliza shouted. There was no panic, no intimation of fear in her countenance. The woman heard what she had said, and calmly instructed the older children to take the little ones back inside. She knew instantly, of course; but Eliza looked back into the distant meadow, over which no birds passed at that moment, so oddly silent, and she understood: these people had lived so long under the powerful thrall of superstition, their existences shaped and reshaped by the inexplicable, that they accepted everything that happened to them.

She needn't have been so worried about what they might see, for when she looked back at the body the face was back to normal. That unexpected metamorphosis into the mundane scared her far more than the face's previous grotesque state.

What on *earth* was going on?

She woke up, to find that her driver had taken her back home.

'My dear, are you alright? You gave us quite a fright!' Mrs Hobbs was fussing over her.

Eliza felt clammy, out of breath. She had no recollection of getting back into the cart, but eventually she must have found her way back, climbed on it, and let herself be taken back home. She didn't want to be seen like that.

'Mrs Hobbs, have you called my cousin?'

'Not yet. Mr Hobbs is about to go to…'

'Please don't. I am feeling much better now.'

Perhaps it was overwork—she was doing too much.

She was writing her monograph on Eunice, intent on lifting the curse of her vanishing; she was taking her regular stroll before breakfast, looking for birds that ought to be there and weren't; she spent hours making copious notes of everything remarkable, beautiful, or simply mundane; she helped with Dot a few days a week; she was also now trying to keep a record of where she spotted the unnatural—no better word than that—greenish hue bursting over the waters some mornings from Wicken Far End, in what seemed to be a triangle formed by the ruined church, the old factory, and the Tudor ruins; and finally, she had at last decided to merge her two notebooks into one another, feeling that the scientific and the preternatural were screaming at her that a dialogue was required at once between the one and the other.

And, to top it all, she was trying very hard indeed to ignore her persistent dead mother.

Too much, that was obvious.

Were Eliza to consult a physician, or physicians, she knew that they would run some tests, take a blood sample. She believed in medicine, hygiene, more than she did in otherworldly manifestations. Or so she kept repeating to herself.

But still, she had to admit it: her belief in science *could* be misplaced after all. For she would only be told the same thing as always: eat more meat and drink more red wine. Take country walks, have a little holiday. That was if she found a *modern* physician. Unmoving quietness, not getting over-excited, not leaving the house, quit reading at once, and what about all that manic writing! That was the most probable prescription for a woman, no matter what ailment she had. Even, she feared, from kind Peter. Old habits die hard… Whatever little scientific knowledge remained in her stupid brain sufficed for her to acknowledge that, at least, she was suffering what seemed to be a strong headache.

There was no denying it. She had seen it, next to the body, as she had seen it in the wretched place. Another tern, dead on the floor.

'Fairy grave,' her driver had enunciated, after they had reached the boundary of Lady Matthews's land, and were getting closer to Old John's house. It was a curious name, but Eliza knew that 'grave' in Norfolk simply meant a hole in the ground. There was, of course, no hole, and no fairy. Or so she had thought until now.

CHAPTER NINE

The afternoon passed slowly enough. Sam went for a drive in his car, and eventually drove it back home. He had been looking for something, or someone, but it was only an odd feeling; if he had been asked he would not have known what. He didn't see Charles, who was attending a committee meeting of the League, and occupied his time alone by writing in his journal, something that he had not done since before the river accident. He read a little of George MacDonald's book. He had learnt that Viola's favourite author was still alive, a very old man living in Surrey, and was trying to decide whether a visit to the writer would be at all possible. He had no idea what he expected to achieve from it: it would not bring Viola back. Nothing would.

Something kept nagging at him, pressuring the back of his head. He knew it was connected with the strange past few weeks, but couldn't put his finger on it. And then it hit him: the beggar. He had seen him twice, he was sure now. The second time, when he was returning from that strange evening at The True Dawn. And the first time it had been in front of Charles's house, the night of the séance. Two strange evenings, on which his senses had been somewhat heightened, or that had brought with them the vividness of the supernatural, had started or ended by sighting this odd creature.

His hairs stood on end, exactly as they did when he recalled the way Lady Matthews had looked at him.

He went out and crossed the street. The gas-lamp by which the beggar had knelt the night of the séance didn't work, and he had the feeling it hadn't since then, although he had not remarked on it. On closer inspection he saw why: the whole long metallic pole was rusty, and the pavement around it, in contrast to the rest of the street, was overtaken by fungus, weeds, rotten leaves. The gas-lamp, newly installed barely two years previously, looked two hundred years old. What *was* going on?

At about eight o'clock, after a lonely supper, someone rang at the main door, and none other than Jim was shown into the library, where Sam sat, trying to finish MacDonald's strange novella, but in truth musing on the recent events. Jim's countenance alarmed Sam a great deal. He looked shocked; his whole face was set in a clenched mask, and he avoided Sam's eyes.

'Jim, what's wrong? You look like you've seen a ghost.' He got up and served two stiff drinks.

'Sam, I've got news.'

'Which news?'

'I thought I better come to tell you in person.'

'Tell me what? Is it about Freddy? Is he alright?'

Jim took the glass and emptied it in one gulp, gesturing to be served another. Sam complied.

'Jim, what is going on?' Sam's heart missed a beat, as he started to realise that, whatever Jim had come to tell him, it somehow involved him.

'It's about Viola.'

Sam caught his breath.

He could hardly mumble, '*What* about her?'

'She's alive, Sam.'

Sam hardly understood the rest of the explanation that followed this initial blow. As he slowly receded and sat on a chair, he half-heard the words coming out of Jim's mouth: Viola had never drowned, apparently, but had appeared somehow upstream, in Wolvercote. *Upstream?* Was that even possible? The family had hushed the matter up almost entirely; Viola was, so the modern doctors said, catatonic, half mad, looked after in a private clinic somewhere in Yorkshire.

'Maybe it was on account of your own disappearance you thought she was dead!'

Sam knew Jim was trying to be helpful. However, he had no

idea what his friend might mean by this statement.

'What disappearance? You mean my coming to my uncle in London?' For the first time, the word 'uncle' felt odd in his mouth.

'I mean your disappearing into the countryside like you did.'

A pause.

'Do you really not remember? You were lost, Samuel. You ran into the wild after it happened. It took days to find you! That was when we brought you here; Mr Bale said it wasn't the first time you had done that, that you ran away once when you were a child.'

Sam's head was filled with Viola's face, with the dark-greenish waters of the Isis, with the ruined Tudor manor in all its decaying splendour. He had no idea what Viola's cousin was talking about, and could only press his nails deeper into the sofa's leather arms, as he tried to grasp hold of reality, and as reality slowly receded away from him.

Grewelthorpe, the village was called Grewelthorpe. Up in Yorkshire. That was all Sam needed to know. The rest of Jim's gibberish didn't matter a bit.

On the other side of the train window, he saw now and then square black buildings through the darkness, old farms and villages resting on slopes, churches stinging the clouded sky, buildings extending their fingers like a dead body lying over the hills. The train left lagoons behind and the countryside became richer in rocks and gradients and uneven slopes, a welcome rest from the eerie, infinite vistas that filled his brain; and then Sam knew that he was going north. And that meant going to Viola. He was angry, thirsty and cold, but would not leave the train for any of the refreshment stops, scared that he would miss the call to get back on board. The only thing in his mind was to see Viola as soon as possible. Not even talk to her, something according to Jim her current state did not allow, but simply to see her face, to reassure himself that she truly lived. He needed to see this, and had vowed not to go to sleep until that was done. Then, and only then, would he think on what to do next.

Unfortunately, his eagerness was interrupted by his anxiousness: he got into a fight with a group of youngsters and had to change trains. Jim's presence prevented the situation from getting out of hand, as he insisted Sam needed to calm down.

The house was a large Regency mansion in the outskirts of Hackfall Wood. It sat alone on a little slope of land, with the woodland shooting up behind it. They arrived on a frosty morning, and the pale birches on the back looked like whitish ghosts. They took rooms in the nearby town, and set off almost immediately. Sam was restless, eager to do something, anything.

They first observed the building from the edge of the wood, hidden among the oak, lime, ash and sycamore trees. He had a strong feeling then of the wood protecting him, of nature bending to his will. Sam kept saying that he would come up to the hospital by the front door, that he would not hide. That he felt that the oak and the lime and the ash and the sycamore trees were on his side, and that this gave him strength.

Sam introduced them, and Jim quickly added that he was Viola's cousin. They were granted access at once.

A nurse offered to take them to her. She smiled now and again, revealing teeth that needed some attention. They traversed some white corridors, through the open doors of which one could glimpse benign inmates occupied in genteel pastimes, all of them lavishly attended by a set of professional-looking carers. Everything was clean and full of light, blessed by a calming whiteness that reflected the peaceful but cold winter sun. The wide rooms and passageways and serious hunting portraits and high ceilings spoke of old fortunes and rich inmates, and Sam silently wondered how Viola's father, a sexton in a minor Oxford church, could possibly afford such a luxury.

The distant wing they reached after a few minutes suffered from a sudden change of mood, for lack of a better word. The woman had directed him into an area very different from the ample corridors and vast wards they had been traversing. The chambers here were decidedly smaller, most of the doors were locked, and the windows weren't in the tall French style that he had admired but rather small, poky and barred. There was another thing that struck Sam, an indefinite stench, an acrid odour that emanated from the mixture of human smells and the medicines and chemical concoctions necessary in institutions such as this one. He found himself in what appeared to be one of the gloomiest and more dangerous wards of the asylum.

Sam suddenly saw that the nurse's clothes were strangely grubby, more perhaps than was fit even for a busy worker in a place like this. Her eyes were clouded by something indeterminate, and were strangely alert, and her nails appeared to be too long and yellowish to be considered hygienic.

He looked around in some trepidation.

'Excuse me,' he said, with all the calm that he could muster, 'but I don't think I caught your name.'

She smiled again, looking down as if she were blushing, an odd gesture.

'Does it matter, sweetheart?'

She advanced in his direction and Sam went rigid, but thought it better to give her a sense of being in control, so he let her take him by the arm and direct him to look into one of the chambers. Jim was already peering through the small opening. Those poor souls looked terribly dirty and haggard, very much, he now saw, the mirror image of the unknown woman they had so foolishly followed.

'They know the land beyond the stars,' said the woman. 'They have looked directly into it.'

'What?'

'That is why they are like this: they looked into that which no human being should ever glimpse…'

'My dear woman!' Jim started. But he didn't know what to say.

'Here you are! Mary, thank you so much for looking after our guests. Mr Moncrieff, Mr Woodhouse, I hope Mary wasn't a nuisance,' said a young-looking doctor, going rather pink at his ears.

'Not at all.'

'Good! I'm Dr MacFarlane. Miss Rochford is right here. Before we go in, I would like to tell you a few things. In fact, if busy-bee Mary hadn't walked you all the way here already, I might have done so in my office. Perhaps you want to see Miss Rochford now, and come and talk to me after?'

Sam could not wait to see Viola; he could not wait a single minute.

'That would be most kind, Doctor, if you don't mind,' he muttered.

'Not at all! I'll wait for you just here.'

The last sentence carried the notion of a visit of a short duration, and the implication of a risk for their safety inside the ward. Reluctantly, they went in.

Viola looked at him, or rather through him, lost on those otherworldly plains where she now dwelt. Sam moved slightly, right and left; her eyes did not follow. She was tied up to a chair with the straps used to physically restrain lunatics, but her posture shifted slightly. Sam thought he could glimpse a flicker of recognition, and said her name repeatedly. Her skin was an odd, greenish hue, and it looked cracked in places; she was strangely aged, as if ten years had passed in a few months.

'Viola, my love. It's me!' Sam repeated.

She was sitting lopsided by the straps, like a broken doll; but she suddenly jerked up with all her might, trying to position herself as far as possible from him. There was no other way to describe the scene: Viola was scared of Sam. She started shrieking, suddenly animated.

They were instantly ushered out from the room and into the care of the young doctor, who conducted them back down the long corridor.

'Miss Rochford has started to sleep more than normal. But that doesn't seem to make her less tired,' he explained, once they were sitting in his office. 'She can hardly stay awake during the daytime, and grows progressively more lethargic.'

'I see.'

'She seems to have experienced some extreme shock, although her development from day-lethargy to a total catatonic state has been progressive, taking place over a few concentrated weeks. But we are helping her here.'

'Why is she restrained?' Sam asked.

The doctor seemed lost for words. 'Restrained? Sir—?'

'Why is she restrained?' Sam could not mask the threat in his voice, and the doctor was quick to sense a change in his manner.

'Sam, please...' Jim interjected.

'For her own protection, of course! Look here, this isn't the hospital from a penny dreadful, but a respectful, modern establishment! What did you say your name was? You are not exactly family like this gentleman here, are you? I'm going to have to ask you to leave, sir.'

Sam understood at once that he would not be allowed back in the institution. The realisation threw him into a fury; he had to muster all the control he could not to succumb to his sudden need to destroy the doctor's office, and hit his complacent face until it turned into a fleshy pulp. But he managed to contain himself. He got up, boiling inside with anger, and left, leaving the door open behind him. Jim made his excuses and went after him.

It happened as they were on the way out, when they were passing next to a set of double French windows. Behind them was a well-kept garden that made one think of nothing unwholesome. Suddenly one of its glass doors inexplicably exploded, fragments of glass cutting everyone at hand, Sam and Jim included.

In a corner Mary was laughing wildly, and cheerfully clapping her hands, a distorted grin on her face.

Sam, however, had just finally understood something about himself: he had broken that glass door, without touching it.

There was some tranquillity in knowing the truth, in accepting it. It had taken its time, but it had finally come to light: for so unwilling had he been to interrogate the mysterious events of his life that it had needed to find other ways to reach him.

Sam had come to understand something in the past few weeks: people think that a burial is final, but this supposed finality is a mockery. If justice so requires, a coffin can be dug up, unveiling its secrets: a child buried with his mother because he wasn't meant to exist; objects one thought gone forever, hidden amid the earth's embrace; empty infant coffins, empty adult coffins. Even the oldest corpses, under proper examination, were capable of pointing a finger at those responsible for their early departure. Nothing, nothing at all, could stay hidden, no secret was safe, no matter how deeply it was buried. No crime was left unresolved, and all truth came to light at the end.

A French window had exploded, and Samuel Moncrieff had finally learnt a crucial truth about himself.

CHAPTER TEN

Lady Matthews had arranged some séances to take place in London before her country weekend. The first one was going to be hosted by Madame Florence. As usual, Miss Clare Collins and Mr Thomas Bunthorne were in attendance, as well as Madame Florence's new pet, Willimina Lawrence, a little American with incredible powers of sight.

'We are all friends here,' Miss Collins began, throwing an odd glance in Mr Woodbury's direction. 'And we can share our greeting to Mother Gaia with you. From here, we invoke the Mother of All, the Earth Queen.'

'Should Madame Florence not be present?' Helena ventured.

'We have a little surprise tonight,' continued Miss Collins. 'Miss Lawrence here will perform, under the blessings of our beloved Madame Florence.'

A murmur of anticipation could be sensed from among

sitters, except the two men who were there, who continued to display brooding moods. Willimina Lawrence, Madame Florence's new protégée, was quickly making a name for herself with her impressive powers of sight. She was also, or so it seemed, the female Messiah. Helena took note of the likes and dislikes that the young woman generated in the public.

Everyone was instructed to close their eyes, and unite in a chain of hands.

No hymns, no prayers, but a regular breathing whose rhythm came loudly from Miss Clare Collins's seat, and which all the sitters gradually followed. Helena opened her eyes one second, just to keep track of proceedings, and saw how the room was much darker, as someone had put out candles one by one, leaving only the one in the centre of the table shining, together with the fire in the grate. That was all she could hear, the fire, the rhythmical breathing, one by one all present falling into a regular way of existing that was similar to a regular thinking, a performance, a moment in which they were all sharing the same thoughts, seeing the same images in their inner eyes. Miss Collins started humming slowly, and then she spoke a series of words intently, with long pauses between each of them.

'Sun. Moon. Light. Darkness. Male. Female. Line. Circle. Clarity. Shadow. Sound. Silence.'

It was hypnotic. Helena had never sat on a séance like this one; but Miss Collins knew very well what she was doing. Willimina, on the other hand, seemed not to be doing anything. Helena opened her eyes and saw her head hanging, slightly lopsided, in front of her, describing little circles. She looked like one of those old-fashioned French dolls. Suddenly, her head jerked up, and she opened her eyes. They were two white balls, surrounded by deep dark circles that hadn't been there before.

'I am so lonely,' Willimina blurted out. 'Oh, my friends… Where are my friends?'

She didn't sound like her at all, but like a much younger girl, a girl who perhaps was pining because a doll had been left out in the garden and the rain had damaged it, Helena thought. It was a dull tone, uncanny, as if they were listening and posing questions to a child talking in her sleep.

'We are all friends here, you are not alone,' Miss Collins answered confidently to whoever had taken possession of Willimina.

'Oh, but I am, miss. For where are Flora, and Maud, and Alice?'

Helena looked up, and everyone around the table had opened their eyes and was looking at each other and at Miss Collins for guidance.

'No one moves,' she simply indicated. 'Who are you, dear?' she asked.

'Dot,' answered Willimina. Mrs Ashby swallowed a gasp.

'Ask her about the girls!' the old lady couldn't help but

interpose. Miss Collins indicated with a serious countenance that she should be patient, and let her continue the proceedings.

'Welcome, Dot, we are all friends here.'

'No!' the spirit shouted now. 'You are not my friends! I don't know where my friends are! Only Maud has come to see me… and you turned her away.'

Willimina started whining like a spoiled little girl, shouting and crying and hitting the floor with her boots, in a veritable tantrum. Miss Collins tried to calm her, and she eventually succeeded. Willimina started talking again:

'When did it happen then? I cannot remember. I remember Baptiste, my favourite kitten of that whole litter. He made friends with me very quickly, followed me around, pushed his little face against mine, caressed my arm with his little paw, scratching. And then, one day, he wasn't there anymore. How I looked for him! How dreadfully scared I was! For there was something there, some thing… In the ruins, it was, that I came upon his broken body, the pulpy grey liquid of his flesh mixing up with the earth and the rubble. Someone had smashed his head with an old brick.'

'The ruins? Who else was there, dear?'

'The man with the long hair. He always crossed the room inside the mirror, you see, never on the other side. On the other side, it was only me, sewing, or writing, or playing, or reading. How handsome he is, I think, with his three-piece suit, his walking stick, his moustache. I feared him; I waited for him, for he always knew very well how and where to find me. I saw him: inside the mirror in the parlour's wall, over the stagnant water of a puddle, sticking out over my shoulders.' Willimina's face was not her own, a shadowy, shaded face. 'I saw him: in the recently cleaned stone floor of the kitchen, buckets of water thrown on it. I felt him: walking all over the house, turning the corners ahead of me. In the garden I saw him often, reflected in the house windows.' Willimina was now twisting her head far to the left and to the right. 'I recognised him in the vanishing of food in the pantry, always liquid things, in the wash stands that appeared filled up of their own accord, because he wanted somewhere to reflect himself, so we could see each other. I talked to him, finally: on the thresholds of badly lit rooms, hidden among the shadows.' She stopped her movements, jerked her head upright. 'And then I learnt what he wanted.'

'And what is it he wanted, my dear?'

'Why, them! Not me...' Willimina deflated, and slumped back on the chair.

Mrs Ashby got up, and fled the room.

'Let's all close our eyes again,' Miss Collins indicated. Everyone did as they were told, and they continued holding each other's hands as she started reciting her words again.

'Sun. Moon. Light. Darkness. Male. Female. Line. Circle. Clarity. Shadow. Sound. Silence.'

It happened then. Something happened to Helena. Images

appeared inside her mind. How was that possible? And then she saw it: the ruined Tudor manor, and Samuel Moncrieff, wandering around it as if he was lost, considering the walls, caressing the fallen stones, in a daze, looking intently into the rotten fungus-clad walls. She saw the old beggar woman, and she could imagine her lying in the foetal position. And then she metamorphosed into a little girl, sleeping in the same way. She saw a man walking towards her, extending his hand. A man who looked like a beast, with a long mat of grey hair and a strange-looking overcoat, big and tall and otherworldly. And Helena saw, *sensed*, that she had been waiting for him, for a long time. And in her mind's eye, the man looked like the two-faced creature with pointy teeth that she had encountered in London, in London of all places, at the estuary.

AUTOMATIC WRITING DEMONSTRATION

NORFOLK, MARCH 1901

MEDIUM: WILLIMINA LAWRENCE

Brief initial statement: Session performed under the presence of impartial witnesses. Miss Lawrence claims that the spirit is called, or calls himself, Old John. She also claims he is now her new spirit guide.

I decided to wait for the young lady in my favourite spot. I hoped that she was not going to ask about that ugly affair back in the big house. I hadn't seen Lady Matthews for some time, but I still respected her. She wasn't like the other lords and ladies who owned the land up and down the county. She had always let me feed my family, on account of how poor she had been when young, and the times when I had come to her and her mother with some game. They never had anything to give me in return. But one day Lady Matthews—or Rosie as she was back then—gave me a fairy stone with a hole in it, and told me that it would keep the devil away. It was shiny and green.

Back in those days, people said that Rosie's mother was a witch. People can be so cruel. They were used to the harshness of life, to be fair. People now are so detached from nature; they do not know where the meat that they eat comes from, for it is prepared for them in abattoirs and slaughterhouses. But they knew it back then, knew how to kill it and prepare it and gut it and bleed it. And I always thought that was something to be proud of.

It wasn't an easy life being a poacher. You need to be a good shot, and move silently, and see game from far away, while hidden among the reeds. And be willing to spend hours waiting in the frozen night, in the whirling snow, mellow with rum. And still not fail when the game approaches you.

Lately, I had been thinking about those days very often, my parents making the effort to send me to school to learn reading and arithmetic, to honour and obey the Queen; the children of the two villages under the same roof, the deadly rivalries, the lasting friendships. My parents had done well for me, for other children were sent to work at such young age! That little one, no more than six or seven, sent to keep the birds away from the stacks of corn. It was such a cold winter, deadly, and they found him nearly perished one day, dead of the cold. He was brought round eventually, and lived to a ripe old age.

For we endured the cold and the hardships—but at least there were no demons who took us.

Life in those days was simpler: the feasts when the last of the fields was cut and got up, and the Lord of the Harvest took his fork with the sheaf of wheat up to the Master's house. The lonely nights in foggy weather, the boiled oats on cold December nights to lure the partridges into the sack, the eternal game of hide-and-seek with the keepers.

I think I saw it first on one of these nights, one of those when the fog is so dense that you may pass next to somebody, and not know until they have left you behind. An out-of-shape double of himself, that's what it looked like to me. Made of wood, or of clay. Unliving. I was a poacher at the height of my powers, and feared nothing. That night I was after a couple of youngsters who had stolen a gun, for I wanted to scare them, to make them think twice about doing things like that, the two silly boys who had stolen a gun and were poaching with it. They would be dead by the next morning, although I didn't know it yet. I was hidden in some holly bushes near a road I suspected they might come by. But I never saw them: it was the devil who came instead, and found me there. It would also be the devil who got to the youngsters before I could scare them back home, poor lads.

I had always known why he let me go that night: the devil was looking for someone else.

But I knew also that one day he would come back for me, for the devil doesn't like being observed, and even less being recognised. And I recognised him, beyond a doubt. It could be nobody else. Who else could that be, a terror with your own face? For I understood then that everyone would see the devil with his or her face, to be ashamed of their own sins.

The creature was bigger and taller than any man ought to be, with broad Viking shoulders and an overcoat made up of vermin and shadows that moved of its own accord. The devil seemed to be carrying a green light around with him, so dense it left behind a trace of a sticky white substance. I remembered then about the fairy stone, which hung around my neck, and I held it as if it were a golden cross. And the devil looked at me, and in that look it told me all that I needed to know.

Not now, John. But one day.

Then came the dreams, in which sometimes I was the devil himself, and sometimes I was his victim. But always, always, it ended with those empty black eyes looking into my skull and putting there the words.

Not now, John.

I hadn't dreamt for years, hadn't thought for years of it, of that night. For the dreams had gone at last, or I would have ended my days in Fulbourn.

I hid myself under the tree, and I woke up, for I had dozed sitting there, waiting for the young lady that was to come. And I had dreamed again. And the devil had said: Now, John. Twenty years later.

I wasn't surprised to see the shadow advancing towards the tree, and gaining consistency as it came nearer. And I wasn't surprised when the world around the devil changed light, and a white sticky substance seemed to impregnate the air around me, bringing rot and decay and death along with it.

Then I looked for the fairy stone, and did not find it, for I had passed it on, long ago, to my own daughter. So I whispered a prayer instead. But I knew somehow that it would not help.

I wasn't surprised at all when the devil opened his mouth and showed me hell inside. And when he beckoned me in.

CHAPTER ELEVEN

'And now, for the jewel in the crown,' continued the guide, 'neither a gadget nor a contraption, but something infinitely more fascinating, ladies and gentlemen: a creature that possessed a life that we can't even imagine, in our era void of magic.'

'Hear, hear!' someone shouted with passion.

Helena had bought a ticket for a tour of The True Dawn's headquarters, hoping to gain some insight, but now she was regretting the idea. The shaman had been preserved in a meditative fashion, sitting with his legs crossed over each other, his palms open and delicately placed on his knees. He was wearing what the guide identified as 'magical robes', with a curious hat, and had a dried snake wrapped around his legs. And open, infinite beady eyes.

Helena needed a second to digest it: she was looking at the

desiccated body of a human being. A wave of profound disgust ran through her. This atrocity brought to mind other atrocities, and she found herself panting heavily, and had to make a huge effort not to vomit then and there, not to shout at everyone present what the hell was wrong with them.

'This shaman,' resounded the guide's voice, 'served on a scientific expedition to the Chita region, in Siberia. After his death, his body was perfectly preserved due to the low temperatures. He was brought back like this, and it is now one of Count Bévcar's dearest possessions.'

'Marvellous!'

'How horrid!' someone thankfully said.

'Is it true he cures wasting diseases?' someone wanted to know.

'Can you all see that he is wearing a necklace of teeth? They are bear teeth. It means that he had the power to transform himself into a bear.' Everyone wanted to say something at the same time, and Helena sensed that the hubbub was gaining consistency on the indignant side. She felt relieved to see that she wasn't the only one horrified by the dismal 'object'; for that was what they had made of this human being.

The drunken man in the estuary guarding the kidnapped boy had been one of Bévcar's acolytes—the visit to The True Dawn's headquarters had been illuminating after all. But other matters were pressing. A baby farm had been dismantled. The case had started, as most cases do, with a seemingly unrelated affair, which had quickly and horridly evolved into something other, something malign. A woman checking into a hotel with a small child, leaving him sleeping, and going out to do some errands. She got lost, of course, in the chaos of the streets, and did not remember the name of the hotel, nor the street where it was located. It seemed to have simply vanished, disappeared. Helena could not take the credit for solving it, for there had been many agents involved, but she now needed to finish the necessary paperwork, to write her report for Scotland Yard compiling the final data. In short, dealing with the low-level administrative duties that would mean she would be compensated. Solving a case was a matter of placing pieces together, and this was also part of the puzzle.

There had been moments recently in which even her rational mind had reacted against the things that were happening in the capital. She had found herself assessing the known city like a huge, unexpected beast, moving around it unsure of how to interpret its signs. For the first time since she had established herself here, Helena thought that she saw it for what it was, a horrid labyrinth, and for once she did not enjoy the challenge; she was not in the mood to solve it. She feared she was starting to lose touch with what was real. Measurable data, facts, things that she could understand. Not strange visions in the middle of séances; not creatures who changed, twisting from a monstrous beggar to a gentleman with a cane.

Everywhere she went, she felt out of place, an oddity for her usual self. It was an unexpected feeling, deeply unwelcome. She sensed that her usual confidence, her determination to get things done, her resourcefulness, were all slowly receding. If she didn't get a grasp on things, she feared she might lose herself. And if something frightened her it was that: she had worked long and hard to attain a freedom she had only dreamed of when growing up with her grandfather, a freedom that was precious to her. She had always prided herself on her rationality, but her thoughts, the new ideas that her mind was rehearsing, were not rational. Her case notes, she observed, weren't rational either. They talked of shape-changing men, and young people either lost or catatonic. Or of children 'used' as vessels for older people, in some strange rituals. She had purchased Bévcar's book, but reading it had not helped. It was gibberish.

She had to admit it to herself: the unusual occurrences she was encountering, roughly since the Queen's passing, were dangerously close to tainting her capacity for rational thought. Still, she had accepted a huge challenge: solving a twenty-year-old riddle, the three vanishings. So she had to pull herself together, somehow. She was very angry with herself, and shocked at her anger.

A knock at the door.

'Miss?' Her maid was carrying a letter.

'Thank you.' Helena opened it.

Information pertaining to the last known movements and current whereabouts of a Samuel Moncrieff, Esquire:

Mr Moncrieff abandoned the house of his godfather, Mr Charles Bale, seventeen days ago, reason unknown. He was accompanied by his college friend, Mr James Woodhouse. They took a train to Edinburgh, travelling first class. There was some occurrence during the journey: he was expelled from a women-only carriage, where it seems he had taken refuge, or was hiding from someone. He used one of the refreshment stops of said vehicle to remain behind in some middle station, and later climbed on another train, this time due for York. Mr Moncrieff didn't stop in the city, but, almost at once after setting foot off the train, he moved on to the village of Grewelthorpe. Stayed a couple of days, after which he reappeared in York. His trace was lost for up to a week. Next seen last Saturday, boxing for money in one of Manchester's illegal rings. He badly beat a man and bolted town. His opponent will recover. Left the city on a third-class carriage bound for London. Please follow key PSALM 137.

The canal and tinker network had outdone themselves. The fee would have to be equally handsome. Before setting off back to Norfolk, she penned a note to her solicitors with the required instructions.

*

The next day Helena reached the abbey shortly after lunch was finished, and was shown into the spacious and impressively stocked library, where Mrs Ashby was taking coffee. Lady Matthews was nowhere to be seen.

Lady Matthews lived in the abbey with only her friend Mrs Ashby for company. Mrs Ashby had come to Great Britain as a rich American heiress thirty years previously, but had never got used to her late husband's northern seat. They were attended by a few servants, and kept some parts of the house shut. The house was crumbling, disorderly, chaotic. In every room, corridor, landing, a bunch of *sempervivums* was slowly dying inside their vases, an old local custom to make sure the devil would not come near.

Later on, Helena would put in writing a few impressions of the abbey itself, a curious building to her eyes, both close to and isolated from the coast, set in a remote area where sea and land blurred into each other. That part of the country, she was amused to find, was rotten with superstition, filled with old women who still buried cider bottles in the marshes as offerings. The region was surely an oddity, as it was rich in rhyolite, not very prominent in marshy areas.

Helena had read about the architect who built the abbey, Mr Williams. He had built the Matthews family a house based upon the ideas of a French château of the time of Louis XI, rather than in Italian medieval architecture. This alternative Gothic Revival style, she was surprised to find, was based on the writings of Eugène Viollet-le-Duc, an artist who had designed buildings heavy with a curious ornamental style, an antiquarian feeling: gargoyles, fanciful crests of arms, unnerving animal heads. James was connected to the development of some metropolitan cemeteries, and Helena could sense a running funereal discourse in the ornamentations, as if she were in front of a large mausoleum. The fantastical and rich display was too much, and produced the opposite effect: she could not really consider each affectation, and, head giddy with detail, avoided to look, preferring to rush inside. In the middle, overlooking it all, sat the odd-looking tower, too small to be of any consequence or use, as if it were a strange folly integrated into the building instead of being put in a meadow, and as out of place as a hummingbird on the English coast.

Once inside the building, the Great Hall with its large staircase revealed at once the effect the place wanted to have on the visitor: that of an oppressive grandeur. At the top of the staircase, before turning right or left, one was greeted by it: an imposing portrait of a younger Lady Matthews in the pre-Raphaelite manner, with long abundant hair, profusely jewelled with strange antiquated things. Something about those jewels impressed Helena a great deal; the painter had made a point of mimicking their maddening green shimmer in Lady Matthews's emerald eyes. The effect of the rhyolite in the painting was simply magnetic.

*

Helena had always prided herself on being a good observer, not only of human nature but of the places humans haunted. It did not take her long to see that the house, which to a passing visitor would seem in perfect order, was after closer inspection under the spell of some form of decrepitude which haunted its venerable walls. If one looked carefully, the cracks and damp stains on the painted paper were revealed, as were the cobwebs shrouding the ceilings, although she had to look twice to notice anything amiss. The tapestries were moth-eaten here and there, costly woven pieces which had obviously been left to their own devices, and the mirrors were clouded from inattention and lack of polish. The oil paintings were darkened by the dirt and dust that accumulated in the corridors, on every surface, even over the books in the library—as she found out to her dismay—and on each one of the items from the collection of mummified birds that was the pride of the household.

As soon as she went out she ascertained the degree of abandonment in the gardens surrounding the property: the ornamental hedges had grown in a strange fashion after years without a human hand to tame them, now transformed into shapeless things.

But only someone who spent a considerable amount of time as a houseguest would have seen through the obvious 'shape-up' that the hostess, or indeed their little group of servants, had effected. It was like a house cleaned up in a hurry, she thought, where the dust had been pushed behind the rugs, and the corridors swept in a frenzy.

Coffee and petits fours consumed, everyone retired to follow their different pursuits. It was time for Helena to leave her observations for a moment, and start with other kinds of pressing matters. Before leaving the room, Helena asked Mrs Ashby for a private word, and the older woman motioned to be followed into a sitting room off the hall, at the right of the main entrance, presumably her morning room. It was sparsely furnished with a desk in its centre as its main feature, a woman's desk on which to write letters or compose menus to deliver to the cook, and little else. Helena was surprised to see something as modern as a telephone hanging from a corner, an interior line communicating with the rest of the house itself.

'Mrs Ashby. I would like to see Lady Matthews at once,' she started. 'I also need to visit the Tudor ruins as soon as possible.'

Although Helena had already visited them in secret, she wanted to see the old woman's reaction to her request. She wasn't disappointed: her face drained of life, turning as white as the parchment diligently set out on the desk for letter writing and menu setting.

'Pray, tell me, why do you *require* to see the ruins?'

'It's an obvious place to start looking.'

'But nothing has ever been found there!'

'Mrs Ashby, I don't expect to "find" anything, exactly; but, all the same, I need to see the place for myself. From what Lady Matthews explained to me in London, the ruined Tudor manor was the usual playground for the three missing children.'

'Wouldn't you prefer to be taken to your room first, and freshen up? The ruins will be there tomorrow, and the day after.'

'Mrs Ashby, please. I do not like being idle when working on a case. There is still light, and no better moment than the present.'

'We should have had the whole thing pulled down. Down!' Mrs Ashby said, with unexpected passion, and added no other word. Helena had what she needed.

The matter of the ruins' reputation was for now resolved. However, her secret trip to visit them earlier in the week had elucidated two obvious questions: who was the woman that she saw there? And what was she doing in the ruins? A few well-placed, discreet enquiries among the servants elicited the information that she was a beggar who kept appearing all over the estate, that she had tried to get into the actual house at least three times, being rebuked and succeeding only on one occasion. She was thought to be a non-dangerous creature, and generally idiotic.

*

The following morning Lady Matthews did not come down for breakfast. Helena had not seen her employer yet, and she needed to double-check some facts that had emerged since their brief interview in London.

'Mrs Ashby, I need to have an interview with Lady Matthews as soon as possible,' she explained. The woman looked frankly puzzled. Helena wondered whether she had any inkling as to how her work was accomplished, and gathered not.

'I will also need to see the children's nursery.'

Mrs Ashby's brows shot up.

'The nursery has been shut for two decades, Miss Walton. Damp problems.'

'I ought to see the places where the children spent most of their time. Please let me know whenever you can grant my request.'

And with this, Helena left, hoping to command some notion of urgency rather than impertinence. She knew from the servants that Lady Matthews had been indisposed, but she needed to see her nonetheless. She went out of the house, and left the grounds at a brisk walk, to all intents and purposes to take the air.

The servants had also provided her with information regarding a recently deceased local poacher. It seemed that there would be no inquest into his death, as he was an old man who had lived a long and happy life. Still, the gathering expected that morning in Old John's house was an invaluable occasion to take the measure of some local characters.

As soon as she was out of the estate, she found herself opposite a long field heaving with activity. It was the planting season, a group of men gathered in the distance around a tatty ploughing engine. A long line of land workers was marching ahead of her in the road. She thought about catching up with them, but they were too far away.

At last she arrived at the cottage. Exactly as she had expected, a few neighbours, the priest, the local historian, and a young local woman who was introduced as a cousin and helper to Dr Wilson, also present, as well as the local constable, had all descended *en masse* upon the little place. Helena was asked how she had come to be in those parts. It sufficed to say that she was a guest of Lady Matthews, interested in the history of the estate, and she had wanted to pay her respects to one of her older tenants.

'Old John surely had many stories to tell about the estate, Miss Walton,' the reverend simply said, and he added, somewhat pensively, 'Blessed Edmund preserve us! Blessed Edmund preserve us all!'

'And St William of Norwich,' muttered the young constable. 'Poor Old John; always knew he would be gone at dusk. "At dusk the devil will come and devour me," he was fond of saying,' he chuckled.

Helena said nothing. The young woman had apparently found the corpse, but Helena wasn't interested enough in a death by old age to talk to her. Still Helena sensed that she regarded her with interest. She had an unruly mat of pale blonde hair, which seemed to stay up without the need for pins, and a nervous and alert gaze that followed her around the room.

One of Old John's granddaughters was serving tea, struggling with the large teapot. She went to help her, and finally served herself a scalding cup that burned her tongue.

'Thank you so much for the tea. What is your name?' asked Helena.

'Rosie.'

'Thank you, Rosie.'

As Helena had expected, the cottage was the closest dwelling to the Tudor ruins. She managed to snatch a few words with the old poacher's daughter outside of the cottage, where the men could not hear them talking. Helena went straight to the point: had anyone seen anything peculiar? Something they could not explain?

'Aye, aye, miss. All that.'

She and the children had seen an 'odd-shaped' version of Old John the previous night, wandering about. Apparently, she was sure that the 'false' Old John would not do anything to harm the children. She said something very perceptive, in Helena's opinion: he looked like he was *made* of mushrooms.

'But you knew he was harmless?' she ventured.

'Aye. But I didn't want the children to see him like that, miss.'

'Why is that?' Helena asked.

''Cause, miss, no one should see anything that it wasn't meant for this world, do it changes you for the rest of your days,' she explained. 'Do' meant 'if it should happen', a much more absolute phrase, Helena thought, than her own clumsy equivalent.

The young blonde woman who had been introduced as Dr Wilson's assistant appeared at the door, hovering over the conversation. Old John's daughter made her excuses and went back into the little house.

'Hello.' It was Eliza Waltraud.

'Hello.'

Helena had noticed Miss Waltraud did not flinch at her Spanish surname, which made her instantly like her. She assessed her to be in her late twenties. Helena lit a cigarette.

'May I have one?' Miss Waltraud asked. Helena offered her a little enamel box, which contained some roll-ups and matches, kept in a clever little contraption on one side.

'This is nifty,' Miss Waltraud pointed, appreciating the object, as she took a deep drag of the fragrant tobacco.

'It is created particularly to fit into the secret pockets in the fold of a dress.'

Miss Waltraud smiled at this.

'Clever! I should get one for myself.'

They both smoked for a few seconds without saying anything else.

Eventually Miss Waltraud offered, 'Have you seen her?'

'Who?'

'The butler's daughter, Dot.'

'No, I haven't. Do you think I should?'

'Are you not the lady detective?'

Helena smiled. 'You have the advantage of me.'

'I apologise. There has been some talk among the servants...'

Miss Waltraud threw the cigarette butt on the ground and stepped on it.

Helena produced a flask. 'Cranberry liquor, from the north of Spain. Would you like to try it?'

'No, thank you.' Miss Waltraud paused for a moment and then took a breath, as Helena took a sip from the flask. 'Around a month ago I found a girl while out walking, wandering around the marshes, and Peter, Dr Wilson, took her under his roof. He looked after her for a few days.' Helena nodded to make her continue. 'Eventually she was removed to a facility in Yorkshire for catatonic cases. You see, she was catatonic, in a very similar way to—'

'You mean like the butler's daughter? Is she also catatonic?'

'Exactly—or, rather, like Dot used to be in the early days. She has improved a little with the passing of time, apparently.'

'I see.'

'Well, most doctors in the area have been here at some point to see Dot, and are aware of her history.'

'So your cousin remarked on the similarities between cases? It sounds strange, certainly, but why should this interest me, I wonder?' Helena said this smiling, trying to put Eliza at ease. She took another sip.

'Dot wasn't born like that; she was found like it the day Maud, Alice and Flora vanished.'

Helena had not expected the conversation to take this turn. She had not expected this at all.

'That is very interesting indeed. What did the doctors have to say? About the cause of her condition?'

'Not much. They put it down to the shock,' she explained. 'It is curious, to say the least, is it not? The way most female maladies are put down to shock, over-exhaustion, hysteria. It almost seems as if the good doctors are trying to find reasons not to worry about our ailments. We are not worth that much to them, I guess,' she concluded.

'And what do you think?'

'Me?' The woman laughed at this. 'Believe me, no one cares to hear *my* opinion.'

Helena felt a pang of sadness on hearing this. It brought too many memories back.

'Well, I do.'

'In that case… I would very much like to show you a couple of places around here. The collapsed church, the factory, and the ruins. Especially the ruins.'

'Oh, I know the ruins…'

'Then you must know.'

'I must know what?'

'That "*there are more things in heaven and Earth…*"' Eliza

210

smiled again. 'Look, would you like to meet Dot now?'

'Now?'

'I help look after her, and I need to give Mrs Burroughs a rest soon.'

Helena agreed. It was an opportunity too good to miss. But she was getting worried about the implications of what she had just heard. Had the child in the estuary been catatonic as well, or merely fainted? She couldn't have said.

When Helena re-entered the house, the butler informed her that Mrs Ashby wished to see her. Helena thanked him and followed him into a room where Mrs Ashby sat behind a gigantic desk that made her look diminutive.

'Miss Walton-Cisneros,' she said. Helena noticed it was the first time she had used her full name since their acquaintance, and knew herself in trouble. 'You have not been idle these past couple of days. I gather you have covered much ground already,' she said.

'I would have covered much more by now if I had been informed of certain things that I've had to find out by myself, Mrs Ashby.' The old woman smiled oddly, got up, and went to a cabinet. Helena wondered whether to continue, but there was nothing to be gained by class-conscious delicacies and, although she imagined she was risking her displeasure, she added: 'And I don't normally accept cases to "be idle", something my clients normally appreciate; when their intention is to find the truth and not to obfuscate it, that is.' Helena felt relieved when the old lady laughed at her words. It was difficult not to feel a little bit imposed upon by her aristocratic demeanour. Helena knew her late husband had been an earl and wondered why Mrs Ashby didn't use her own title. She opened two gold-gilded panel doors to reveal a collection of decanters and glasses.

'Too early for a sherry?' Mrs Ashby ventured.

'Thank you, I'd love one,' Helena replied, and the old woman indicated by a gesture that Helena should sit on one of the chairs by the fire. She was a bit damp from a light rain outside, and welcomed the opportunity to dry out a little and ingest something revitalising. It struck Helena that she had never seen this woman perform any task, no matter how minor, and it was odd to see her serve the drinks and bring them to a side table set between both chairs with her little bird-like steps. She wondered if she should have offered to help her.

'Where is Lady Matthews?'

'Lady Matthews has a slight headache. She'll be down for dinner.'

'Really?' Helena had not seen her hostess since she got to the abbey. 'Mrs Ashby, if I may, I was engaged by Lady Matthews, and I would like to report directly to her. I have not seen her since I got here. I have many questions for my employer, questions that have arisen during this investigation. I do not know what you may think my work entails, but I assure you, in order to test and retest the ongoing theories that may arise, it is advisable to remain in contact with one's employer. Obviously, if there are difficulties, or if the person who engaged you is detained, or indisposed, it is a shame, but it would be much better for me to acknowledge this fact at once, instead of being led into this absurd game of hide-and-seek. Pray tell me, will I be able to see Lady Matthews at all while I'm here? I do not normally abandon my cases, but let me tell you that my approach to this investigation will vary a great deal if my employer does not make herself available to me.'

Mrs Ashby remained silent a few seconds.

'Is that all?' she simply asked.

'It is certainly all I would like to say to you, yes. But, if you really are going to act as the true mediator between your friend and myself, I advise you to memorise to the slightest detail all her movements and impressions of the day the children disappeared, because I need a first-hand account, in her own words.'

Helena could not tell in truth why she felt so frustrated by Lady Matthews's lack of interest in her progress. Perhaps it was because the woman had seemed interested in her methods back in London, perhaps it was because Helena was starting to sense something darker in her refusal to cooperate. Why had she not mentioned the factory at all? What was she hiding?

A sharp sound pierced the air, and it took Helena a moment to understand the telephone on the desk was ringing. Mrs

Ashby got up with determination, and walked towards the little device with more energy than she had yet seen her display. She picked it up brusquely.

'Yes?'

Someone spoke at the other end of the line, but Helena could not hear a word they were saying.

'I see. Please inform Dr Wilson. Do the usual.'

Her business-like manner, handling such a modern machine, was somehow baffling, like an anachronism. She put the receiver down.

'May I ask what that was about?' Helena hoped she understood that she was conducting an investigation, not simply being nosy.

'Nothing you should worry with. However, I would appreciate it if from now on you avoided asking questions of the child. She is having a very difficult afternoon.'

'The child? Do you mean Dot?'

'That's right.'

It was odd how she didn't say her name.

The old lady looked intently at Helena, finished her sherry in one gulp—not a very ladylike gesture—and put the empty glass down.

'Very well, I'll see what I can do for you. Wait here, please, Miss Walton.'

*

It had not crossed Helena's mind that she was going to be summoned there and then, but something of what she said had struck a chord with Mrs Ashby. She stayed sipping her sherry, expecting the American woman to come back to let her know when she could expect a private interview with her hostess. To her surprise it was the butler who appeared.

'Miss Walton, Lady Matthews will receive you now. If you would be so kind as to follow me.'

Helena got up. They climbed up the main staircase, and took a turn to the eastern wing, the opposite one to where Helena was staying. They climbed one more floor, reaching a large corridor that had the faint feeling of not being much used: some pieces of furniture had white sheets covering them, some windows were shut with that finality one expects in abandoned houses. The only sign that the place was in use was the eternal *sempervivum* in their little vases and china saucers. The butler stopped in front of one of the doors, and he knocked in that soft butlerish manner, opened the door, stepped inside to murmur something Helena didn't catch, and held the door open for her. As she entered, he, with a deft servant's movement, left noiselessly, closing the door behind him.

It was the anteroom parlour adjacent to the lady of the house's bedchamber. It was decorated in pastel colours, with frills, and faded oil paintings of floral arrangements. But it also had the faint air of a room hardly ever used, as if it were lacking ornaments somehow. And it had a particularity not very common among landed ladies: the walls were covered in a profusion of little framed black-and-white photographs, competing for the available space among the oil paintings. They were all haunting, and they were all like the three Helena had been entrusted with in the folder Lady Matthews had given her on the day of their first acquaintance.

The Broads, the mirrors of water over the fenlands, the fragile and barely standing wooden windmills, the miniature bridges, the little boat with its square sails over a water so quiet, so smooth, horses and carts ploughing the fields, the eel catchers considering an osier eel trap, the huge corn stacks in the middle of a long field. A canal, endless. And everywhere that flatness, that sense of a land without end.

The photographer Peter Henry Emerson had stayed in the abbey shortly after its construction in 1875, and then again in 1881. He was not interested in photographing buildings; he went out every morning to capture the land and its occupants. Helena in truth had not followed the notion of researching the photographer; and in any case she would not have found anything to share with Lady Matthews: she seemed to have his entire *oeuvre* hanging inside this room.

'An impressive collection,' she offered.

'That series over there.' Lady Matthews pointed with a shaking hand at the photographs on a back wall of the room. 'Those are the pictures he took while he was here for the hunt. It has taken me twenty years to find all these.'

Some of the images were as clear and haunting in their quiet, unmoving quality as the land itself they were representing. About half of them, however, were too foggy to clearly represent anything, and it surprised Helena that anyone would have thought them worthy to be displayed.

'Some were discarded, you see. The "moved" ones; I think that is the term they use. But to me they are the dearest.'

Helena could get a glimpse of a figure peering through the fog; she could even see the girls themselves if she half-closed her eyes. They looked like the photographs of ghosts, a long-discarded *memento mori*. But Helena knew these were fancies, and she needed facts.

'Why has he not been invited?'

'Peter Emerson? Oh, he is abroad, I think.'

'Lady Matthews, if I may—'

'Would you allow me to begin, my dear? I have been told you want to hear my "impressions" of that morning; as if I hadn't repeated them to the police over and over.'

Helena ignored the slight rebuff.

'By all means. I also wanted to let you know that Old John is dead. I went to his family's home this morning.'

A tremor crossed the old face, but Lady Matthews maintained her detachment while she asked, without looking in Helena's direction, 'Who, do you say?'

'Old John, one of your older tenants.' The old woman

offered no reaction to the news. 'Lady Matthews, I do not want to overtax you, but—'

'You would like to know it all, everything that we have ascertained over the past twenty years.'

'Yes, that would be most useful.'

'However, Miss Walton, you must realise that hasn't helped us at all. The children have never been found.'

'Still, if you want me to cover more ground in less time than, let's say, another twenty years, it would speed things up a great deal if you were to trust me.'

'Yes, but you are missing the point, my dear. I wanted someone to look at this mess with a new perspective… Poor John—he knew very well one day he would come back for him at last. He named one of his granddaughters Rosie, after me, you know.'

'Who, Lady Matthews? Who was going to come for him?'

But she feigned not to have heard the question, so Helena decided to try another one:

'That beggar woman, the servants say she has tried to get into the house several times.'

'Three times,' she corrected; so, she was aware of the situation. Now it was Helena's turn to smile: she would not be able to feign she didn't know what she was talking about.

'Do you have any idea why?'

'Not in the faintest.'

'Did she ever manage to steal anything, take anything, to your knowledge?'

'Well, it was curious…'

'What was curious?'

'The only time she managed to actually get in—she went there directly.'

'Where, Lady Matthews?' The old lady looked at Helena. She looked almost like a child, happy with a secret knowledge no one else had.

'To the nursery. She was found there, on the floor, sleeping curled up, like a baby in the womb.'

Helena wondered why the servants had not shared this piece of information with her.

At last, Helena got her version of events: on the morning in question Lady Matthews had wanted to get up earlier than usual, not wanting to miss the excitement of the dogs, let out of their kennels, all the preparations contributing to their monstrous eagerness. It promised to be an excellent hunt.

She also had another task to perform: to make sure the girls didn't wander into the ruins. What she could not understand was why her husband had not demolished them completely and built the new house closer to the sea.

'You see? I hated the ruins. I cannot think of a place in closer communion with the shadows.'

This comment struck Helena as singularly perceptive, and very much in accordance with her own impressions.

'But you haven't demolished them either, Lady Matthews—'

'I couldn't now, with the girls gone, could I? What if they are still hiding there, somehow?' It was an odd comment, but Helena knew what she meant.

Afterwards she would always remember how quiet that day was, the eerie silence that crept down the stairs from the old nursery rooms at tea time, when normally a flurry of girlish feet would sound noisily on the treads. She would remark on the closed wardrobe doors, on the closed books, the pencils and colours quiet in their china pots, the glue pot shut forever, the cuttings and postcards and decoupage littering the polished surfaces, the silent dolls which could not give away the sisters' secrets, no matter how much they wanted to betray them. All those treasures left behind forever. The abandoned mousseline dress hanging behind the door, an empty replacement of the self, discarded, looking more than ever like a costume.

Breakfasting in bed, Lady Matthews had run through the various adjustments and last-minute requests in her head: the absence of Lord Caister's valet; the need to provide refreshments to those who, to her husband's dismay, had expressed a desire to stay behind. One could judge the lady of a house on the attention paid to the smallest detail, she said, and she would not be caught out. It was her first hunt at the abbey. She knew that the men would be eating down in the depths of the cave-like kitchen. It was customary to do so on hunting days. She still had a few minutes, a short interval of welcome solitude. The dogs would already be out in the yard at the back waiting, while the men sipped their coffee and brandy and ate their eggs and kidneys surrounded by huge pots and oversized baskets.

She finished and got ready without her maid's help, going straight down. The house was oddly silent. She failed to see any of the houseguests, any of her servants. She went onto the terrace and looked out, but there was no one in sight: the kitchen was empty, a rare occurrence, and the dogs could be heard in the distance.

She felt confused. What time was it? She thought she was doing what had to be done. But more peculiar than anything else was the deserted servants' quarters, where one could always be sure to find someone bustling about with their duties. She recalled now being woken up by the noise of guns, and how she had dismissed the notion: it had to be a dream, she had thought, the shooting would only start later. But *where* could they possibly be? Were they all playing a joke on her? Had her silly maid woken her at the wrong time on purpose? She had expected that, some kind of revenge on the young bride who had been a governess shortly before.

She knew where the hunting party was set to begin and started walking in that direction.

She did not expect the mist rising from the ground; it wasn't so hot after all, and it wouldn't be for the whole rest of the morning. Some dark clouds closed over where she was, and she felt a strange anxiety. The mist rose slowly, and she could not see her feet for a moment.

The hunt would cover the whole estate, but the eastern side would offer the best shooting for the wild ducks and geese, not to mention the pheasants. She knew that's where they were bound to start.

But once out of the house she felt disorientated, by the elusive hour, by the elusive hunting grounds. What *was* happening to her?

Some birds flew above, and she heard the guns firing. The beaters were making their rattle, walking in her direction. She realised her precarious situation, and rapidly moved on. But she didn't know exactly which way to do so. Left, or right?

She saw a little copse and ran there, and, without knowing why she did it, she hid beneath a tree, catching her breath. It was then that she saw it: the white muslin of a light summer dress, a girl, running along like a little dove. She thought it was Maud, her eldest stepdaughter.

'Maud? Darling?' she called from the empty copse, and only the branches moving repeatedly, and only the birds shooting up into the sky, and the smell of gunpowder, offered their silent acknowledgement. She was there; had Maud been?

The girl was nowhere to be seen, and she wondered if she had seen her after all.

Later on, she would recall that moment, trying in desperation to fix it with the utmost precision regarding place,

time, and whatever else was needed or asked by the constable.
For that would be the last time she would ever see the girl.

'There was an odd energy floating around that morning. It
not only affected me, but all of us, everything. The hunt was a
disaster; they kept getting lost and could not find anything to
shoot! Unheard of! Malcolm, my husband, was incensed.'

'Lady Matthews, you mentioned that Old John knew that…
somebody would come back for him—' Helena dreaded how to
put the next question, but Lady Matthews anticipated it.

'Yes. That's around the first time he saw him.'

'Saw who?'

'The devil, Miss Walton. I'd guessed you would have had
ample experience of him, with your Catholic roots.'

Helena ignored the comment. She had, in fact, been raised
as an Anglican, but she had no desire to explain to this woman
that she didn't profess any faith.

'You are saying that Old John saw the devil at the time the
girls went missing?'

'That's precisely what I'm saying, my dear. And now he
is back. Do you really want to know everything we know?
Perhaps you can start with this.'

She walked towards her bedside table and produced a
little key, which she used to open a drawer; from this she
took out a piece of paper. She walked back, handed it to

Helena, and sat down again, heavily this time.

It was a list of names, seven names in total. Next to them, ages, none older than fourteen. The last three names were those of Maud, Flora, and Alice:

Michael Farrow, fourteen years
Benedict Hobbs, nine years
James Proctor, twelve years
Rosalind Proctor, six years
Maud Matthews, twelve years
Flora Matthews, ten years
Alice Matthews, eight years

'Lady Matthews, I'm afraid I don't follow—'

'Don't you? Well, then perhaps I have overestimated you, my dear. Do you imagine *our* children were the only ones taken?' She looked at Helena with disdain. 'Of course he took others! Only those didn't make the papers, did they? The police said they had run away, or gone to find work in London, or whatever excuse they deploy for not looking for the missing children of the lower classes.'

Helena looked at her in dismay.

'Are you saying that there were *more* disappearances?'

Lady Matthews laughed, and her laughter, loud and manic, filled the room with so many things: her sadness, the frustration of many families, and, Helena feared, her own incompetence.

'My dear, there were twenty years ago, and there are now again!'

'You mean that another child has vanished *now*? Are the police involved at all in finding him, her? Lady Matthews, I beg you, no more riddles. I need as much information as you can give me about this case; and I need to see the child's parents. Was it in this area—'

The old lady cut her off with a hand gesture.

'His family will not tell you anything. They are convinced he has run away to join the Navy, of all things.' She laughed again. 'Simply because the poor boy was fond of sea stories! Can you think of anything more ridiculous than that? They don't want to know the truth, and I can't blame them. This is a ghastly business, Miss Walton. It's tainted us all. But I know, and Old John knew, and Mrs Ashby knows—'

'What do you know?'

She looked at Helena in disbelief, as if she were a little girl that needed everything explained to her.

'That he took them, Miss Walton. And that it is happening again. And I trust that you can help us.'

'Lady Matthews, what do you mean by tainted?' There it was, an averted look that, in Helena's experience, meant guilt. She insisted: 'Lady Matthews, if I may, I would like to know about your business venture with Charles Bale.'

The old lady looked confused. 'The factory?'

'Yes. What was the business trying to do?'

'Nothing much, I don't think. Harness the power of nature: the sea, the sun, the wind. Oh, it was nonsense, I know.'

'Why did it go under?' Lady Matthews looked at her and, for a moment, Helena expected an answer. Silence. 'Lady Matthews, if I may insist, I am only trying to get a general idea of the local context at the time of the disappearances.'

'Well, as far as I know, the technology did not work… as we had been led to believe. There were some problems. The venture had to be abandoned. And now, if you excuse me, my headache is back with a vengeance.'

'Jenkins, I would like to see the nursery. Could you please find me the key?'

The butler did not stir.

'I've got Lady Matthews's permission.'

'Ah. Very well, Miss Walton. I don't normally go to that part of the house: my knee, all those steep steps…'

'Perhaps you could ask Miss Waltraud to come with me, if that is convenient?'

'A splendid idea.'

'That would be most helpful, thank you very much.'

The butler started moving away, so Helena called: 'And, Jenkins!'

'Yes, miss?'

'The beggar woman.' She saw his expression change.

'She was found in the nursery, sleeping.'

He said nothing. But two could play this game. Helena stared at him in silence; she would not move until he gave her an answer.

'That is right, miss.'

'Any idea of why she went there?'

'She just wanted it back, I think.'

'Wanted what back, Jenkins?'

He had spoken without looking directly at her; butlers were apt at communicating while staring at walls and halls and the general universe.

'The doll, miss.'

And with that he turned abruptly to go.

The eastern wing: so, the nursery, probably, looked out onto the distant sea.

Helena was told to wait for Miss Waltraud in a little sitting room, and there she appeared shortly, with a bunch of keys in her hand.

'I hope you don't mind the climb,' Eliza commented. 'I'm told it is rather narrow in places.'

'And how did the children manage?'

'Apparently they had their own exterior access, to come and go, so as not to disturb the house.'

An odd arrangement, in particular for children fond of

going where they were not meant to.

'Could we take this external route? I'd like to see it.'

'I don't think so. I'm afraid the external stairs have been condemned for the past decade at least.'

They climbed up, took a corridor, went up another set of stairs, came into an upper landing, and climbed once more. Helena had lost count of the steps they had gone up, but thought a distance like that must surely be off-putting for both children to visit their parents and vice-versa. She imagined them stuck in this upper part of the house, *very tired with nothing to do*, and knew that, if they were clever, inquisitive children, *curiouser and curiouser*, they would have hated to conform to this imposed idleness.

'Here we are, I think…'

Eliza had her fair share of trouble making the key turn in its lock; but turn it did, eventually. The door would not give, and they had to push it a little. A flutter of dust got to their eyes and their nostrils, and they both bent down, coughing wildly.

When Helena could look up, she saw the reason: the room was infused in that same whitish substance she had seen in the meadow, although thankfully in a much smaller measure. It did float still, sticking itself to the surfaces, like oversized dust particles.

'This is not what I had expected,' said Helena.

'Me neither.'

'When was the last time anyone was up here?'

'I've no idea. Mrs Burroughs looted the place looking for books to read with Dot. But she hasn't been back in years. She says this place is unnerving.'

'Did she explain why?'

'It was mostly the dirt, I think. It gave her a severe headache, apparently. I assume it was even worse than that.'

'Let's carry on.'

They entered the little sitting room. All was painted in white peeling paint, the doors and the different pieces of furniture and the walls. There was a round table where Helena guessed the children ate, a miniature fireplace, a chair tumbled down on the floor. A cupboard with its two doors opened and askance, and the crunchy dirt and the dead leaves that one always wonders how—how on earth—they get into an empty place; until one spots the open window, the curtain moving wildly on a corner of the room, the air chilling one's soul. Cobwebs aging, long and distorted, dust obscured by frost.

But none of this was different from any other abandoned place. What made this space so wrong was the fungi.

The walls and the furniture pieces were strangely swallowed by it. It infused everything with its wrongness, forcing the wood into wrong shapes, collapsing the paint on the walls. It made everything look as if it were made of pasteboard, strangely provisional. Helena thought that, if she were to touch that wall, she would make a hole in it; she was certain she could grab the table with her own small hands and bend it.

'How did it get to this stage?' Helena muttered, disbelieving.

'Who knows.'

'And why is it concentrated in a few places?'

'It's like the ruins...' Eliza ventured.

Helena looked at her. 'You've seen them?'

'Oh, yes! Everyone knows about the ruins... Although you wouldn't believe that if you were to ask about them.'

'People like to pretend as if they are not there...'

'Exactly.'

They advanced into the next area.

'Let's carry on.' They entered the little sitting room. 'There is a schoolroom over there, and that must have been the bedroom they shared.'

They walked into the schoolroom. There was a standard map of the Empire and another of Europe, and a blackboard. Nothing remained of twenty years ago, no hidden messages or puzzling scribblings. It was therefore strangely empty and useless and black, with specks of sticky dirt. The bookshelf wasn't entirely empty, although it had the unavoidable feeling that someone had ransacked it in the course of the years, and that what remained in it was only the discarded bits and pieces of unwanted books and notebooks. An assortment of the expected lesson books, a faded French dictionary. The floor was littered with bits of paper, mixed with the sticky substance. Helena opened the school cupboard: nothing remarkable. Pencils and standard inkpots abandoned on the shelves, sheets of paper, cuttings of flowers and cherubim and ponies, postcards and decoupage littering the floor. She took up a postcard: someone, perhaps a maid, had wished them to be where she was, from Scarborough of all places.

'Let's see the bedroom,' she indicated.

'Wait!' Eliza had spotted something. The map was hanging from a clay decoration, and she moved it to one side, revealing something stuck to the wall behind it.

'How did you notice that?'

'I don't know. Maybe I have the makings of a detective myself.'

Behind the map, stuck to the wall, was another map, this one crude, painted obviously by children. Helena couldn't at first work out where it was, but then she understood the reason for her confusion: it was a map of the estate and a stretch of coast. However, it did not include the abbey, and therefore it was difficult to interpret it on first glance. At its centre was instead the Tudor manor house.

'Look, what is this?'

The children were awfully clever. The map had little flaps of paper stuck to it, and so, lifting one of them up, it was possible to see the two versions of the tide.

'That is very nifty,' Eliza said. 'What is under the other flap?'

That was a very interesting question, as the second flap replaced the Tudor manor with—what? Helena could not tell. It looked like an alternate landscape. One of the children had painted a beautiful bird, a hummingbird, blue and green, to signal, in the manner of old-fashioned maps, the beginning of a foreign land.

The sentence, '*This is how it starts*' was written below.

Was the map indicating that there was another exotic land *underneath* the Tudor manor? Although exotic was perhaps not the right word for it. It was a kind of citadel, with standing stones and crooked buildings, very similar to the drawings that Eliza had found in Dot's room when she'd first arrived, a sort of wrong landscape.

Eliza had mentioned the drawings, originally made by Maud, that she had found among Dot's things. All this was odd and intriguing.

'I need to hold on to this. Let's see the bedroom now.'

The room had nothing remarkable on first inspection. The beds had been removed. Then Helena had an idea.

'Eliza,' she said. 'That beggar woman. Lady Matthews told me that she sneaked up here the one time she managed to get into the house.'

'Oh, yes! I've heard that from Mrs Burroughs. That was odd indeed.'

'It is, isn't it? I wonder where did they find her, exactly.'

'I beg your pardon?'

'She was apparently found lying in the nursery rooms, on the floor and in the foetal position.' Helena had an idea: 'As if she was sleeping. On a bed.'

In one corner there was a wardrobe, and she walked in its

direction. The smell here was faintly decaying. Helena opened it. On the floor, next to the usual dirt, there was a pile of books and papers surrounded by paper roses and a collection of stones and minerals, and other little things she didn't recognise. She took out the little magnifying glass that she carried around her neck, ostensibly to help her read newspapers, and picked some up between her fingers.

'What is that?'

'I'm not sure—I would need a microscope to be certain. But they look like dry petals.'

'Oh! I didn't know that was there!' More children's books. Eliza took them in her hand and the dust went everywhere. They both covered their mouths again.

They sat among a collection of scribblings and drawings. Helena took them and quickly considered them: strange four-legged creatures with long limbs, knights, maidens. The alternate landscape again.

'These children...'

'What about them?'

'They really liked George MacDonald.'

'Who?' She looked at Helena.

'These books: *The Princess and the Goblin*, *Phantastes*, they are both by George MacDonald. How odd that they put them here—even this collection of fairy tales, *Dealings with the Fairies*, they are all by him.'

Helena's mind considered the pile of books and the papers.

'Eliza, I'm thinking—'

'Yes?'

'Don't you think this is odd?' Helena realised at once that she had said something stupid; what wasn't odd about this place? 'I mean—they look as if someone had—'

'As if they had been studying them,' Eliza said, reading Helena's mind.

'Exactly!'

'As if they were a pile of books and papers one finds in the college library once it has shut, because someone has abandoned them in a hurry to go punting with her boyfriend.'

'Which college? St Hilda's, Girton, Newnham?'

'St Hilda's,' Eliza answered.

'Yes but—they had no boyfriend.'

'And they took the precaution to hide them here—'

'Unless—'

'What are you thinking?' she asked.

'They had no boyfriend, but I wonder: who was their white rabbit? Who did they follow down the rabbit hole?'

'Alice—'

'Alice.'

'*Down, down, down. There was nothing else to do,*' Eliza quoted.

'*She walked sadly… wondering how she was ever to get out again,*' Helena quoted back.

'My God—'

'What?'

'Look.' Eliza had found some papers folded inside one of the books.

'What is it?'

There were some loose pages, three in total, written in compressed handwriting.

'Helena…'

Eliza passed on the pages, and Helena saw that they were signed 'Maud Matthews, 1881'.

She started to read:

'*Something very wonderful happened when I was little…*'

'Is it a diary?'

'I am not sure… but we need to take it with us. And the books as well.'

'George MacDonald's books? What do you need them for?'

'I can't explain it, Eliza, but I am sure that they are the clue to all this.'

They took it all and left the place, locking the door behind them.

CHAPTER TWELVE

When Mina was little, there was a fairy story she liked very much to read, and she also had a favourite spot to read it in, like children sometimes do. The story was called *The Blue Light-Shade*; the favourite spot was a bench in her back garden. In the story a couple of twin sisters entered a haunted house, and only one of them came out again. The sisters were called Raven and Rose. The house stood at the other side of their garden, quiet with secrets.

Sometimes a blue light could be seen glimmering over it. The twin sisters saw it floating around the house and its surroundings, moving from room to room, illuminating window after window, pouring into the starry sky through the chimney. Leaking from beneath the main door. Hovering over the ceiling like a lost cloud from another world.

The Blue Light-Shade was one of those stories where

'something horrible happened'. Mina had liked those stories very much when she was a child, she had explained to Eliza, and they had laughed together about it.

The blue light vanished Raven away. It had to do with her name, Mina said. She didn't really belong *here* but *there*. The sinister light had come to claim her back.

Raven was never seen again; she was lost forever. From then on, Rose always left a space between herself and other people, as if there were someone standing next to her.

It was so painful to think of Mina. For a long time Eliza had hoped that their quarrel would resolve itself; but she had also fallen prey to one of her least endearing qualities: a certain immobility, which resulted in her expectation that the issue would resolve all by itself somehow. She had been the one leaving their shared home, but simply because she had her family carstone cottage; she had a place to go. But she had always hoped that Mina would come to find her one day, or would write her a letter perhaps, explaining how wrong she had been, how much she missed her, how impossible it was for her to be apart from her. None of this had happened. And time had now passed, irrevocably.

At the time it had seemed to Eliza that they had quarrelled about something minor; it had taken her a long time to realise the importance of the issue for Mina, how much it mattered to her. Indeed, it had probably been the most important thing of all, as it directly assaulted the only thing that mattered in Mina's life: her writing.

Mina wrote strange stories, and poems in the fairy fashion, and had, always under the cover of a pseudonym—sometimes the name of a man, but more often and more comfortably a simple set of rhyming initials, N.N., X.X., B.B.—published them in several places. *St James's Gazette. Home.* One long poem, once, in *The Yellow Book.*

For years she had been trying to write a novel. Her writing desk had been covered with reams of dusty paper, all written over with her cramped but enthusiastic hand, which she had never let anybody see. Until she met Jane Howard. They had seemed to complement one another perfectly. Mina was a writer, and Jane was a reader. Jane had not, as so many other women had, mocked Mina for her choice of topic, her fairies and elves. She had seemed to have a genuine curiosity about them, although, as she always said, it was not a topic she knew anything about, or one that she would choose herself. She read Mina's stories and poems in a disinterested way, mostly to tell her how much she liked them, and how they would never sell in any quantity.

What happened then was unacceptable. And predictable, like a plot twist in a book. Jane Howard herself sold a novel she had been working on in secret. And it turned out, after all her protestations, to be a novel in the 'fairy' fashion, and to incorporate many of the topics that Mina herself had been working on. Jane was invited to speak to various groups, to write long articles for the magazines where Mina had only, with trouble, placed a short story every now and then. In a public talk about her book, Jane mentioned the poem 'Goblin Market' as her inspiration for the novel. A poem that was apparently dear to her, but which she had not known at all before Mina had shown it to her. This was never mentioned. Mina, as friend and confidante, had suddenly disappeared from the literary sphere.

As luck would have it, the world at that time was gasping for a novel of elves and goblins, and Jane's book was extremely successful; so successful that it pre-empted any complaint on Mina's part: anything she said would be taken as pettiness. And what, exactly, could Mina protest about? Mina understood her hopeless situation: nothing criminal had happened. She did not have the exclusive use of 'fairy' or 'Celtic' topics. But something was wrong, nonetheless. She could hardly bring herself to read the novel, aware from the reviews she had read of the familiar ground it might cover, and also scared that, unfairly, Jane would turn out to be a better writer than her.

Jane had come from wealth, had married wealth, and had the confidence that went along with wealth, the easy confidence of those who knew the world was for their picking, the charm and the know-how of the rich. Jane's novel became the talk of the season. It was made into a play by the impresario Wybert Reeve, translated into French, German, Italian, Spanish. She was said to have '*remade the fairy tale*', this woman who knew nothing about them that she hadn't learnt from Mina.

But that wasn't all, far from it. For Mina realised that she had to start again rewriting her own work. If she were to finish and publish her novel, that dusty heap of papers that seemed somehow now to threaten her from the desk drawer, there would of course be too many similarities in themes, approaches, to Jane's book. Mina feared that *she* might be accused of copying *her*. The irony. Jane Howard was a woman made for success, elegant and beautiful; she was now on her way to a fame comparable to that of Marie Corelli herself. Mina was not: she was mousy and insecure. Her looks were all wrong, her parentage disputed. It was quite possible that, even being the talented writer she knew herself to be, she would never publish anything.

The whole situation was a perfect exercise in manipulation: there is always someone weaker than you around, someone you can abuse. And Mina, poor Mina, had found herself too often on that receiving end.

It was embarrassing for Eliza to admit it, but she had not positioned herself readily on Mina's side. She remembered that day all too well; they had gone to visit a church attached to a neighbouring estate. After admiring the building, inspecting the stained windows, they were taking a stroll in the brief, unkempt cemetery, Mina in particularly low spirits.

'Whatever is the matter?' Eliza knew what the matter was, but the truth was that she had avoided talking about the topic for as long as she had been able to.

Mina, as if waiting for the right occasion, burst it all out, expecting some compassion, no doubt. But Eliza was ruthless. Partly, she was ashamed to acknowledge, out of cowardice, for Mrs Howard was now so successful that it would be impossible to confront her. But also, as she pointed out, there was nothing 'exact' to confront her with. She had not copied any of Mina's work; her only sin had been, perhaps, the lack of respect for a fellow writer's imagination, a very vague thing indeed. Eliza explained that she ought to be pitied, presumably because she lacked any ideas of her own. There was nothing more terrible for an artist. It was her opinion that, quite possibly, Mrs Howard would not write another book. And even if there could be some kind of acknowledgement, an apology would be unlikely, for Mrs Howard would still win: she would have at her disposal all the greatest platforms to defend herself, her publisher being extremely well-connected in Fleet Street. She would destroy Mina's reputation, Mina's career, before this career had even begun.

This was not all she said: Eliza also called Mina childish, absurd, self-centred.

On the way back home, Mina hardly spoke, answering only with monosyllables.

They quarrelled that evening, and the next morning. Eventually, Mina threw some of the pages of her novel into the fire. It was obvious that she was hurt, but it was equally obvious to Eliza that there was nothing they could do. And she thought at the time honesty was the best she could offer.

Eventually Mina asked Eliza to leave the house. And Eliza went, not thinking that Mina was serious about a proper separation. She was. Eliza went off with a smile on her face, sure that her lover would ask her back soon. She didn't.

Mina had never written again; the experience had broken her. And Eliza knew it to be her fault. She wondered sometimes if that was the reason why she had chosen Eunice Foote as her subject: another woman erased, whose ideas were put to better use by others. But Mina's experience was shocking in that a woman, bent on success at whatever cost, had done that to another woman. Perhaps that was the reason why she now wanted to help Helena.

The truth was perhaps more complicated, for every time that Mina came into her mind, Eliza looked at the list of things that she had offered to help Helena with. She was good at research, but she also knew why she was putting all her efforts into solving this particular mystery: she felt she had something to atone for.

Her successfully completed first task had been to unearth the local account about the church at Wicken Far End. It was baffling to say the least. According to the records, the building had collapsed in the 1770s. However, the local people were sure that it happened a whole century later. For a legend it was an odd one; for something so solid as a building to carry two accounts of its demise, it truly was peculiar. Eliza dug a bit further, asked Mrs Hobbs, visited some local record offices, wrote to a couple of folklorist friends of Peter's. The report of one of them was surprising to say the least. For he wrote back that the church, at least in people's minds, was 'here but not here', and that for a long time it looked from the distance sort of 'put together', as if a green hue or light sustained its stones. There was no record of services or of any activity going on in the actual building, but the general sense was that the place was sort of 'held together', at least in people's imaginations. What could all this mean? It was almost as if the 'real' church had in fact collapsed, but for a long while people could get a glimpse of its sister building, one that still stood, in a sort of mirror realm from their own, conjured up by the light itself.

'This is not helping. I need solid facts,' complained Helena. They were in Eliza's sitting room, eating Mrs Hobbs's fruitcake.

'I agree. Why don't we go to the factory?'

'I thought you said that you and the good doctor could not make it there!'

'We can try again…'

And so they set off that very afternoon in the pony and cart.

Ahead of them, the tired green and dark brown marshy soil stretched towards the grey, leaden waters, receding almost to a mudflat, but still separating them from the island.

'How long have you been a lady detective?' asked Eliza.

'I am not any lady, Eliza,' Helena replied.

'Well, a detective then—'

'Tell me about this bit of land, please,' Helena cut her off.

'Well, it is not as deadly as the Broomsway; you know, the one that the papers call "the Doomway". But you can get disoriented here, I assure you.'

'Has that happened to you often?'

'I wouldn't say often, for I try not to come this way if I can help it. But in rainy weather anyone could lose their way—Look!'

A green light shone from the island.

They climbed down from the pony and cart into a reed swamp. On the other side of the water stood the ruins. There were a crumbling heap of derelict constructions that looked as if they had been washed ashore by the tide. They did not look as if they had ever been standing in any way or form. The island resembled a nowhere place, neither land nor sea, and it had probably been like that for centuries for the church to end up like it was now, a collection of stones scattered by the hand of God over that mound. It had happened, eventually: a gale that lasted several days, which submerged this bit of countryside entirely, cracking the stone walls forever, breaking the windows, collapsing the little tower as if it had been made of gingerbread. And then the church had fallen, and the bell had stopped tolling forever.

'The factory is ahead, down the coast. We may need to cross while the water is down. I am not sure of how to get into it from the forest. What do you think is happening here, Helena?'

'I'm not sure yet,' she conceded. 'But the ruins are significant somehow, obviously.'

'And the sleep illness?'

Helena looked quizzically at the young woman. 'Is that what you think it is?'

'Well, it has to be something like it. They are in a sort of suspended state, as if—' She didn't finish the sentence.

'As if their souls are somewhere else, caught up in some limbo, and only their bodies remain here,' Helena ventured. '*Down the rabbit hole we go*—'

Eliza didn't reply. She feared Helena remained sceptical about it all.

'Do you believe in that?'

Helena didn't reply immediately.

'I am beginning to understand,' Helena offered, 'that the particulars surrounding this case ask for more open-mindedness than usual. Especially after seeing the children's nursery.'

Eliza shivered.

'Look! There is something, someone, moving on the edge of the island.'

Helena took out her binoculars from her pocket, had a long look, and sighed heavily. The list of names that Lady Matthews had provided her with felt heavy in her pocket.

She had problems swallowing before she said:

'It's Rosie, Old John's granddaughter.'

'Rosie? What is she doing here?'

Helena remembered the scene by the estuary, the two-faced beggar man, the uncanny light, and the dead boy. She did not feel that she could offer a reply.

'How long till we can cross?' she asked, kneeling down next to the gurgling mudflat.

'It's frankly hard to know. We are going to be able to do a crossing fairly soon; but mind you, the path would be hardly visible, and still very dangerous. It would be almost impossible to spot steady ground.'

Helena considered the salty water, slowly receding, leaving the muddied bed behind.

'Any quicksand?'

'Here? I don't think so.'

That seemed to make her decide.

'Then we ought to go now.'

'You could drown anyway!'

Helena sighed deeply and looked cross.

'Look, this will not do. Not knowing the terrain as well as I should could put Rosie in danger. I'm going, Eliza.'

'And I'm coming with you.'

'No. You are staying here!'

'What? I've brought you this far!'

'And I am very thankful, but this could be dangerous—'

'I'm not staying behind!'

'Suit yourself, then.'

They started walking over the wet sand, incapable of seeing the little gradients under their feet, formed by the ferns and liverworts, the little rocks, the bits of damp wood, the fallen reeds. It was hard work, and Helena had to fight against her boots being at least a little sucked by the damp ground to make steady advancement impossible. When she thought they had been walking for a long time she stopped; her spirits sank when she saw that they had covered less than half the distance.

They touched the elusive shore eventually, but she was feeling exhausted. They climbed the little headland, looking for places to put their feet, almost touching some of the fallen stones of the ruin. They were damp and clammy, with extensive lichen and fungi covering them in many vibrant colours.

'There she is!'

'Yes, that's Rosie.'

Something wasn't right in that scene, Helena thought. She couldn't get the estuary to the south of London out of her mind. On that occasion, a huge bearded man had appeared seemingly out of nowhere. And now Helena realised, weeks later, what she had actually seen.

His movements had been all wrong; he had been walking as if he were doing it behind a mirror, every single one of his actions suggesting some parallel natural movement which was nowhere there, the slow motion an uncanny, demonic dance.

And now here, in Wicken Fen island, as far away from London as she could imagine, she was seeing a repetition of this. How was that possible? The fact was that the shadow of a gigantic man had moved into the moonlight. Helena swallowed a gasp: it was the same man.

'We need to get to Rosie now,' Helena muttered. A green light was shining from the fallen stones of the church, from the scattered rocks, and it moved, solidifying itself into a quiet pool of darkness: a mirror of sorts. On the other side, it was almost possible to distinguish a cloudy, crooked landscape.

The man walked in front of the light; and, indeed there was a reflection there, smiling demonically at them. But the reflection was a 'version' of the man, not how they were seeing him. In that image, the beggar-looking giant was an expensively dressed gentleman holding a cane, with long sleek black hair. But, for all his glamour, he looked like the horrible beggar's twin. The demonic figure had now crossed the light, and Rosie started to move towards him.

'Eliza, we need to go now!' All Helena was thinking of was that other boy in London, falling dead in her arms. She and Eliza grabbed Rosie and forced her into the marshes.

The journey back was slow, exhausting, and by the time they had reached the pony and cart Helena was sure that the scenes in both cases were mirrors of each other. Did that mean that both cases were interconnected somehow? She knew that Bévcar's acolytes had been responsible for abducting the children in

London. Were they also involved in the Norfolk mystery?

They were panting, lying on the ground, their clothes completely ruined. Rosie had fallen on the grass and seemed to be sleeping peacefully. At least that was something.

'Look!'

The green light seemed to have moved, and now it shone from further along the coast.

'I know what is there: the old factory... Helena. What is the matter?'

'This scene, everything about it. I have seen this before.'

'Where?'

'In London, not so long ago. I fear the two issues may connect.'

'What does that mean? In practical terms?'

'I am not sure yet, Eliza. But I suspect we will know very soon.'

At Old John's daughter's cottage, Rosie lay on a bed made up by the fire. She had fainted on the way back, but that was good, as it meant that she had been responsive at some point. Eliza had feared that she would be somehow catatonic. Helena had managed the reins, a dark expression clouding her face, and had not spoken all the way back. But their fears seemed to have been misplaced, for Rosie had awoken eventually, miraculously; she was tired, but otherwise looked unharmed in any way.

'She is going to be fine. How is it possible?' Eliza asked Helena discreetly, as they prepared to leave.

'Eliza, think: what is different from Dot? From the girl you found in the marshes? What does she *have* that they didn't?' Helena said.

Have? Eliza thought. What could Helena possibly mean? These people had nothing, nothing at all.

And then it hit her; she looked in the child's direction once again. Around her neck, the fairy stone with the hole in the middle shone her green, uncanny hue.

They made their goodbyes, and Helena left her card for Old John's daughter, with instructions to write to her in London immediately were any developments to occur.

Eliza invited Helena to freshen up in her room. She guided her upstairs, and opened the door.

'Please, let me know if you need anything,' she asked. Helena went silent, looking around her at the many dolls, then to Eliza, who was already at the door.

'This is a bit unnerving—'

'My mother bought them for me. They come from many different countries. She was a great traveller, an explorer of unknown places.' It was the story she repeated, to whoever cared to ask. Although in truth how she hated the dolls. Those dozens of eyes looked intently at her, black eyes, blue eyes, green eyes, all glassy and dead, little synthetic things, guarding over her dreams. The dolls made her think of little girls. The little girls made her think of big girls. Of being taken, used up, put in places where one doesn't belong.

'Anita Waltraud? The famous traveller? That was your mother?' asked Helena.

'Well, yes. I didn't know her, really. She died giving birth to me.'

Helena frowned, deeply. 'But then, how—' She waved a hand around the room.

'Oh! No, she started collecting the dolls before I was born. I guess they were hers, really, came to me when—'

'Come on, we have a lot to do,' Helena cut in. It was obvious that Eliza did not enjoy talking about her family.

Downstairs, Eliza showed Helena her scientific tools, and she was sure they would be enough to run some simple tests. The fungi present in the ruins, and presumably in the disused factory could, when breathed, cause alterations in perception, confuse the mind.

'This,' she said, 'could explain the disorientation, the sense of loss, the feeling of dread. This could conceivably cause hallucinations, visions, dreams, nightmares. It doesn't kill you, but it alters your perception.'

'Of what is real?'

'Precisely.'

'Are these conclusive results?'

'Yes, I think so. It is quite possible,' Eliza continued, 'that the children breathed too much of the fungi, so perhaps got lost, disoriented, wandered too far away from the house, fell into a ditch, or got into trouble. Perhaps the intoxication was so deep that they could not remember their names, or how to go back home. This is an explanation that fits all the facts.'

'Does it? In that case, please, tell me, where has the fungi come from in the first place? And what about the light?' Helena was thinking again of the recent scene in the estuary by the Thames marshes, of the similarities in the scene they had just witnessed. There was much that they did not understand. The factory had meddled with the seabed and the rhyolite, that was a fact, but it was almost as if those actions had awoken something more sinister in the landscape. 'The problem with this scientific solution is that it is all too neat; and it does not answer all the questions.'

'Perhaps we will never answer all the questions, Helena.'

'But, these oddities of nature and place we have seen—'

'Are there oddities of nature?'

'Of course there are! There must be. Otherwise, please, tell me, why do you look over your shoulder when we are out in the marshes? What are you expecting to find?'

Things had rarely been this horrific: the beggar woman, found in the place where a child's bed had been, which according to the servants had been Maud's, holding a ragged doll in her hands, the implications of that narrative simply too horrid to contemplate; Old John's corpse, disfigured by a strange fungus, or by something even scarier; the ruined little Tudor house, tainted by some strange connection with the shadows, as was the nursery; that evil creature, both horrid beggar while in this world, pointed-teeth gentleman while in the other...

'I am finding it very challenging to understand this place,' Helena burst out in frustration. 'As impossible as it would be to understand a landscape in the middle of the moon! I can't reconcile my idea of the coast, of the sea—for wasn't it little more than an idea after all?—with this bogland, the black bits of peat, the gurgling holes, ready to suck a human being into their sinking muddy embrace. And all that continuously moving water, endlessly coming and going, and never ceasing to speak and speak and speak; and what is it saying? It's like a dead thing, galvanised into unnatural life.'

Eliza understood what she meant. The marshes of the olden days may have been a beautiful landscape, as her father had explained. But this wasn't all true; there was darkness underneath, a wilder nature that needed to be tamed, day after day, and there was death, and there was disease. She knew well what the fetid waters could do when allowed to stagnate. In Lincoln, in the slums, she had seen children with the life sucked out of them, ravaged by cholera. Here, after the floods, there were always fevers, and the sky filled up with fat swarms of black flies, on account of the rotting animals, of the dead fish.

The bad air, and the black, unmoving waters meant 'marsh miasma': malaria. And the wetlands had been full of it.

There was also the matter of the papers and books collected from the nursery for them to reckon with. The books had all been heavily underlined with pencil, for it seemed that the children had studied them thoroughly. One of the underlined sentences caught their attention: *Some little girls would have been afraid to find themselves thus alone in the middle of the night, but Irene was a princess.*

'This will not do. We are going to have to read the whole thing!'

The Princess and the Goblin wasn't really about a princess and a goblin, but about a princess and a miner boy called Curdie she liked. The goblins were creatures who lived inside the mountain, depicted horridly. Their plan was of course to kidnap the princess, and marry her off to their own heir.

The princess displayed a lot of ingenuity, even saving Curdie at some point from inside the mountain, which made Helena understand what the three little girls saw in the book. There was a discourse about perception running through the book, about believing without seeing, or choosing not to do so.

Phantastes was a very wordy book for such little children, she thought. A youth enters Fairy Land on his twenty-first birthday, where he lives many adventures, even killing a giant and becoming a sort of knight. All the characters in the children's drawings were there: Sir Percival the knight; another knight on a horse, dragging the dead body of a dragon; the White Lady; the Maid of the Alder Tree, and the spirit of the Ash Tree, whom Eliza gathered were evil. What Anodos, the hero, had to do was to go *beyond* reality, leave behind its limitations, believe… in what, exactly? Eliza feared that that was precisely the question that eluded her; she was not a literary critic. The dream-reality at some point overlapped the reality, *becoming* the new reality. The book was so boring, so utterly dull; it didn't read like a work of fancy, but like a real travelogue, where one cannot truly leave out the most boring parts.

No… it cannot be.

A youth enters Fairy Land on his twenty-first birthday, where he lives many adventures, even killing a giant and becoming a sort of knight. What had Helena explained about Samuel Moncrieff?

Samuel Moncrieff will turn twenty-one this year.

There were no coincidences.

Eliza shivered, set the book aside.

'Helena, Mr Moncrieff.'

'What about him?'

'A youth enters Fairy Land on his twenty-first birthday… but in many ways he is returning back home…'

'Blimey,' Helena replied. She seemed to consider something. Eventually she asked, 'Where did you say that the catatonic girl had been sent?'

'A sanatorium up in Yorkshire. In a village called Grewelthorpe.'

She rummaged and found the report from the canal and tinker network.

Mr Moncrieff didn't stop in the city, but, almost at once after setting foot off the train, he moved on to the village of Grewelthorpe.

Helena sighed, showed the report to Eliza. Meanwhile, she added to her case notes:

New and Revised Facts:

At the time when the Matthews children disappeared, other children were being abducted. Why this was not followed up by the police is irrelevant now. At the time, a poacher known as Old John claims to have seen 'the devil'. The children liked playing in ruins. Alice's Adventures in Wonderland *was one of their favourite books. They had a play companion; she did not disappear, but lost the capacity of speech, perhaps thinking, on that same fateful day.*

Points needing clarification:

The connection between the ruins and the disappearances; who truly is the beggar woman—is she Maud; the exact cause of Dot's affliction and others; why some people go catatonic and some simply vanish; supposed protective 'powers' of rhyolite; Mr Samuel Moncrieff's true origins; is what happened to Mr Jim Woodhouse's cousin similar to what happened here? And, in that case, is Samuel Moncrieff its cause; how can a house built twenty-five years previously get so decrepit so soon; where does this sticky substance come from; connection of all this to the Alice books, to George MacDonald; implications of a further place—Wonderland? Fairy Land?

She read the new notes to Eliza. The younger woman had something in her hand: the list given to Helena by Lady Matthews:

Michael Farrow, fourteen years
Benedict Hobbs, nine years
James Proctor, twelve years
Rosalind Proctor, six years
Maud Matthews, twelve years
Flora Matthews, ten years
Alice Matthews, eight years

Eliza had been wondering whether Mr and Mrs Hobbs thought often about their son, Benedict. Did they say a prayer for him every day? Would they hope to see him again, if not in this world, in the next? Did they visit an empty grave? She wished so much to have something to tell them, to reassure them; but the truth was, they had nothing.

Helena was fetching something from her bag, the pictures that Lady Matthews had given her in London, in what seemed like a lifetime ago: a cart, all blurry, the Tudor manor at the end, and, floating on top of it, three little lights.

What were they?

Will-o'-the-wisps, jack-o'-lanterns, corpse candles.

Those are normally on the ground, not over the roof of old ruins...

So not corpse candles, but three little figures, uncannily floating away, three children who would not come back home.

*

That same night, while Helena and Eliza pieced together the last pieces of the puzzle, Mr and Mrs Burroughs sat to an early supper in the kitchen of their cottage, happy to enjoy the peace and quiet at last. Soon, they would be leaving their duties behind, and keeping a place only for themselves for the first time in their lives.

Outside the sky looked ashen. A solitary nightjar flew over the house, the trees whispered to each other, the peat rustled, complaining of the late hour, the day quickened to an end.

In the distance, from the old factory beyond the marsh, a green mist softly lifted and swarmed up, covering the black waters. It moved like a pair of ghostly arms, caressing all within their reach, reaching the priory ruins, and moving forward along the coast, and reaching the tree trunks, the fields, the fens, the dykes, getting to the water mill two miles ahead, covering its willow, its eel traps, in its uncanny embrace. And the queer curls of mist lifted and fell, lifted and fell. It seemed to suck up the water as well; and the water lifted with it, and with it fell, starting to move like a shapeless shadow.

Mr and Mrs Burroughs had gone to bed by then, and did not see the water creeping in, animated by the mist, which secreted into it its obscure power. They had not been asleep for long when Mr Burroughs awoke to a distant sound, like someone sounding a metallic pipe amongst the thickets. Only then did he realise that the sound was a toll, a chime, a non-existent bell, echoing through the night. And then he thought he heard a dog barking somewhere, although they had no dog, and no neighbour. He woke his wife up, and told her to listen—the last thing that Mr Burroughs ever said. For, at that exact moment, thousands of tons of water crashed violently against the cottage, washing it from the face of the earth and taking them both, and Dot as well, quiet in her sleep.

All the green-tainted water ran over the fields, and rushed into the fens, even though the banks of the dykes and the rivers remained intact, for this was no natural water pouring in. The flood washed away the houses and the animals.

The water moved around the Tudor ruins, as if trying to avoid its dark power. As if it was part of its secret plot. It almost reached the estate, but before doing so, it killed the beggar woman, the one whom Eliza and Helena feared to be Maud, her body prematurely aged after her journey to the other side. It dug up the bones of Benedict Hobbs, lost to his parents twenty years earlier, murdered and hidden in a ditch. And it carried on, the water, unburying the treasure left by the Danes hundreds of years before. On it surged, as though it knew where to go, animated all by itself, a creature resurrected in all its cruelty, as only the waters can be when they come, pouring their destruction over the world, covering all, and forcing the land to regurgitate all its secrets.

MAUD MATTHEWS'S DIARY
1881

*S*omething very wonderful happened when I was little. I must have been very little, for this was before Alice, before Flora. My nurse put me down on an edge of the garden, next to a hedge. I understood later that she used to meet her beau in that hedge. Her beau was a stable boy, and they would laugh and smoke and kiss, all the while keeping an eye on me, lying on a blanket. It must have happened one of those days; she must have moved to the other side of the hedge to be sweet with him, and left me alone for a little time. My nurse wasn't a nasty sort; she was young, I fancy, and she was fond of me. But she must have done so once, or else how did they know where to find me, all alone?

For it was then that they came, that first time. There would be many other visits, throughout the years. I never knew whether I had imagined them or not. They had luminous faces, sickly white, and shiny, but they were not beautiful. Their smiles were all wrong; they did not go with their weary, ancient eyes. I do not know what they wanted from me. But they *were always there. What was it that they taught me, what was it that I learnt from them? A secret language, I guess, like an incantation. New names for the trees and the birds and the sky, words that ought not to be spoken. These were the most secret of all secrets, and I used to write them down, and hide them very far away, in the most secret of all secret places, some places in the woods, the old house. I would find crevices there very easily, and there I put my things. They left little gifts for me in these secret places: strange sweets, colourful feathers. Once, a green stone. I was their special friend, even after Alice, after sweet little Flora. I was not to tell the secret of their coming, or his coming, for they were hailing the advent of someone else, someone all-powerful.*

I am sitting in this room. I decide that what I really need, what I really really need, is to lie back. So I do that. I find a way of being comfortable, and lie back on the floor. I am now seeing the ceiling. I am now seeing through the ceiling. I am now seeing all the little doves that are sleeping on the ceiling. And I am now seeing the sky. The sky is my friend, I know it. I decide I am not scared of the sky. So I go up, willingly, like falling but the other way around. So I go flying, up and up I go. And I fly directly into the void, directly into the dark. And I come out the other side of the dark, and I am now over this round planet; I pass the moon in a second, and I carry on going. And there are galaxies all around me, and stars, constellations, many little shining dots that grow big as I pass them by.

I am one and only with the Universe. I know and understand it all. I know and understand the meaning of everything. How awfully clever of me! He has taught me how to do this.

I wasn't meant to come here. I must go back, to the meadow, and the house, no craggy hills, no snow-bound peaks. Openness, whiteness, vastness, conspiring to make me dizzy.

I go back, past the constellations, past the moon, past the sky and the stars and fall deeper and deeper into the darkness below... I am in a meadow. I don't know if it's the right meadow. But it is a meadow. I am tired and I sense a warning, a danger the colour of blood; and then, I see the birds scattering themselves all over the sky, painting them in so many colours... I can feel them, fleeing in a panic at the advancing beaters, and I smell the gunpowder.

Dread. Confusion. Someone is holding my hand, or my paw. Who is it? But then he lets go, and I find myself completely alone, with no clear idea if I am hunter or prey.

Thick fog.

I cannot remember how I got here.

There is a man on the grounds; he has come for me at last.

He looks at me, and looking into his eyes I'm reminded of it all: of fathers, of uncles, of guardians; of wolves, the moment they jump over their prey, that second before they spring.

CHAPTER THIRTEEN

The Open Door, *Journal of The New Occultist Defence League*
April 1901

MADAME FLORENCE WAYFARER UNMASKED!

~*Trapdoors, sliding panels, concealed by darkness, assistants wearing costumes, make-up and even wigs!*
~*Items concealed on the false back of chairs found in her Gower Street house.*
~*Small balloons used to convey the impression of spirits floating around the room, manoeuvred with fishing rods.*
~*Full report of the fraud inside!*
~*Extra pamphlet available in interior pages: 'Tricks of Mediums'.*

*

Report on Madame Florence Wayfarer's two last séances in New York City in the autumn of 1900. Printed in London, The Little Haunted Press, April 1901.

This report covers Madame Florence Wayfarer's two last séances in New York under Miss Clare Collins's management, in which they charged the fee of fifty dollars per séance.

The investigation was brought over by a Mr Kantaris, honorary secretary and psychical researcher. It is suspected that Madame Florence fakes at times, whereas at other times she manages to produce genuine telekinetic manifestations. It is also noted that more than one individual seemed to perform under the name 'Madame Florence', and that the person who performed under that name is not the same that did so five years ago, as explained by many witnesses.

Madame Florence, or the individual calling herself Madame Florence, had initially agreed to perform with two hands holding her down, one visibly on her knee, a hand on her shoulder, and a stuffed handkerchief in her mouth. However, once she arrived at the séance, she claimed to have no recollection of having agreed to such a course of action, and refused to follow these instructions. Eventually, she agreed to comply.

Declaration by first witness – Against
I feel absolutely convinced she is a trickster from beginning to end. While her right foot remained on the foot of her right neighbour, and her left shoe

remained on my foot, she obviously deploys marvellous skill in removing her foot from the shoe without giving me the slightest suspicion.

Before the séance started Madame Florence was stripped to her underclothes in the presence of women, but nothing was found upon her person that could in any way be used to help her in her séance. She was then reclothed and escorted into the front room. I feel compelled to inform the committee that a number of suspicious objects were nonetheless found in Madame Florence's proximity after the events.

The light when the séance began consisted of six eight-candle power lamps, which gave the room what might be called an almost brilliant illumination. This light remained until after one or two of the complete levitations, at which time the medium called for less light. I am sure that this is in order to hide her features, for by now it is clear that some of the sitters do not recognise her as MF.

Declaration by second witness – In Favour

MF had no knowledge, nor had her managers, of the room in which the séance was to be held, a square parlour. A corner of the room was chosen. Across this corner a piece of clothesline was divided in the middle. Behind this curtain were placed a small stool and a small four-legged table. On the table were placed a tambourine, a flute and a music sheet. Neither the medium nor her managers brought any paraphernalia with them. The table and the stool were both built especially for this occasion, and also the curtains. The medium had not seen any of these until she was led to her seat.

Séance Diary: Séance starts at 9:17p.m. At 9:27p.m., the table starts to come up on two legs. Those near MF look carefully to see if there is any connection between her and the table, but find none. It is now 9:35p.m. The table rises on two legs. Mr Curtis and Mr Kantaris both say that they are in control of her. The first complete levitation of the table takes place at 9:45p.m.; that is, the table rises clear off the floor about twelve inches. It is now 10:08p.m. At this time MF complains of the light and asks that all lights be extinguished but one. The room is quite dark now. At this time, another complete levitation of the table takes place. Mr Kantaris explains that he can feel her left leg pressed tightly against his, her hand is clasped in his and she is clear of the table by at least three inches. Mr Blanchard, who has taken Mr Curtis's place, also states that he has complete control of MF's leg and hand. It is now 10:11p.m. MF now seems to direct her powers towards the curtain. She begins to appeal to the mysterious being whom she calls Kitty. Three or four complete levitations of the table occur. Kantaris is now behind the curtain and he says the small table there shot directly towards him and struck him in the elbow. He says he can see this clearly and at the same time the things on the table fell to the floor with a crash. The table rises on one leg. Then comes a complete levitation, the best of the evening; everybody stands up and the table raises fully three feet from the floor. The table stayed up for a few seconds and then dropped with a crash and one of the legs of the table broke off. A few of the complete levitations occurred when there was no contact with the table on the part of the medium.

Preliminary conclusions: The result may seem inconclusive in Madame Florence's case; however, it is difficult to justify the conditions that she imposes upon sitters. All we can do is guess at her methods. The blowing out of the curtains may be explained by the use of a very thin rubber hose about the thickness of a lead pencil, and painted black so as to be invisible, which is attached to a bulb, or possibly a small steel flask containing compressed air, under considerable pressure. The curtains are very thin and it wouldn't take much air in motion to move them. I have talked with some of the men who attended the first séance here and find that most of the newspaper accounts were inaccurate. As near as I can learn, Madame Florence and her sitters took usual positions about the table. After some contortions, she lunged forward and there was a violent tremor of the table. I suggested the use of a black cord dangling from Madame Florence's neck, with a small blunt hook fastened to the lower end of the cord, and thought that when she pitched forward that the hook swung under the edge of the table, which gave her a connection to it. Now it was after this preliminary movement of the table that complete levitation took place, and the lights were lowered after the first tremor of the table, and before the complete levitation occurred. Moreover, before the complete levitation, Madame Florence had the free use of her hands and held them out of sight part of the time, between her abdomen and the edge of the table. There is also the matter of Madame Florence's appearance. Many witnesses that attended her séances even two decades ago claim that MF was blonde—she is now dark-haired—and that she now looks younger than then, which is surely impossible. This hints at the possibility that MF may be a role played by different people at different times; this suggestion came as a genuine surprise to Miss Collins, newly employed by MF, presumably, after her last 'change' into a new appearance. Miss Collins claims not to know anything about the tricks, etc., etc.

The Open Door, *Journal of The New Occultist Defence League April 1901*

STRANGE FLOODING EVENT IN EAST ANGLIA!

~Read everything about the Green Water's Flood.

~Graves upturned, buildings collapsed, treasures unburied.

~Strange Hybrid Seen, Half Whale, Half Seal, the Huge White Creature now roams East Anglia.

~Strange shiny city seen in the horizon, where the North Sea and the Land touch.

~Read it all here!

The Society for Psychical Research was located in an imposing building in the Marylebone district, a dark and huge residential block which was not in fact occupied by any tenants but by different offices and departments of the Society, which attested to one thing: vast amounts of money at its disposal. Helena was surprised to see she was expected. She was escorted up a set of badly lit staircases and asked to step into what was referred to as the small library. The clerk shut the door behind her and momentarily left her there. The small library turned out to be a high-ceilinged room with a gigantic mahogany table in the centre, surrounded by locked glass cases and cabinets, containing books, memorabilia and several objects. She was admiring the ectoplasm, and deciding it looked like a cheese cloth, when the same clerk reappeared and asked her to follow him through a further set of doors, leading into an unexpected narrow and heavily decorated corridor, until a further door was opened, and Helena was ushered inside.

She found herself in the middle of an office, where John Woodbury, celebrated vegetarian, bookseller and chairman of the SPR, was waiting for her, not sitting behind the desk, but on one of a set of black leather sofas in front of the fire, to which he motioned she should join him. There was a tea set and some cups and saucers on a little table, as if Mr Woodbury had just entertained someone.

'My dear Helena. How good it is of you to come and pay us a visit.'

'Mr Woodbury.'

Someone moved in the corner of her eye, and Helena saw that Charles Bale was standing at the other end of the room, looking out to the park below.

'Mr Bale.' The older man did not move. 'How kind of you to be here. You have saved me the walk to Holborn.'

'Miss Walton.' The older man acknowledged her with a curt nod.

'I hope you will call me John from now on,' indicated Mr Woodbury. 'It is time that we dispense with the formalities, don't you think? After all, much has happened in this strange affair.'

'I know that you know that Sam's being here is intimately connected with the girls' going there.'

'Why, Miss Walton, could you not leave him in peace!' Charles blurted. 'He was only a baby, when—'

'Mr Bale, please, if I may. If this business is true; if we are prepared to accept that theory—' Charles did not reply. Helena continued, '*If* we accept that theory, Maud, the elder, possibly managed to come back.' This caught Woodbury's attention. 'I will get to it in a moment. But first, Sam.'

Mr Woodbury smiled manically.

'*If* we accept that theory… it would seem that Samuel Moncrieff is a sort of… *changeling*.'

Bale's face went yellow; he looked about to vomit. Woodbury said nothing; then, half-smiling, '*A changeling?* But, my dear, that is a term borrowed from literature, no doubt. A rather romantic way of putting it, if you ask me. What Samuel is or isn't is far more complicated than that.'

'I am aware of that. But you have to allow me some… shortcuts. I do not possess an idiom to speak about these portents, I'm afraid. Until now my only language has been the language of rational thought.'

Woodbury pointed at her with a finger, as if he were going to scold her for being a naughty child.

'And yet… palmistry, isn't it?'

'Sir, I trust by now our cards are plainly laid on the table. If I am not mistaken, you clearly know a great deal about me already.'

'No, you are not mistaken.'

'Still, you chose to expose Madame Florence, and not me. Why?'

Charles Bale snorted.

Woodbury said, 'You ask why? You, who have been helping the police with the children's disappearances from the beginning? There was not much we could in truth do; she had been too clever covering her tracks! All we could achieve was humiliating her in the eyes of her many followers, so as to not cause a major uproar. Her crimes are bad enough. Sad, so very sad. She has been apprehended for fraud; no doubt your friends from Scotland Yard will devise a clever way to keep her locked up for a very long time.'

'I see.'

'All we do is our public duty, my dear.'

'And now you are doing it again, setting the trap to "unmask" those poor academics.'

'Ah! The Little Trianon affair! Time-slip! Time travel? *I* could accept that much, but *meeting Marie Antoinette*?' He was trying very hard to contain a laugh. 'My dear friend, we will not need to do much at all to ridicule the two ladies; they are perfectly capable of managing that all by themselves.'

'Why?'

'Why, what?'

'Why do you like to see them ridiculed? And why is it that there are always women who need to be ridiculed, Mr Woodbury?'

He looked at her, momentarily at a loss.

'Women, you say? I certainly have no idea what you may mean! We do unmask whoever needs to be unmasked—'

'I spent the whole of yesterday going through my past issues of *Light*, *Two Worlds*, *The Open Door*. I could not find a single case in which a male medium was reported, "unmasked", or simply accused of being a cheat.' Woodbury did not say anything. He was looking at her with what seemed like fury. Nevertheless, she continued. 'It is a curious coincidence, is it not, Mr Woodbury? *Curiouser and curiouser.* As if being curious was a disease, a malady, that needs to be remedied. Only when it affects women, that is. Although, I'm sure you both will agree with me: there are no coincidences.'

'My dear Miss Walton! What we do here follows the scientific method! We—'

She dismissed him with a wave of her hand.

'That is not why I am here, John,' she cut across him. 'Have you not tried to find out how to help Samuel Moncrieff?'

The old man sighed heavily; Charles Bale moved uncomfortably in his chair.

Eventually Woodbury spoke, 'Miss Walton, let me ask you a question: do you know when Charles became interested in Spiritualism? Exactly when Sam appeared in his life. It is true that, with the years, he had covered much ground in the sciences, become interested in many of the different strands of knowledge, and certainly helped a great deal of people in the community. But it all started that day, and with only one idea: *to help the child one day.* That was foolish, you see,' Woodbury paused. 'Sam could never be happy, not here,' he concluded.

This made Helena think of her complicated feelings about her grandmother, of her fantasies of abandoning everything to go to Seville, her recognition that she would not entirely belong there. Not fully belonging here did not mean she would fit in that world either.

'That doesn't mean that you can decide *where* he will be, Mr Woodbury,' she said presently. She felt exhausted.

'Miss Walton, if I may, do you know how I myself became interested in the Spiritual world? Perhaps I will tell you the story one day. It suffices for me to say now that I was very much like yourself, you see. Not an inch of anything connected with the supernatural, only a science-led young boy. But then something inexplicable happened, something that worked to explode my pompous highblown stupidity. Afterwards I did what I could to organise this knowledge, sort it out the best I could. I needed to return to a world ordered and understandable, one that made sense, where that event could be classified into one more category, be studied and analysed.'

'I see.'

'Perhaps it won't have a place in the Round Reading Room with its cubicles and the clerk seated at its centre. But it does in a place like this,' he waved his arms around, indicating the SPR headquarters. 'It *can* be rationalised in a place like this. Or at least we are trying to rationalise it. The necessary accumulation of knowledge, the order carved out of the chaos… Our society demands it, the political and social events demand it, the scientific discoveries, exploration, even the Empire demands it!'

'I'm sorry. I'm afraid you've lost me.'

'It is possible that I am talking nonsense; I am old, after all. But the years have also taught me some things. For example, it is always easier to solve a labyrinth when you see it from above, don't you think? What we are doing here is to domesticate that other nature, to classify it, to impose different categories on our individual achievements; and in the process we give solace, we give comprehension.'

Helena had to make a tremendous effort not to get up and leave; she needed whatever information she could obtain from the man. But the narrative was an old one, heard so many times before: *order, chaos, domesticate…* Words that only meant one thing: men like Mr Woodbury, desperately trying to keep control of women like herself.

'Although there is so much still that we don't understand, that perhaps we will never understand,' the old man was saying.

'What about Sam? How can we understand Sam's nature?'

The old man laughed shortly with a sad face.

'We do have a theory.'

Helena's face brightened. Woodbury's grew sombre.

'You will not like it, I am afraid.'

'Try me.' She sounded fiercer than she had intended.

'I do not doubt your capacity for processing shocking information, Miss Walton, that is not what I am saying. I am just trying to stress that you may find it difficult to accept our theories; but also, importantly, that they are only theories.'

Woodbury walked slowly towards the desk, grabbed the handle of some kind of communicating machine, pressed a button, and talked to someone on the other end of the line. Presently the same clerk who had ushered her into the room appeared, so quickly that he must have been waiting in attendance in the adjacent room, with a presentation folder.

'Everything we know is there.'

Helena took the folder and weighed it in her hands: it was so light, so thin. Too thin to contain, as it did, the truth. She tried not to laugh: it amused her to see that it was red, and very similar to the one that Mr Bale had put in her charge not so long ago.

'Mr Bale, your factory,' she said, finding her overcoat and preparing to leave. 'It is polluting the coast; it may be closed, but there is something still coming out of it. It is vomiting a pernicious substance that is affecting people, places. You need to do something about it.'

'It has already been dealt with.'

Helena was surprised.

'How? When?'

'The flood. The factory doesn't exist anymore.'

'But, my dear sir… even if I and my associates haven't been able to draw final scientific conclusions, we do know that whatever you were doing there twenty years ago was connected with the strange occurrences, perhaps even the vanishings…' Helena stopped talking. By the manner in which Charles Bale sat there—motionless, holding his hands over his lap, avoiding looking up at her—she knew it immediately: he was aware of this. And perhaps he and Lady Matthews had been aware all along.

'I'm sorry, I need to know. What were you trying to achieve there, Mr Bale? Before you felt compelled to close it down, that is.'

'Energy,' was all Bale said. Suddenly, his face changed, and Helena had a brief glimpse of lunacy dancing upon the old features. 'Do you not know? Heat-death, Miss Walton! The world is going to end, but not before we use up the sun! We were very lucky to have the stone; the stone was all we needed, the stone was the future!'

'What stone? Do you mean the rhyolite? What happened then?'

The man sounded so tired when he spoke.

'We could not harness it, as simple as that. We were looking for energy, and found instead… something different.'

So that was it.

'Good luck, my dear,' put in Mr Woodbury. 'I am sorry to say that I, we, cannot help beyond this point. Where you are heading is a dangerous place, uncharted, a veritable *terra incognita* we surely do not possess the necessary means to venture into.' He paused for a moment. 'Miss Walton, would you consider working for us?'

Facing the world under the power of the SPR's patronage would surely simplify things a great deal, Helena considered for a second. Then she thought about what she would be representing: *order, chaos, domesticate*.

'I am truly sorry, sir, but I prefer to make my own way.'

Mr Woodbury doubled himself in a little bow, with great trouble. Helena left the room, opened the folder almost at once, and found herself, all of a sudden, alone with the truth.

Helena tried to calm down, and to gather her thoughts. After perusing the folder, she had felt that she simply could not breathe, and had to run outside of the building as fast as it was possible. She knew she was close to Regent's Park, and started walking briskly in that direction. She needed to see trees, green grass; she needed to breathe pure air.

She was also trying to keep a grasp on the world somehow. In Celtic mythology, she remembered for some reason, fairyland was just one step aside from the human world; one didn't need to open any hidden door, go deep into any mountains. There were no mountains in Norfolk either; but still, she thought, a place did not exist anywhere where one could feel more acutely that one was crossing unseen thresholds, where the boundaries were as capricious as the tides, where the churches and the dwellings that today sat in our world could be swept away by the mist tomorrow.

She was walking mechanically, in a sort of trance. Or something similar, a kind of numbness that quenched the pain.

She reached the park breathing heavily, and looked frantically for a bench to rest. She was asking herself if Sam knew, if he *could* possibly know, the horrid truth that she had just learnt about him.

It was that evening when Helena and Jim met again. At the appointed time, Helena arrived at a disused train station in a borough at the south of the capital. It was an eerie suburb, a liminal space not yet swallowed by London, but almost deprived of any identity of its own. She had no idea where she was to be taken. They both greeted each other briefly, and Jim led the way.

'What do you suppose you are going to learn with this meeting?'

'To tell you the truth, I am not sure. But Sam and I need to talk.'

Jim had not managed to delve deeper into Sam's mystery, but he had recounted to Helena in a letter the events that happened in Yorkshire. This document, although fascinating, proposed more questions than answers.

The two men were staying in a half-derelict building occupied in greater part by workers and immigrants, and Helena followed Jim there. Outside a man was roasting chestnuts, and he gave Jim a little packet and murmured a brief thank you when he passed by. He received the offering in silence and put it in the pocket of his coat. The canals divided the street into little islands, their black water shining in the darkness. There were fewer street lamps here, pouring a little bit of light over the filth formed by the recently fallen rain.

Once inside they climbed a steep set of stairs into a main passage, lit by a single oil lamp. It smelled of spicy food being cooked in a stove that ought to be behind one of those grim-covered walls. Jim opened the door to an attic room and motioned her to enter. When she did she found herself inside a large space in semi-darkness. The smell inside was a strange mixture of alcohol, herbs and sweat, and something else that she couldn't identify. She could hear pigeons very near, and assumed she was smelling their droppings. It was very cold, and she kept her coat on.

Samuel Moncrieff was sitting on a wooden chair, with his feet, still with his boots on, upon a desk, reading a book by a candle. As they entered he pushed the chair forwards, and stared fixedly at Helena. She eyed the book he was reading. It was *Towards a Science of Immortality*, by Bévcar. It made Helena shiver.

'What is she doing here?'

Jim did not reply. He crossed the room, and started lighting a little fire in the grate. Helena rubbed her hands, trying to revive her numb fingers. Jim took out a little pot from somewhere, and soon the smell of coffee filled the attic. He started busying himself with bread and cheese, roasted chestnuts, eggs and butter. He continued to prepare the meal in silence. Helena felt she had been abandoned to the explanations. It did not matter now.

'Mr Moncrieff, we need to talk. Whatever happened to you in Oxford, and whatever happened in Norfolk all those years ago, is all somehow connected.'

Sam seemed to find this amusing.

'You don't know anything, Miss Walton.'

'I know that you are scared of ruins.'

He turned to look at her; she had finally gained his attention. He considered her again with a curious expression. Meanwhile Jim produced a cup of steaming coffee in her hands and a plate of cheese and bread next to her.

'I can help you, and you can help me,' she insisted.

'Ah. You were always a great talker, Miss Walton,' he offered.

'Please, call me Helena.'

She took in her surroundings. There was an impressive

assortment of glass bottles and jars, dried flowers and herbs hanging in odd receptacles, stones on the windowsill of a little round window, laid out like a dark smile. The walls, an indeterminate light-brown colour, were covered by complicated diagrams in which the sun and the moon and the stars took prominence. A tree of life was painted on the wall in one corner, each of its branches sprouting what she identified as charms, against the evil eye, perhaps. She didn't know really what they were, but some lost knowledge stirred softly within the deep crevasses of her mind.

'What are these?' she asked.

He answered without turning to face her:

'A prayer to quell the pain of unrequited affection. The means to come back to life. Other things as well.'

From the walls hung more charms and amulets made of twigs and dried leaves and pieces of rags and birds' claws, and other things impossible to name. A table was covered in the wax of candle stubs, which Jim was now lighting. Old newspapers and books littered the floor. On a shelf, next to some books, a skull.

'How did you get that?' she asked, pointing at it.

'A friend of a friend of a friend,' he said, turning towards her, and fixing her with that odd stare once more. 'And for everything you ask me, I will give you the same answer.'

'Sam,' Jim intervened, 'there's no need to be rude.'

Samuel Moncrieff laughed.

Now that some candles flickered a frail golden light, she could see the floor at the centre of the room. It was carved with some kind of round maze pattern. Some twists and turns were punctuated by little offerings, and she moved around it carefully, not wishing to disturb their silent meaning. She recognised the dry *sempervivum*: not only were they Dot's main pastime according to Eliza, but the abbey had often been dressed with bouquets of the flower.

'What is this for?' she could not help herself asking.

'Protection,' was the answer.

'It is meant to keep away the demons.' This time it was Jim who replied.

The silence was dense.

'Mr Moncrieff,' she started.

'Sam,' he corrected her. He was serving three drinks and presently came back holding a shot glass with something darkly red. 'I apologise, Helena. I'm not used to visitors these days. Please, take a seat,' he said, and she saw he was pointing at the only armchair, a tattered piece of furniture that surely had been thrown out in the street. 'I think we are going to need something stronger than coffee, don't you think, Jim, old man?' Jim did not answer, but took a sip of his mug.

'I don't mind where I sit,' responded Helena, and sat down on the floor exactly where she was standing, cross-legged beneath her ample skirts. Sam chuckled, and sat down in the same position, right in front of her. He had brought the bottle over and left it on the floor next to him. The label was in Cyrillic.

'*Za zdorovye*,' he said.

They drank, he at a gulp, what turned out to be some kind of berry vodka.

'What do you want to know?'

'I think I have connected most of the dots.'

Sam laughed at this.

'Sam, please, listen to her.'

'What happened in Yorkshire?'

The two young men exchanged looks but did not answer. Eventually, Sam served himself a second glass, clicked his glass against hers, and looked directly into her eyes.

'You had better run, run far away from here, from me.'

'Why?'

He served himself a third glass, in silence. Then he said, 'Because I'm dangerous. I cause harm. Even to those I care for.' He offered this odd answer without looking at her. Jim had got up and walked to the other end of the room, where he busied himself with something.

'Go away, Miss Walton,' Sam repeated.

She sighed. Behind her, Jim spoke.

'Show her the book,' he said.

'Which book?' asked Sam.

Jim had rekindled the fire, and it now burnt cheerfully. He walked in the direction of the little collection of books over the mantelpiece, took a copy of *Phantastes* from the shelf.

'What are you doing?' Sam asked.

Jim did not reply. He threw the book on Helena's lap.

Helena went to her light travel bag and rummaged inside it. She picked something from it, walked towards Sam, and dropped it in front of him. It was a tattered copy of the same book.

'It's the Matthews girls' copy,' she said.

Sam looked at her puzzled, and then at the book.

'They were *studying* it. Look, it's marked everywhere.'

It looked as if she had finally managed to grab his attention. He flipped through the pages briefly, and started inspecting the notes and the underlined sentences. Eventually he said:

'It seems as if they *almost* got the point of it,' and threw the book back at her.

'The point of what?'

'That book is not a work of the imagination, it's a *travel guide*.'

She couldn't deny it: she and Eliza had discussed the same possibility. It was unnerving to have it corroborated. 'I know it is *dull* at times, but—' Even then she was trying to hold on to some kind of rationality.

'Have *you* read it?'

'Of course I've read it! I care about what happened to those children. I care about what is happening *now* to other children—'

Sam was looking at her but said nothing. He sighed, and bit his lips. He didn't say anything for a moment. Eventually, he asked:

'Other children, you said?'

'Yes.'

Sam reached for the bottle of berry vodka. It was almost empty.

'We are going to need a bit more than this,' he said.

'Good boy,' Jim said.

'Something happened in Norfolk,' Helena said, 'something I don't have a rational answer for—no, that's not entirely accurate. *Several* things happened in Norfolk I don't have answers for. And my business, Samuel, is about finding answers, no matter what they might be. I would be a very poor investigator if I were to let my prejudices cloud getting to them.'

He didn't reply.

'I have been trying to find a rational solution for all of this. There must be a connection, with the factory, with the fungi. We, Eliza Waltraud and me… Eliza is a young scientist who is also looking into this. She thinks the infestation originated in there, and it extended somehow.' She got up, found some paper and a pencil, and started drawing. 'Look, the factory is, was, here. The fungi got to the ruins by the coast, and the children, somehow, may have transported some spores back to their nursery.'

He was looking at her with attention, but somehow she knew he didn't believe what she was saying.

'Like a form of pollution. Eliza ran some tests with the fungi. Some places are completely taken over: the ruins of the church, the nursery, the ruined Tudor manor…' He looked at her suddenly. 'These are the places where the… hauntings, or whatever you want to call them, manifest themselves more fully.'

'Hauntings?' asked Jim.

'The fungi was enormous in these places, monstrous.'

'What does it do? Kill you?'

'It makes you see things, feel things… Things that are not there. We could have lost our wits, suffered loss of memory, lost our way completely to never return.'

'Is that what you think happened to the children?'

She looked intently at him.

'We are not very sure what happened to the children.'

'I see,' was all he said. He got up, and walked slowly to the other end of the room. 'Go away, Helena,' he repeated.

'There's more to this, so much more.' She thought of the demonic figure in the estuary, of Mr Friars's statement about young Mr Chapman. She thought of Bévcar, which the SPR's report connected horribly with the young man in front of her. And she thought of the three pages of Maud's diary, so brief and so revealing. It was all connected; Bévcar might have been trespassing into East Anglia for decades, taking children with him.

'Tell me, Mr Moncrieff, have you ever seen a strange-looking beggar who kept appearing in the places where you happened to be? A strange-looking beggar who is also a gentleman when you see him beyond the veil that separates us from his world?'

Sam turned furiously in her direction. 'What do you want from me?'

Helena didn't reply immediately. 'I was hoping that you would help me understand some things.'

He looked at her intently. 'Why me?'

Helena and Jim exchanged a look. 'You will be turning twenty-one soon, am I right?' she offered.

'So?'

'We are not very sure of what happened to the children,' she repeated. 'But, like I say, we do know it is connected with your being here.'

She turned to face him, and she saw it then. The patterns on the floor, the jars with strange liquids, the little bits of twigs, the butterfly wings, the moth wings, the little green pebbles of rhyolite, so similar to the one that Rosie had... *used*. That was the word. She realised that now.

'Magic. You are doing magic here.' It wasn't a question.

He started walking towards her, slowly, and Helena started walking backwards.

'I have remembered some things. Some things about myself.'

'You are doing magic, aren't you? You know it; you know who you are.'

'I have remembered some things. Some things about myself. About my home. And about my father.'

He picked up Bévcar's book, threw it on the floor. So the

SPR's report was correct at least on that.

'I know,' she said. 'I know. And I am truly sorry, Samuel.'

Eventually she left them, with the promise of coming back the next morning.

She could not sleep that night; she kept turning and turning in her bed. At that moment between consciousness and oblivion, her tired, overworked brain was still placing the pieces, one by one, next to each other, each different hindsight revealing hidden meanings in the next. She thought she understood, but needed confirmation.

The next morning, she woke up to a stillness that didn't anticipate anything good. Almost before arriving, she knew it: Sam had gone. On top of Bévcar's book there was an envelope addressed to her, and inside it the last clue.

> *Dear Helena,*
>
> *I can hardly write these lines. Here I am, sitting and trying to focus on the blank pages in front of me. There's so much I have to tell you that I hardly know how to start putting the words together. I think I hoped that if you solve this mystery, I would be allowed to stay. But that was a fantasy, I see that now that I truly know who I am, now I've come to understand the horrid truth that simmers beneath the surface of Mr Samuel Moncrieff.*
>
> *I have no doubts that by now you understand it—the thread that ties me to the other side, endlessly pulling, how*

deeply its dark currents run through my veins. There is a reason for that; there's much about myself that I have come to realise in the past few weeks, and I'm still unsure of how to process this knowledge. But, first of all, allow me to tell you a story—how one day changed everything!

Viola played with me mercilessly during that whole summer. By the autumn I was in a frenzy, utterly miserable. The weather was unseasonably warm—it was as if I were provoking somehow this oddness, this late heat. And who knows? It seems to me that perhaps I was, since I didn't want the summer to end. Unseasonable weather or not, that would be our last outing.

Two other people came with us that morning, a friend of Viola's and a boy, I think it was the girl's little brother. Their faces blur; they were, are, unimportant. We were on the river; I punted. We saw it by chance, we almost missed it in fact: a little chapel of Cotswold stone lying in ruins in the middle of what looked like a deserted meadow, entirely unexpected. We all agreed it was a perfect place to have our picnic, and abandoned the punt.

It happened there, among the ruins. We kissed, finally. The friend's brother was nowhere to be seen; he was an amateur botanist, and went looking for some kind of reed or other—I can't recollect the particulars, for I truly did not care about them. Her friend was close by. Suddenly, Viola started laughing at me. Her friend joined in, and they both *laughed and laughed at my expense. That is all our kiss had been to her, a schoolgirl joke.*

It was too much to bear. I got up, and stumbled clumsily, and, in order to prevent myself from falling, supported myself on one of the chapel stones. It was then that I saw it, my true self. Some energy travelled through my fingers, and infused itself into the stone I was holding. A strange fungus, yellow and brown and lukewarm, sprouted where my fingers touched the stone, as if by magic. I don't know what I was feeling exactly: anger, at having been a mere puppet for her fun. Selfishness. A disproportionate sense of my own entitlement. It was as if I had assumed she had to be mine simply because that was what I wanted. I am ashamed of writing this. In any case, something exploded inside me then, and a green light, dense as a cloud, descended upon us. A kind of door, for lack of a better word, opened in mid-air, and I got a glimpse of what I now know is my home. To Viola or to the girl I don't know what happened, exactly, for I stepped in, or shall I say I stepped back into it, for the first time in nearly twenty years.

Yes, Helena, my home. Like I say, I do not desire to keep any more secrets. The mere word, secret, makes me gag with disgust.

And now let me tell you what I infer happened all those years back. It is my belief that, as you may have guessed, the three Matthews children managed to open a portal of communication to what they must have believed to be some kind of fairyland, or perhaps Wonderland, perhaps aided by him, Bévcar. He somehow lures children into doing so, tricks them. It is also my belief that some kind of exchange took place on that occasion, perhaps because it was needed—I am still not privy to which rules apply, if any—that meant that I, somehow, crossed back over the threshold here. It all happened in the Tudor manor, the one that I have seen in my nightmares since childhood.

What about the fungi? Although I am sure that your friend is correct, it is clear to me that it came from that other world, that it doesn't truly belong here.

So, Helena, I could not blame you for all that you might be feeling: shock, disgust.

Now you see it is me who is to blame for what happened, to Viola at least; who knows what happened, or is happening, to others, now or in the past or the future. I need to stop this somehow. These two worlds were never meant to touch each other, be it ever so lightly. So much pain is produced by it. I see now that my stay here was a little sojourn of no consequence. I don't belong in this world, not really. And soon I will walk back forever into the other.

So I'm going after him. I believe that my only chance against Bévcar, my father, is on our common soil. That here, where he only appears in the guise of the demonic *beggar, he is untouchable. I'm going after him, and I don't expect to come back.*

It seems cruel to think that my life here is finished, when I feel it had only just started. But I owe it to Viola, and to who knows how many others. I take this thought with me to give me strength for what is now to come, as I cross to the other side.

Yours faithfully,
Samuel Moncrieff

CHAPTER FOURTEEN

St George's Wood
Haslemere
Surrey
May 1901

Dear Miss Waltraud,
Thank you for your letter to my husband of last week, and
please excuse our slight delay in replying. I must confess I
was a bit baffled by it. We do not normally allow visitors,
as my husband's advanced years make it difficult for him
to spend the days in relative comfort. However, since you
say that it is a life-and-death situation, we would welcome
you to visit him any afternoon of your convenience this
week. My husband usually has his tea at half past three,
and retires shortly after sometimes, and therefore I advise

that you come a bit earlier than that. I am not sure how
much help he will be able to give you, but he has personally
requested your presence. Please let us know your plans, and
we will send a car to pick you up at the station.
    Sincerely,
    Louisa MacDonald

The man sat alone at the bottom of the garden, underneath a willow. He was covered by a woollen rug and didn't look up when she approached.

'Ah, Miss Waltraud… Did I pronounce that right?'

He had a leonine white mane, entirely unexpected, that reminded her of portraits of Tolstoy she had seen in a London bookshop. Eliza also hadn't expected such a cheerful pale eye, or such a broad smile, after reading such serious fairy stories. Sure, they contained humour, but one could tell it was the humour of someone who was controlling how much he used it, and with a specific purpose in mind.

'You pronounce it perfectly, Mr MacDonald. It is very kind of you to agree to see me at such short notice.'

'Short notice, long notice… I seldom see anyone these days, so it doesn't signify.'

'What doesn't signify?'

'The notice, of course.' He smiled again, and motioned for her to sit in a white iron garden chair, which she did, as straight as a bird on a branch. It was uncomfortable, and the discomfort reminded her instantly of what she was doing there.

'Mr MacDonald, if I may…'

'Please, call me George. I am too old for formalities,' the old man said.

'I have been reading your stories with interest…' He looked at her, frowning. Eliza continued, 'There are some things that puzzle me a great deal. I'm not a literary critic, but still—'

'Ah!' he interrupted. 'I see. The wording of your letter led me to believe that you may want to discuss something… of a slightly different nature.'

She was lost for words for a moment.

'Mr MacDonald—George. It struck me that your fairy stories and novellas possess a further meaning, that there is a dark, sinister current running through them…'

'Well, perhaps that is due to the fact that I don't write them for children in particular.'

'I beg your pardon? Surely they are books bought for the nursery, sir.'

'I don't write for children, but for the *childlike*, Miss Waltraud. There is a difference, whether one talks of a human creature of nine or of ninety-nine.'

'But, the darkness in them, sir…'

'We give very little credit to children, my dear. They are more used to darkness than we might think. They do not need to be segregated, cut off, from every experience that threatens their sense of wonder and their innocence. Sometimes children are much more perceptive than adults about death, for example,' he said, and Eliza thought he was reflecting on some specific occurrence. 'Miss Waltraud,' he continued, 'if there is something I dislike, it is having to "explain" my stories. Explanations, explanations and more explanations... that is all that is ever required of me. If someone does not understand my tales, why am I going to write a signpost to indicate my meaning? And what is my meaning, anyway? Children are much more used to this as well, to the fact that there are no settled meanings—that is a fallacy created by the modern world in order for a few to establish what is right and what is wrong. And some things are not so clean-cut, my dear. We are surrounded by grey matter. Well, the same can be said of my tales.'

'I am afraid I don't follow, sir.'

'Think of this, then. Does a sonata possess a fixed meaning for everyone who hears it? Does nature? Are sonatas or nature *failures* because we cannot grasp their ultimate meaning? The same happens with the world, and with my stories. Children are much more perceptive than us in that sense, I find. They have no compunction in accepting that meanings are unsettled, that borders are porous, that each person will create their own interpretation. The best thing one can do is to rouse somebody's consciousness. Show them that there are no fixed ways to look at the world. We are but guests here, and only for a limited time.'

That last sentence gave her the courage to say:

'Are children also more able to open doors, or walk across unseen thresholds, Mr MacDonald?'

The old man looked at her in alarm. His face was a rigid mask, and her words had cut short his verbosity.

'My dear Miss Waltraud…' he said at last, his eyes fixed on hers, his voice lowered.

'Is that what you mean by *porous borders*? Does our world possess *porous borders* of the kind you describe so often in your tales? Because I need to find one.'

'Do you mean… *crossing over*?'

'That is exactly what I mean.'

'But surely… if you know about the other side and if you have read my books… surely you know.'

'What?'

'That it is no Wonderland you are seeking, but Hell.'

Eliza used the silence to look up, and considered the clouds for a second. They had fantastic shapes, as all clouds do, and she reflected on what a strange little child she had been; hardly any friends, no favourite dolls named with pretty little names, no fondness for playing at cloudsight. What had she done to keep herself entertained, if she had not followed these childhood pursuits? She could not remember. Nothing special, surely.

'I don't care,' she said at last. 'I have to go.'

He looked at her, horrified.

'And I don't know the way, Mr MacDonald. It is as simple as that. I need your help.'

'But, my dear child! You have misunderstood everything I wrote!' the old man protested, clearly worried now.

'I thought you just said there are no fixed meanings.'

'I was talking about allegories! Literature! My young friend, what you are saying, what you are trying to achieve, it is very dangerous, more than you can imagine.'

She sighed, fearing nothing would be obtained with her visit.

Eventually, the old man said, to her surprise, 'Well, if you are here, seeking this knowledge, you *must* know enough already. I won't patronise you by explaining the possible dangers.' She turned to look curiously at him. 'But surely you must see that my stories are cautionary tales, *precisely against going there*, or anywhere near there?'

'Mr MacDonald, some children have disappeared, and what I am trying to do—'

'Exactly! Some children have disappeared, and will continue disappearing, until we teach them to recognise the dark, and to keep away from it.'

She decided on a more direct approach.

'Mr MacDonald, can you help me cross the threshold or not?'

He looked at her with infinite sadness.

'My dear, I have been trying to cross it myself these past thirty years.'

Eliza sighed. Considered once more the clouds over her head. 'Someone very dear to you?'

The old man did not reply, but there it was, plainly written on his face, everything that ought to be read about it. His wife was still alive—someone much younger then. A boy. Or a daughter, more likely. 'I am so sorry for your loss,' she said, realising that she had used the formal mode of consoling the relative of a deceased. But then again, just as the meanings of the old man's stories were unfixed, she couldn't really tell if they were talking about a death in the family or a disappearance to the other side; or perhaps it was both things at once.

'There is only one thing I can advise you, and it is this: in my experience, as indeterminate as thresholds arc, it is clear that there are moments in which we ourselves generate that indeterminacy as human beings. In those moments we are closer to it than in others.'

'Which moments?'

'Death. I don't mean your death, particularly. But the death of somebody. When death is present in the room. It is only between life and death that *It* has power over us mortals, and can carry us away.'

She smiled. This knowledge was more than she had expected to obtain.

'You may remember one more thing.'

'Yes? What is it?'

'That, sometimes, the way of finding the way is to lose oneself.'

'I truly thank you, sir.'

'But, my dear, that is only *going there*… Even if you succeed, how on earth are you planning to *come back*?'

Eliza didn't reply, for she didn't have an answer for this.

'Ah! I see our tea is coming… I hope that you will humour an old man like myself and have the tea out here, now that the sun has finally graced us with his presence.'

'It will be my pleasure.'

The old man looked pensively at her. When tea came, he asked the maid to bring something back. The young girl returned with a book in her hand. The older man opened it and started reading.

There was a boy who used to sit in the twilight and listen to his great-aunt's stories. She told him that if he could reach the place where the end of the rainbow stands he would find there a golden key. 'And what is the key for?' the boy would ask. 'What is it the key of? What will it open?' 'That nobody knows,' his aunt would reply. 'He has to find that out.'

The house was entirely surrounded by followers of Madame Florence, sporting banners claiming her innocence, wielding huge bouquets, halfway between funeral wreath and distorted, enormous offerings. The women were also wearing elaborate flower garlands on their heads, and were dancing in circles.

The police were present. Some of the banners declared that Willimina was the female Messiah they had all been waiting for, and implored her to save them.

That kind of demonstration unnerved Helena a great deal. They reminded her of another one, a few years back in Cambridge, that still brought an unsavoury taste to her mouth: male students protesting against the campaign to allow women to be awarded a degree, a campaign that had started a decade earlier, when a young girl called Philippa Fawcett topped the exam results in the university. There had not been progress in ten whole years, when Helena, already a student, witnessed the ugly scene. It was a hot day. Some male students had gathered outside Senate House, where a committee voted on the issue. The students threw eggs, rockets, and even burnt the effigy of a female cyclist in Market Square, an oversized doll that was meant to represent all female students, that was meant to represent *her*. Perhaps Willimina was not the female Messiah all those people were waiting for, but Helena really hoped she would arrive one day.

Miss Collins had requested Helena's help. She intended to take Willimina somewhere to be safe. She looked shocked, upset. The revelations about Madame Florence seemed to have affected her a great deal. Miss Collins had not been found at fault, unlike Mr Bunthorne, who had accompanied the medium for decades. She had no idea that Madame Florence wasn't who she thought she was. She had trusted her implicitly.

'I could not believe it. Madame Florence is only a name, can you imagine? Different people have been Madame Florence. How could nobody realise the trick earlier?'

'Oh, but they did at the end,' said Helena sadly. But inside herself she thought of the young woman called Willimina, and her lucky escape; and of other young women throughout the years who had 'received' Madame Florence's soul, if that was what had happened. She could not confide in Miss Collins any of this, but Helena offered her sympathies for what she was going through. Miss Collins was an intelligent woman; perhaps she had worked it out by herself. She smiled bravely back, she was a professional after all, and Helena did not doubt she would land on her feet.

The living room was full of half-made cases and bundles of linen, hatboxes and a couple of expensive-looking travel trunks. Everything was imbued with a manic urgency. Helena followed Miss Collins upstairs. Willimina was lying in a canopy bed in a bedroom overlooking the garden, perfectly coiffured and with rosy cheeks.

'What is wrong with her?'

'I am afraid she has been in this comatose state ever since our last séance for Lady Matthews.'

Helena could not believe it. Still, Willimina was the very image of good health, and simply looked as if she was sleeping.

Then she saw it, something moving on the other side of the window in the corner of her vision. Willimina was outside, in the garden, looking back at her, leaning against a birch tree. Helena took a deep breath, and turned slowly to look at the bed.

Willimina was *also* lying on the bed, peacefully sleeping.

Helena looked back at the window.

The second Willimina said hello with her hand, and indicated that Helena should come and meet her.

Helena excused herself and went out into the garden. The girl, or her shadow, spirit, projectal matter, whatever she may be, was waiting for her.

'Hello,' the second Willimina said.

'Hello. Are you well?' answered Helena.

'I am perfectly well, thank you very much.'

'You are… the real thing.'

'I do not feign my Spiritualist trances, if that is what you mean,' the girl said, with a charming and proud smile. 'Madame Florence thinks I am some kind of Messiah… She is wrong, of course. I am not that important.'

'Why are you here?'

'I have to talk to you, explain things. The girls have asked me to.'

Helena did not have to ask to know she meant Maud, Alice, Flora. Willimina continued:

'I am the key, at least for now. Like Sam was the key, *is* the key. Come on! I will wake soon; there is not a moment to lose.'

Willimina took her by the hand, and they started walking

to the bottom of the garden. The light changed suddenly; but instead of night falling like a curtain dropping it settled into what seemed to be an eternal dusk, as if they had entered a realm in which the sun was forever setting. This reminded her of the meadow with the Tudor house. It was a country of shadows, all of a sudden.

Helena did not know if she was now dreaming. Perhaps she was. Perhaps she was awake.

Willimina took her towards a tunnel made of trees, which got narrower and narrower, until they had to crawl down, and eventually they came upon a little door; she opened the door, still holding Helena's hand, and what was on the other side of the door was a staircase spiralling down, and down and down they went... It looked to Helena as if the tunnel was never going to end.

Some birds flew around them. Although they were not birds, she noticed, but winged fish.

It was a landscape from a dream, made by the mist itself, an invented scenario put together by the gathering dusk. And then they came upon it, the little copse of birches she recognised, and behind it, the Tudor manor.

'Here we are! The country whence the shadows fall,' announced Willimina. 'I hope you recognise this place,' she said. 'You are meant to always enter by the first place in which you traversed between. From here you can access the rest. I did not realise immediately. Do you understand, Helena?' she insisted.

'Understand what?'

'That no mortal or immortal being can tell where one place begins, and the other ends.'

Willimina let go of her hand, smiling, with such longing that Helena thought for a second that she was saying goodbye.

'Wait! How do I get back?'

Willimina seemed to consider this, but she didn't reply.

Helena continued walking, firmly into the other world. Or so she thought; she was sleeping in an armchair in Miss Collins's house, next to Willimina.

In the dream world, eventually, Willimina vanished from view.

Lady Matthews arrived at the abbey later that night. She had read several times the short, final report sent by Helena Walton. She had never felt so tired. It was the report of a lunatic. If she thought she would get the agreed fee after these raving propositions… Lady Matthews did not finish her train of thought; she punctuated it by an action that surprised even herself: she took the delicate china mug she had been served tea in, and smashed it on the floor of her room.

She was panting, eyes wide open, amazed at how relieved she felt after the futile gesture. If Miss Walton was right, Maud had been trying to get back to the house all those years and had been rebuked; whereas the other two children were, presumably, lost for all eternity. But she knew it well; she had always known it, what those horrid pages said.

Oh yes. She had known all along. She had always known. But she could not admit it to herself. She needed someone else to show her the truth.

That wretched place by the coast, its poison reaching out into the ruins, and into the eerie countryside. And into her home, into their lives. She was to blame. Charles was to blame. To even imagine that they could have succeeded; what fools had they been.

She took the saucer and smashed it with sudden fury. She took the milk jar and smashed it next. She grabbed with both hands the teapot, considering whether she would dare to do it; after all, it was a much bigger object. She let it drop; and, after that, there was no stopping her.

Lady Matthews suffered an apoplexy while smashing the third row of framed photographs. By then she was full of cuts, bruised, slightly manic, her perfect coiffured bun out of place, her face distorted, amazed and full of grief. In her last effort, an oil bedside lamp crashed against the floor with her.

No one heard her when she herself fell on the carpet as the flames spread.

EPILOGUE

The Reverend Harry Cecil-St John was an exile in a strange land. He had been sent to that dismal stretch of coast by his bishop six months back, and still had not got used to the wretched place. During the trip there, his heart had contracted slightly while considering the never-ending blackness, expanding queerly. Those big open fields, the still regularity of their tired greens, and then the dark soil, darker and darker as you got deeper into the county. The Fens had always looked to him exactly what they were: a made landscape; or rather, one could say, 'made-up', giving the impression that someone had just dreamed it. It was an impossible thing; even in the blackness of the night the sense of land without end was palpable, forcing one to reflect on one's own insignificance. And then it hit him: nothingness was what truly stretched between oneself and the horizon, so distant that it looked like a thin indeterminate line

309

dreamed up by the overwrought brain, a mirage of sorts. The light was also something improvised by a mind that needed to impose shapes and forms in order to stay sane, when truly, really, the eyes were incapable of elucidating any object or gradient or slope, for there were none.

A deceitful landscape, dishonest. It spoke of clean lines, its man-made angles reassuring the viewer of its symmetry, its order; but its ditches were cut out of the mud with so much sorrow, so much suffering. Whatever poor soul was caught poaching, or had committed an even minor infraction, was sent to remove the sand, clay, gravel, until the fatigue was too much and they ended up underneath the land themselves. And here, in this bitter, awful land, was where he had been put, in a parish by that uncanny coast, with its monstrous tides and collapsed churches. True, he could have fared much worse; for he ruled over a Norman church with a pretty little tower, and the proud air of a fortress, an atmospheric miniature vestry of dark wood, and a couple of treasures paid for by the wool trade, all those centuries back: a little Nottingham alabaster panel representing the virgin saints (Katherine, Ursula, Helena, Barbara), and a quaint panelled window overlooking the marshes, depicting Etheldreda herself, the Saxon princess, presenting a treasure to those who would lay the foundations of what would in time become Ely's cathedral. At least he had not been ordered into a phantom parish by his bishop, he thought—small triumph! But he saw them in the distance, in his wanderings—for what was there to do here but rambling and bird-spotting and daydreaming?—and he knew all their stories by now. St Agnes's was still visible, its tower a beacon in the mist, the pole of a ship in the middle of water when the tide covered it all. The shoreline had shifted here, all those centuries back; and now the little building had been abandoned to the capricious movements of the sea, neither here nor there. The life around it had gone with the transformed landscape dreamed by reclamation, and its parishioners had vanished, as forcefully as if the fairies had taken them. The marsh dwellers had insisted on staying for a while, but at the end the ghosts had been too much, and they had been forced to move a stretch inland, all the way to his parish. This had happened generations ago, and still he could sense their bitterness.

On windy, bleak mornings like that one, they said that the tolling of a bell could be heard coming from St Agnes's direction. These were mornings when ghosts went out to air themselves, protest their existence. For it was a haunting, no doubt; it had been a long time since there was a bell perched there. High tides and strong winds had crashed with the force of a mighty gale against its crumbling walls, and the little construction had finally collapsed, forever sinking into the marshes. Other churches had collapsed, and were still collapsing, as the waves were intent on recovering their kingdom. Only six years ago Eccles Church had disappeared, swallowed up by the sea.

And so, this was his final domain: vast dark-soiled fields, wide never-ending skies, sea mist, wet, marshy ground, and howling winds; birds to watch and sermons to write, and absolutely nothing else. Unless one were to write about the disquiet of the soul on certain mornings, the eeriness of the ruined churches standing in the midst of the tide, the unusual quietness, the unbroken, hellish landscape. The unwholesomeness of it all. Even the beach nearby felt oppressive, claustrophobic, with its leaden sky and its furious gales, pushing the birds higher into the clouds. The knowledge that the ancient buildings that now stood proud could be gone at any time and without warning.

The church of Wicken Far End had suffered a different fate, for the storms of the 1870s had finished it off completely, scattering around all its stones. And there it had remained, for a very long time. Until the Green Flood, that was. Now, there was nothing. The water seemed to have changed the shape of everything, and even now, many weeks on, it was still possible to see the destruction that it had brought with it. For one thing was clear: the paths had been altered somehow, the usual landmarks were all wrong, even more than they normally were.

In the past, the reverend had got not exactly lost, but somehow disorientated in those fields. Now, he looked again around him, and realised the copse he was in.

'Oh dear,' he said out loud, as much to himself as to the trees and the leaves and the bushes. It was oddly quiet, and he could not see any birds, or anything that indicated the presence of some other living creature.

He came out of the copse, and found himself there, in that place which he had avoided since his arrival. He would not have been able to explain why, he did not know why he did it, although he knew that the ruins were unwholesome, unholy: his instinctive reaction when he found himself there was to take his hand to the cross that he carried in his pocket.

A woman appeared out of nowhere. She was suddenly at the door of the ruined Tudor manor. Next to her, a green light was gaining weight, consistency, forming a small cloud which seemed to advance next to her. The face was familiar... Yes, he had seen her before, in Old John's cottage the morning after he died.

'Miss!' he called, but she didn't reply. She looked behind her for a second, directed her gaze to the place where he was, but, oddly, she seemed not to see him. Surely he, a priest, wasn't invisible; something felt queer.

The woman wasn't from these parts. He wanted to tell her at once to run away, to leave that place. He thought that he could direct her safely back away from the meadow.

He was gasping for air now. The light had become more leaden, greyish. And suddenly he could not breathe.

'Miss!' he called again. To his horror, the woman entered the house.

This would not do. That place was better left alone. Muttering a few words unseemly to a clergyman, he advanced towards the building. He would have to go and fetch her. And what could she possibly be doing in that place?

He hadn't been inside before, and was surprised at the amount of rubble and stones; he was surprised at the whole bricks that had become dislodged from the walls. What no one could understand was why the flood had not taken this place forever. It was almost as if the waters had taken a conscious turn here. It made so little sense. A shadow moved, and he saw the woman had made her way into the very last room.

Something started pulling him now, and something else was urging him to go. The two forces were equally powerful, and for a few seconds the reverend stayed, unmoving, on the spot. Then, shaking his head, he took a step into the unknown. It was only with a profound effort that he managed to get to the last room. Everything was covered in mould, and, worried, he took a handkerchief to his nose.

'Miss!' he tried again.

The woman was kneeling in front of a wall at the end, a wall with a particularly worrying mouldy patch, on which a kind of green energy, or light, seemed to be vibrating. She wasn't alone. Next to her sat Eliza Waltraud. The younger woman was unmistakable, with her unruly mat of blonde curls. What in God's name were they doing? They had some objects around them, the most prominent a large green rock.

'Miss Waltraud!' The younger woman did not seem to hear him either. By now the reverend was feeling rather impatient.

He wanted to leave that place, but the feeling of dread also meant that he felt he had a moral duty to take these absurd women back with him. He advanced in their direction, raising his voice: 'My dear, this will not do! I insist! You—' but the reverend did not finish his sentence. He was now behind the women, very close to them, and his hand had moved towards Eliza's shoulders; and, to his utter amazement it had passed right through them, as if she was a ghost.

With a cry, the reverend fell backwards, and hit his head. And everything went as black as a well, a canal, a destructive flood.

He got up to the woodpigeon cooing, and to darkness. He didn't know how long he had been gone. There was a stale taste in his mouth, and he knew that he had been breathing the mould and the rubble and the dirt.

Eliza seemed to be breathing, he could see that; she also looked more solid, felt more solid, thank goodness, when he rushed to her. There was, however, something odd about her.

'Miss Waltraud! Please!'

Eliza was hanging in the air in a strange posture, as if someone or something invisible was grabbing her by the shoulders. Presently, she fell flat on the floor, and started whining softly. She opened her eyes. She was conscious.

What there was no sign of was the other lady, and he could not remember her name.

Miss Waltraud looked at him; she gave the appearance of not being able to walk very far, and he didn't think he could carry her back. He thought it better to go for help; he hated the idea of leaving the young woman alone there, but could not think of anything else to do. Before he left her he saw she had a pendant hanging from her neck, another green rock. He had an idea; he took out a cross from his pocket, and put it also around her neck. Asking her to stay calm, reassuring her that he would be back soon, he left the Tudor ruins and ran for help.

He didn't get very far. As he left the copse the reverend saw two girls playing. Who could they possibly be? They were dressed in a fashion long gone, even in that backward place. Their hair was twisted into precious curls.

'Flora!' called one of them to the other. The smallest child turned back just as she was about to leave the meadow, walked over to the other child and took her hand. And they both advanced towards the reverend.

'Please, sir, we are tired, and hungry.'

'My dear, what is your name?'

'Alice Matthews.'

Matthews? It had to be a distant relative of Lady Matthews, visiting perhaps. How odd he had not known this. They looked past him over his shoulder, and he turned towards the house. Eliza Waltraud was coming out, walking by herself.

'Well, I need to go and get help. Could you children please stay with Miss Waltraud here?'

The children smiled and nodded, and started walking in the direction of the house.

'Don't go inside!' the reverend shouted without thinking. 'Please, stay out here…' He stopped. Something was not right. What was it? The reverend realised it then, the smell: a huge fire. With incredible effort he ran, coming out of a meadow into a field opposite Lady Matthews's estate, to see the abbey engulfed by the flames.

By the coast, on the sand, the water slowly receding from their feet, were two other bodies, lying next to each other and holding hands.

Samuel Moncrieff woke up to a grey indeterminate mass that he understood slowly to be the sky. Instinctively he looked to his hand, holding another. Next to him on the sand Helena Walton slept. How long had he been away? The woman lying next to him looked like Helena, but at least twenty years after he had met her, in her mid-forties.

Sam got up and heaved this new old woman into his arms, and thus carrying her, he started to walk out of that solitary stretch of the beach, back to the normal world.

ACKNOWLEDGEMENTS

This book has existed in many forms and iterations. It first entered the world as a short story in my Clarion workshop: I am thankful to all my Clarion classmates from 2014 and in particular to our teacher Catherynne Valente, who saw its potential and encouraged me to carry on working with it. As it grew into a novel it became a part of my master's portfolio in the Cambridge University Creative Writing MSt. I am thankful to my classmates from my cohort (2014-2016) for indulging me and teasing me in equal measure during the two years of the course for being the only person in the class writing genre fiction, gothic fiction. As the facts show, I ended up not being the only person writing gothic fiction: I felt very proud to have inspired someone to come over to the dark side. Of my teachers, special thanks are due to Sarah Burton and Jem Poster, who were always accepting, of my writing but also of me. Michael Womack drove me around the fens whenever I asked him to, and James Womack introduced me to the work of George MacDonald. All these experiences have enriched the book, but special thanks need to be extended to my editor at Titan, Sophie Robinson, who transformed an inchoate story into something with meaning and purpose. Thanks also to my agent, Alexander Cochran at C&W Agency for excellent advice at a crucial time: here's to the next book.

Many books and archive collections, talks and chats, in England and in Spain, have inspired this story, from an article in the *Times Literary Supplement* about reissued female detective novels, to my experience working at Cambridge University Library, which holds the magnificent SPR archive and collection. I am grateful to Cambridge University librarians for their support and time. Anything that makes sense in this book is down to the people listed here, and anything that doesn't make sense is entirely the result of my own intransigence.

PS. The reader will forgive me for having taken one historical license. The Petit Trianon affair is mentioned in the spring of 1901, when it actually took place in the summer of that year and wasn't reported until several years later, when an account was published. I have taken the decision to keep it like this, a decision which should become clear if there are further installments of Helena's story: reader, this will depend on you.

BOOK CLUB QUESTIONS

What themes stood out to you?

What is the link between the faerie tale *The Golden Key* by
George MacDonald and this novel?

Share a favourite quote. Why did this quote stand out?

Why do you think Lady Matthews waited so long to
investigate her stepdaughters' disappearance?

How are Helena and Eliza usual women for their era?

How did Helena and Sam change through the novel?
How did your opinion of them change?

At the end of the novel, Helena and Eliza attempt to reach Sam through the portal. Would you have done the same?

Who could you imagine playing the main characters in a screen adaptation?

ABOUT THE AUTHOR

Marian Womack was born in Andalusia and educated in the UK. She is a graduate of the Clarion Writers' Workshop, and she holds degrees from Oxford and Cambridge universities. She writes at the intersection between weird and gothic fiction, and her stories normally deal with strange landscapes, ghostly encounters, or uncanny transformations. Her debut short story collection, *Lost Objects* (Luna Press, 2018) was shortlisted for two BSFA awards and one BFS award. Marian teaches literary genre fiction at the Oxford University Creative Writing Master's degree. She lives in Cambridge, at the edge of the Fens, with her husband, their son and two aging Spanish cats. When she is not writing she can be found working in libraries, or editing books and pamphlets in her indie publishing project, Calque Press.

marianwomack.com

@beekeepermadrid

For more fantastic fiction, author events,
exclusive excerpts, competitions, limited editions and more

VISIT OUR WEBSITE
titanbooks.com

LIKE US ON FACEBOOK
facebook.com/titanbooks

FOLLOW US ON TWITTER AND INSTAGRAM
@TitanBooks

EMAIL US
readerfeedback@titanemail.com